Airships, Aphrodisiacs, & Other Love Problems

CATHERINE STEIN

ISBN: 978-1-949862-55-3

Book cover and interior design by E. McAuley:
www.emcauley.com

For notes on content please visit

catsteinbooks.com/content-notes

Contents

Kiss Me,
I'm Incorporeal

Kiss Me, I'm Incorporeal

A Samhain Ghost Story

For seventeen years, Diarmuid Burke has wandered his decaying castle, cursed to a solitary, ghostly existence. But when the castle's new owner arrives, Diarmuid is shocked to discover she can see and hear him. Even better: She's not afraid of him.

Shunned from society for her "hysteria," Molly Hanover is resigned to living out her days as a spinster in a remote castle. Horrified to discover her new home neglected and filthy, she takes refuge in the one clean room—only to find it occupied by a ghost. But Diarmuid is kind, handsome, and as much in need of a friend as Molly is.

Together, Diarmuid and Molly begin to set the castle to rights and probe the secrets behind Diarmuid's curse. With affection growing between them, will one of them choose to sacrifice for the other? Or will the magic of a Samhain night provide the chance for love to conquer all?

Prologue

Ireland, 1880
Samhain, November 1

Diarmuid Burke had fae blood. He must. Every Samhain his skin prickled with excitement. Tonight, as he surveyed the endless wild nothing from the castle's highest window, he felt only peace and joy. This was his world. His home.

Diarmuid had been born in the waning days of the Great Hunger. He'd grown up in the aftermath, watching people continue to leave Eire for faraway cities like New York and Chicago. This land—*his* land, now—had once been thriving farms, a fully civilized area. Was it wrong of him to bask in the way nature had reclaimed it? Wrong to take such pleasure in the complete lack of other humans?

He was fae. It was the only logical conclusion.

"The perfect place for a railroad, eh?"

Diarmuid whirled around. If only his fae nature gave him heightened senses, to prevent people from sneaking up on him.

"Keane." He nodded at his cousin and oldest friend. "I thought you'd gone."

"Before seeing the view from your penthouse bedroom? Hardly. Besides, I had to show you the fancy trinket I found in the library."

Keane held out a hand, and a pendant trickled from between his fingers. A round green stone set in a circle of gold flashed and shimmered in the lamplight.

A rush of ice shivered through Diarmuid's veins. "Put the damned thing away. It's probably cursed."

Keane gave a bark of laughter. "Nonsense. I can't believe a modern man like you would believe in superstitious prattle."

Diarmuid turned back to the window. "Take it away. Next time you visit you can tell me of all the bad luck you've been having."

"Oh, I'll have excellent luck. I'm going into the railroad business. Or maybe mining. You should join me. All this empty property. It's the perfect solution."

"No. Thank you, but I'm happy with the inheritance as it is."

Keane heaved a sigh. "I hoped you wouldn't say that. But I can't say it's unexpected. It's been fun, Diar, but progress calls. I'll miss you."

"What?" Diarmuid looked over his shoulder to find his cousin holding the amulet aloft, using it to catch the light from the closest gas lamp. "What are—"

A spear of light shot from the amulet, striking Diarmuid directly in the heart and knocking all the breath from his lungs. He collapsed, clutching at his chest and gasping for air as searing pain tore through his body.

"Progress, cousin," Keane said solemnly. "I'm sorry it has to be this way."

Diarmuid tried to speak, but not a sound escaped his throat. The pain twisted and burned inside him, as if invisible blades were slashing his body to pieces. Screaming in agony, he curled into a ball, hugging himself tight against the unending torture.

Except his screams made no sound. And his body lay stiff and straight.

The pain began to subside, and he uncurled enough to look around. He had to be hallucinating. That couldn't be his own body lying beside him, growing smaller and smaller, then rising toward the amulet Keane still held in his backstabbing hands.

With a final flash, the body vanished into the green stone, leaving the gem slowly pulsating with a soft internal light.

The pain vanished. Diarmuid staggered to his feet, lifting his fists to pummel his ex-friend.

"What have you done to me, you bastard?"

Keane didn't respond. He smiled down at the pendant, then looped it over his head and tucked it beneath his shirt.

Diarmuid charged. "What have you d—"

He passed directly through his cousin, then fell, flailing, onto the chest of bed linens. *Into* the chest of bed linens. He pushed himself onto his hands and knees. His semi-transparent hands and knees, halfway in and halfway out of the chest.

"Dia ár sábháil!"

Diarmuid leapt to his feet, grabbing at Keane, desperate to get hold of something with his incorporeal fingers. Keane walked right through him and strode out the door.

"No. No, this can't be." Diarmuid held up a hand, wincing as the bright gaslight penetrated the space where flesh and bone should have been.

He was here, and not. Alive and not.

He let out a howl of fury.

A ghostly moan echoed off the castle's stone walls.

1

Ireland, 1897
October 31st, an hour before sunset

Her castle. Molly Hanover stared up at the imposing stone fortress in front of her. Untrimmed hedges ringed the structure, some rising high enough to hide the first floor windows. No gardener, apparently. At least the windows she could see had been enlarged sometime in the past. The interior wouldn't be entirely gloomy.

It's better than an asylum.

How many times had she repeated that to herself on the way here? Hundreds? Thousands? She forced a slow, deep breath and stepped up to the massive wooden door.

I can do this.

This was her opportunity. Here, no one would call her "hysterical." No one would see her peculiar habits or wonder why she avoided so many ordinary things. She could make something of herself, turn this castle into a beautiful retreat where she could craft her soaps and lotions.

For a moment, she let herself bask in the dream of running her own business, with no one to scoff at her or interrupt her work.

The footman behind her cleared his throat. "The key, Miss Margaret?"

"Oh, yes. Thank you." Molly plucked the weighty iron key from the man's grasp, taking care not to touch his hand in the process.

The key slid easily into the lock. Molly turned it and the door swung smoothly inward. Good. Someone had been taking better care of the castle than the gardens.

She stepped inside and froze.

Maybe not.

The enormous Great Hall that took up the entire ground floor was a mess of dust and cobwebs. What had once been a long dining table was a pile of splintered wood. An insect as large as her thumb skittered across the floor in front of her.

Molly jerked her handkerchief out of her pocket and clapped it over her nose and mouth. No. No, no, no. She couldn't stay here. She could see the cobwebs waving in the breeze that now wafted through the doors. Her skin tingled from the dust that was surely settling on her this very second.

Tightness clenched around her heart and her stomach flip-flopped. Awful things were seeping into her body. Microbes of all sorts. Microscopic insects. They would invade her. Infect her. Leave her bedridden, dying a slow, agonizing death.

The thoughts pounded in her brain, as they always did, no matter how she screamed for them to stop.

"We'll take your things upstairs, miss," the footman said, hauling one of her trunks through the door. "I'm sure the rooms above will be better."

Molly managed a nod, then raced for the stairs. She needed to get somewhere clean. Somewhere she could strip off these awful clothes and scrub her body head to toe.

The first floor was no better. Drawing room, library, study, parlor. Not one was devoid of dust and decay. Furniture stood draped in musty, moth-eaten cloths. Grime caked the floors and walls.

Molly ran up another set of stairs. She'd memorized the floor plan. Second floor: bedrooms. Four of them, plus two water closets and a large bathing room. None were usable.

Molly thought she might vomit. Tears dripped from her eyes, moistening the handkerchief she still held to her face. She trudged up to the top floor, the small, rectangular turret that contained only a single bedroom with a private bath. Her last hope.

God, she felt so ill. She was dying already, either from the filth or from over-exerting herself running up the stairs.

The door to the room was closed. Molly put a tentative hand to the doorknob and turned it.

As the door swung open, the handkerchief fluttered from her fingers.

"Is… is this a dream?"

Molly took a tentative step through the doorway. Golden light from the setting sun streamed through the tall windows. Perfectly polished and swept floors gleamed beneath her feet. A gorgeous stone fireplace dominated one wall of the room, flanked by a cozy chair and a bookshelf stuffed with leather-bound volumes. Opposite stood a high four-poster bed, carved from dark wood and covered with clean bedding in a pale green color.

"Maybe I'm dead," she whispered. "Or else this is some kind of miracle."

"Miss Margaret?" the footman called from below.

Her parents' servants were eager to be rid of her. While they'd never be openly rude, their expressions and tones of voice conveyed enough. She was a burden, like she was to her family.

"There is a clean room up here," she answered. "Please have my trunks brought up."

Molly stepped further into the room and began to explore. The sturdy chest at the foot of the bed held additional linens, all old, but clean. The attached bath chamber was spotless, the taps and the water closet fully functional. Even the gas lights worked. Someone had been living here, clearly. But why only this room?

She pulled open the closet, the last unexplored part of the room. Men's suits hung in a tidy row along one side of the space, while shelves opposite were arrayed with shoes, hats, and other accessories. All the pieces were in excellent condition, hardly worn, but they looked outdated. By at least a decade.

She shut the closet and sat down to rest in the chair

by the hearth. She was no expert on the subject of men's fashion. Perhaps she was simply mistaken. And perhaps fashions were behind the trends this far from Dublin.

But why does a caretaker dress like a gentleman? Stealing the money that should have been used for castle upkeep?

Molly was too exhausted to fret over it. She could find this lax caretaker tomorrow and get answers then.

She surveyed the room again. The beautiful, cozy, clean room. She would have a long bath, she would have a crackling fire, and she would celebrate Samhain with the spiced cider she'd brought from home and some divination games.

For one night, at least, she would have peace.

2

Samhain, midnight

There was a woman in his room. A woman. Here. In his room.

Hours had passed since she'd first arrived, and still Diarmuid roamed his castle in a state of shock. A woman. In his castle. In his room.

Who the devil was she?

The paltry staff employed by whomever had claimed this place had given up on caretaking years ago. Not that they'd ever done much beside checking that the structure hadn't crumbled. And now an apparently genteel lady was occupying his damned room! Had ownership somehow fallen to her?

"Ownership," Diarmuid growled.

He owned the accursed place. He was still here, stuck in this half-existence, fully sound in mind, if not in body.

He trudged up the stairs, unable to enjoy the solid

feel of his footsteps like he usually did this time of day. Unfamiliar physical sensations assaulted him. A prickling of his translucent skin. Butterflies in his non-existent stomach. Feelings of agitation.

Or maybe excitement. For the first time in ages he wasn't alone.

Diarmuid walked through the door and leaned against the wall, folding his arms over his chest and crossing his legs at the ankles, pretending for a moment he was only a carefree lad gazing upon a pretty woman.

The woman in question was indeed pretty, with wild red hair semi-contained in a long braid and emerald eyes that sparkled in the gaslight. But it was her behavior that most enchanted him.

In the time he'd been stomping around the house, she'd taken all his old books down from the bookshelf and replaced them with her own. Now she sat on the floor in her nightgown, drinking cider straight from the bottle while sorting his books into tidy piles.

"Too old," she said, tossing a book onto the messy heap that must have been her discard pile. "Ugh. Too boring." One of Diarmuid's old school textbooks joined the pile.

He chuckled.

The woman paused, cocked an ear and frowned for a second, then shrugged.

He sucked in a sharp breath—or would have, if he'd had lungs to store the air. Even after seventeen years, his ghostly form had entirely human reactions.

The woman went back to her sorting, placing books she wanted into alphabetized categories.

Diarmuid let out the not-breath he'd been holding. She hadn't actually heard him. Most likely she'd responded to a shift in the air caused by his semi-corporeal state.

The woman took another long swig of her drink, then picked up a slim battered volume.

"*The Secrets of a Lusty Shepherdess?*" She flipped to the first page.

Oh, bugger. Diarmuid had completely forgotten he had that book. He'd tired of jerking off to the same illustrations a decade ago.

"That book is not fit for a lady," he blurted.

She dropped the book. Her head whipped to the side to look at him.

"Oh!" she exclaimed.

The woman gaped at him. Not through him, not around him. *At* him.

Shite and bugger. No one had ever encountered him at midnight, when he felt almost alive. No one had seen him during the past sixteen Samhain nights, when the Otherworld overlapped with this one. Now if she ran off screaming into the dark, cold night, it would be his fault.

The woman's surprise faded, and she tilted her head to one side, considering him.

"You're a ghost," she said, her tone entirely devoid of fear.

"I..." Diarmuid became suddenly tongue-tied. He hadn't spoken with another person in so long. Oh, God, so long. "I..." He sank to his knees.

The woman's brows lifted in concern. "I'm so sorry. Did I scare you? I certainly didn't mean to."

Had *she* scared *him*?

A laugh burst out of him, growing louder and harder until he was clutching his belly from the force of it. He hadn't felt so gloriously alive in seventeen years. A person could see him! A person could talk to him! And she was kind and curious and unafraid of him.

"My… apologies," he choked out. "I was… startled. But not scared. As you clearly are not. And, yes, I am a ghost. Or something like it. Allow me to introduce myself. I'm Diarmuid Burke. This is my castle."

Diarmuid settled himself into a seated position. He ought to have stood, perhaps, to make introductions, but nothing about this situation was ordinary, and his… guest seemed disinclined to stand on ceremony.

The woman's brow wrinkled. "The Diarmuid Burke who went missing all those years ago?"

"Yes. Except I am not missing. Simply… not all here."

She winced. "People call me 'not all here.' Though your plight differs from mine, I can understand something of how you must feel. I'm Margaret Hanover, lately of Dublin, current owner of your castle. My friends call me Molly."

Diarmuid extended a hand. "A pleasure to make your acquaintance, Miss Hanover."

Molly stared at his hand, her mouth twisting in an expression of doubt, or perhaps distaste. Diarmuid yanked his hand back, cursing his foolishness. Obviously she wouldn't want to touch his spectral form.

Her gaze dropped to the floor, her shoulders slumping. "I must apologize again. I…" She took a deep breath and straightened up. "I didn't intend to imply that you were scary or unpleasant in any way. It's me. I have difficulty… touching people. Especially those I don't know well."

A deep sadness lurked in Molly's eyes. The sort of long-suffering sadness Diarmuid knew all too well. By God, such sorrow did not belong on so compelling a young woman. He would do what he could to drive it away.

"Is this why people call you peculiar?" he asked gently.

"In part. My mind is always warning me about germs. People are dirty. They don't wash enough, or they sneeze in their hands. If I touch them, those germs are all over me. I'm terrified to leave this room because of what might be lurking in all the dust. And if I do touch someone or something dirty, then I need to wash my hands twice. Once doesn't make the feeling go away. I don't know why I'm telling you this. You'll think me strange like everyone does."

"I don't think you strange. I think your problem sounds challenging."

Her entire face lit up. "Yes! Yes, it is. And I do try, but I can't make the feelings stop."

Diarmuid extended his hand again, slowly. "Perhaps you could teach yourself to accept the feelings. I had to learn how to accept the stillness and the loneliness when I first became a ghost. With practice, those things became easier to ignore. I think you can do it too. And I'm incorporeal, so I have no germs. Touch my hand and see how it feels."

"I won't go right through you?"

"I don't think so. I can touch things when I am most substantial, so it stands to reason that I can also touch a person. I couldn't say how it will feel."

Molly seemed to consider his words for a moment. Then she straightened her spine, set her jaw, and shook his hand. For a second, her warmth seeped into him, like a hot drink on a cold night. And then she was gone.

"My brain says my hand is dirty now, even though I know that's nonsense. It's telling me to wash away the germs."

"See how long you can resist," Diarmuid suggested. "It might be longer than you expect."

Molly lifted her hand up in front of her face. Her brow furrowed in thought. "It's like lifting something heavy. Each time I will get a little bit stronger. Someday I'll pick up a rock that once was hard to lift and realize it's easy now."

"Exactly."

"Thank you. Can we shake hands again when I'm ready for a second try?"

Diarmuid grinned at her, his entire spirit brimming with pure joy. Maybe it was only for one night, but he was no longer alone. "You can touch me any time and any place you like."

Molly turned pink and giggled. "I assume you didn't mean touch you like the pictures in the *Lusty Shepherdess* book?"

He hadn't, but if she wanted to touch him like that, he certainly wouldn't say no. He gave her a shrug and an awkward smile.

"Perhaps someday I could manage to hug you," she offered. "You feel almost human."

"It's near midnight." Diarmuid leaned against the wall, taking a moment to soak in the experience of the wood at his back. "I'm always more substantial near midnight. And it's Samhain. Today I will be like this until dawn."

Her frown returned. "Does that mean I will only be able to see you near midnight?"

"I don't know," he admitted. "I hope not."

"I hope I can see you at any time." Molly reached out and touched him again, this time for a moment longer. "It's nice to have a friend."

Diarmuid's chest tightened, as if something had seized his heart and wouldn't let go. Something like... love.

Damnation.

He'd finally been struck by the power of Aengus Óg. Seventeen years too late.

3

They talked all night. Molly chattered on, swept up in the euphoria of speaking to someone who didn't think her broken or hysterical. They swapped descriptions of books they'd read, and she recounted events from the years Diarmuid had been trapped in the castle. She didn't care one whit that he was a ghost. He was kind and interesting and quite handsome, to be perfectly honest. When she crawled into bed at dawn, half asleep, she murmured a prayer that the night hadn't been a dream.

Only when she awoke, hours later, did Molly realize her mistake. This was *his* bed. And he was in it.

Molly shimmied to the edge of the bed. Last night hadn't been a dream, because it was definitely Diarmuid beside her, even if he was now a faint shadow of his former self. Molly could see every detail of the sheets beneath him, but when she focused, she could make out the slight curl of his thick hair, the long lashes framing his eyes, and the little notch in the center of his chin.

Did ghosts sleep? Or had he become inert due to the daylight? Good heavens, had he died in this bed? Was she going to be infected now and become a ghost too?

The sound of approaching footsteps startled her out of her speculation before panic set in, thank God. A fist pounded on the bedroom door, and she jolted upright.

"Lady!" an irritable voice called. "Your breakfast went cold, and now your luncheon will too. If you won't eat, I'm leaving!"

The cook! In the wild up and down of emotions last night, Molly had forgotten her father had arranged for a cook and a maid for her. Any other staff was to be her own responsibility.

"I'm so sorry," Molly called. "I will be ready shortly."

The woman in the hall harrumphed. "I'll leave your tray here, then."

Molly scrambled from the bed. She yanked open the door and pulled her lunch tray into the room to prevent it becoming covered in dust or rot. She was making a hash of everything already. How could she run a household when she feared to leave her room?

She glanced back at Diarmuid. "He can keep this room clean," she murmured. "Perhaps he could clean other areas of the castle? If only I had a way to pay him to do so."

Diarmuid sat up. "You can still see me?"

"Oh, you're awake! Yes, I can see you. You're very faint, but still visible. I thought perhaps you would be asleep all day."

He chuckled. "I'm not a vampire. Though I do tire easily and cannot leave the room. But I can still touch things if I concentrate, and as you see, I've learned how not to sink right through the bed."

"Useful, if you wish to rest."

"It is indeed. So, you would like some assistance in cleaning this castle?"

Molly's cheeks grew hot. "I do, but—"

He held up a hand to stop her. "I would be happy to help. Spending time with someone who is both able and willing to converse with me is a finer payment than anything I can think of. Although, I might be especially grateful if we could begin with the library."

"The library? Why?"

"When my cousin did this to me…" Diarmuid gestured at his transparent body. "He used an amulet he claimed to have found in the library. If there is any hope of freeing myself from this prison, the information I need would be in the library."

"I will help you search," Molly replied emphatically. No one deserved a lonely half-existence for eternity. Especially not someone as considerate as Diarmuid. "We will find what you need."

"Thank you." His shoulders slumped, and he faded to barely more than an outline. "I should warn you, I have searched before and found nothing. But that was when I was newly a ghost and in a state of complete despair. And before I'd mastered the art of manipulating physical objects. But we may well discover nothing but mold and dust."

Molly shuddered. She didn't want to leave this room. She didn't want to touch a single thing in the entire rest of the house. But Diarmuid had befriended her and even showed her she could be brave enough to touch him.

"I may need to go very slowly, because of my… issues. But I swear I will help you."

"And I swear to help you in return. As you can clearly see, I suffer from issues of my own."

Her entire body warmed, and she couldn't stop a giddy smile from spreading across her face. "This must be why we've become friends so quickly. We understand one another. I hope it's a sign that our friendship will continue to grow."

A flash of something that might have been wistfulness passed over Diarmuid's face, but as insubstantial as he was, she couldn't be certain.

"May it be so," he said firmly.

Molly walked back toward the bed, extending her hand. Perhaps she couldn't feel him like this, but she wanted to make the offer. Touching him still frightened her, but each time she did it, she felt a little bit stronger, a little more the master of her own body.

His fingers closed around hers, at first nothing more than a tickle. Within moments, however, his grip had solidified into a handshake as firm as any man's, albeit slightly cold.

"It is a bargain, Miss Molly," Diarmuid declared.

A spark of green light burst from their joined hands. Molly let out a yelp and sprang backward.

"What was that?"

"I…" Diarmuid stared down at his hand, but as far as Molly could tell, it was as incorporeal as the rest of him. "I fear I may have bound us together in some fashion."

Molly gaped at him for several seconds before finding her voice. "I can think of worse fates."

Truly, if she had to be bound to someone, she was glad it was the one friend she'd had in years.

"Aye." Diarmuid looked up and down his translucent body. "Worse fates indeed."

4

Imbolc, February 2

The ormolu clock on the library mantelpiece struck midnight. For the first time in seventeen years, a fire crackled and danced in the fireplace. Molly spun in a circle, her swirling red dress mimicking the cheerful flames. Utterly enchanting.

Diarmuid's chest ached where a beating heart had once been. He'd wondered if his initial infatuation might fade as he grew accustomed to her presence. But, no. Three months with her had only solidified the feelings, until they were more substantial than he was. He loved her. Irrevocably.

"We did it!" Molly cheered. "It took me forever, but with your help I did it!" Her twirl came to an abrupt stop. "Oh, I'm sorry. I probably shouldn't exaggerate that way. It's insensitive to your situation."

If he'd been alive, Diarmuid's heart might have burst. This was why he loved her. Not only was she joyful and adorable and a good listener, but she truly cared about the feelings of others. She did all she could to make him happy, despite his strange semi-life. She even treated her ornery cook kindly, despite the woman's disagreeable temper and rude comments on Molly's mostly-nocturnal schedule.

"You're wonderfully sweet." Diarmuid gave her his best roguish grin. The one that lately had been making her blush. He may have started overusing it in the last few weeks. "But you needn't fear words like 'forever.' I can cope. Besides, now that our library is spotless, we can begin our search for information in earnest."

He'd been trying to maintain a realistic perspective, but now every time he looked at Molly a spark of hope jolted through him. If they could find answers…

No. No, he needed to be calm. He would try, but he would not let himself become carried away with fruitless dreaming.

"I can look through the moldy books," Molly declared. The blush on her cheeks was pure perfection. Rosy and radiant, especially when paired with her delightful smile. "I won't like it, but I'm confident I can do it."

Diarmuid glanced at the pile of damaged books, stacked and ready to be carted away. Molly had stacked them herself. She called her progress slow, but he had nothing but admiration for her. She'd come so far. They could take walks through the dirty parts of the castle together now, and she wouldn't panic. When she cleaned, she could go for hours without stopping to wash. Every day she grew stronger.

And on days when strength was harder to come by, she was learning to give herself grace to just be. To love herself as she was.

Yet one more reason for *him* to love her.

"But we should start with the rare books," Molly clarified. "We want to be certain none of them are useful to you before I sell them."

Diarmuid nodded. "They all belonged to my great-uncle. I can't imagine any of them would be of use. He liked mathematics, not folklore or the occult."

Molly shrugged. "Some of those mathematical formulas look so cryptic they could possibly be directions for an arcane ritual."

Diarmuid laughed—something that had become an almost daily occurrence. "A fair point. But since we'll never understand them either way, we may as well sell the books." He winked at her. "In all seriousness, they ought to bring you a tidy sum."

"I know!" She twirled again. "I'll be able to pay to have the rest of the castle cleaned. It's going to be so beautiful. And I can finally set up a proper workshop for making my soaps." She danced across the room to a shelf of curios and knickknacks, all dusted and polished. "And now when things get dusty, I can wipe them off without being afraid. Well, without being *completely* afraid."

If Diarmuid had been able to drink, he would have offered a champagne toast. "That's something worth celebrating."

Molly turned the small crank on the side of an ornate music box, then flipped the top open. A tiny ballerina inside began to spin as the notes of a waltz tinkled.

She held out a hand. "Dance with me."

Diarmuid swept her into his arms. If she wanted to dance, he would dance with her until he faded too much for her to hold. He'd always liked the waltz, and he'd particularly liked dancing it scandalously close with pretty ladies.

What a shallow fool he'd been in those long-ago days. He'd never considered that any dance might be his last. Or that he'd never touch another pretty lady again.

Until now.

If these phantom years had taught him anything, it was never to take a single moment for granted. He pressed his hand against Molly's back and pulled her body flush against his.

Molly gasped at the contact, but instead of flinching away, she shimmied even closer, her eyes sparking. "We are perfectly wicked!"

As one, they began to move to the music. Diarmuid would have sworn he could feel his heart thundering in his chest. Molly had progressed from tentative touches to comfortable touches to confident touches. But this… This was an eager touch. This was her wanting to touch him. Delighting in touching him.

Maybe he was no longer a ghost. Maybe he was in heaven.

Around and around they spun, from one end of the library to the other. The warmth of Molly's body poured into him, suffusing him with an energy beyond anything he remembered. He couldn't merely touch things tonight. If she asked him, he could move mountains.

The music box wound down, but they danced on while Molly hummed the tune. Diarmuid let his hand slip lower, settling on the small of her back, tantalizingly close to her lush arse. Cleaning the library had been a lesson in self-control, as he'd watched her bending over time and again to pick up books.

Thus far, he'd managed not to make any advances. He'd

valiantly kept to his side of the bed during those bright daylight hours when he slipped into a state of semi-sleep— even when she rolled close, as if she had an unconscious desire to snuggle. Only a good man deserved this remarkable woman, therefore Diarmuid was determined to live up to that ideal. Whether he could have her or not.

This dance, however, was pure temptation served on a silver platter. He could feel the soft curves of her body. Hear her gentle humming, and the musical peals of joyous laughter that occasionally interrupted it. He could smell the scent of the orange blossom soap she'd crafted herself in his—her—bath chamber. Taking his eyes off her beautiful face was an impossibility.

All he lacked was a taste.

A slight turn of his head. A subtle dip of his chin. That was all he needed. He wasn't much taller than her, so her mouth was already only inches away. How could he resist? How could he stop himself from pressing his lips to that tiny freckle on her cheek before sliding down to delve inside her?

Gods, he was a reprobate for even thinking it. He needed to stop. He needed to run far away until midnight was long past and touching her at all would take a concentrated effort.

They stumbled to a halt. Molly's right hand remained tight with his. Her left hand stroked down his shoulder to his chest. Their eyes locked.

Diarmuid's body froze in place. Her emerald gaze blazed hotter than the fire crackling nearby. The tip of her tongue swept along her lower lip, leaving a moist sheen. If it had been any other woman, he would have taken these as a sign she wanted to be kissed. But Molly had only recently adjusted to touching him. Kissing went far, far beyond anything she'd ever done. He would *not* be the source of anxiety for her.

"Diarmuid," she breathed.

"Molly." Her name came out almost as a groan. He dropped his chin so their foreheads pressed together. This would be enough. He would soak in the magic that had put her here, in his arms, at the midnight hour when he could hold her. "I want to kiss you."

Damnation. A few months and he'd gone from not speaking at all to speaking too much. At least now he'd scare her out of his grasp.

"Yes."

Diarmuid blinked. "Pardon?"

Her fingers clenched on his lapels, as if the suit he wore were actually made of more than air. "Kiss me. Please."

He was moving before his mind could fully process the words, his lips brushing over her cute little freckles, then claiming her mouth.

Some part of him remained rational enough to go slow, thank heavens. He needed to savor this. He needed to please her. This was the best thing to happen to him in all forty-five years of his existence, and he wanted Molly to love it every bit as much as he did.

He caressed her tenderly, keeping the pressure light as she adjusted to the feel and taste of him. When she didn't pull away, he pressed harder, sipping at her lips and even letting his tongue tease her with little light strokes.

She copied him. Dear God, she licked at him. Curiously. Playfully. When their tongues touched she jolted, but she didn't stop. Her tongue swept a full arc from one corner of his mouth to the other.

"Explore me," he panted, pausing only long enough to get the words out. "Taste me. Put your tongue… inside me."

Molly did as he asked, tentatively at first, then more boldly as he responded with noises of pleasure. The kiss deepened into something ravenous, almost desperate. In this moment he could truly believe she had been yearning for him as much as he'd longed for her.

They kissed and kissed, until nothing seemed to exist but this glorious sensation of coming together. He taught her his mouth, his sighs, his shivers, and learned from her in return. He drank every new gasp from her lips as if it were a divine elixir. As if he could become a part of her, or her of him.

"Eep!" Molly stumbled backward, her hands falling from his shoulders straight through his body. "Diarmuid, you're fading."

"A dhiabhail!"

He looked himself over. He was indeed fading, and faster than usual for this time of night—especially on a cross-quarter day.

"I, uh… I think perhaps I put so much effort into making that kiss as corporeal as possible that I over-exerted myself."

Now that he'd stopped, exhaustion set in. He guessed he could make it until dawn before being forced back into his room, but only if he avoided acting as if he were still mortal.

"I hope it was worthwhile for you?" Molly asked. Her cheeks turned bright red and her lashes lowered. "I thought it was rather wonderful."

"It absolutely was." He could wink out of existence right now and die happy. "And if you are amenable, I would like to practice until I can kiss you for hours."

She lifted a hand to his chest, her fingers sinking into him where his heart ought to be. "It would be my pleasure."

5

Beltane, May 1

"Diarmuid?"

Molly stopped beside the bed and placed a hand on his shoulder. He was more solid than usual this soon after sunset. The cross-quarter days were always special. First Samhain, when they'd met, and then Imbolc, when they'd shared their first extraordinary kiss. They'd kissed and hugged at midnight every day since, but it never lasted as long as either of them wanted. Perhaps today they would have time to linger.

She nudged him harder. "You should get up."

"Are you telling me I've been a slugabed?" he jested. "Or is today's task particularly time-consuming?"

A flush warmed Molly's cheeks. "You enjoy having something to do every day. Don't deny it."

He sat up, chuckling. "There was a reason this room was spotless when you arrived."

She touched a finger to the tip of his nose. She may as well take advantage of his semi-substantial state. In six months, touching him had gone from a challenge to a thrill to a daily need that brought her both joy and comfort.

"I greatly appreciated your attention to cleanliness." Molly stepped back, but kept her hand extended toward him. "I have something to show you. The workers found it in the wall while restoring the gas lighting in the Great Hall."

Diarmuid grasped her hand and rose to his feet. "A pirate's hidden cache of jewels? An ancient sword from the days when fae walked the land? Ah, wait! I know. The fragile remains of a prehistoric squirrel."

"Possibly better. Come. It's in the library with the books."

She didn't need to specify further. The two old journals were the most promising of anything they'd found during their months-long search. They'd been working to decipher the scribblings and arcane formulae written inside, with a growing sense of certainty that they would eventually learn *something* relevant.

Maybe that would be what made today special. Maybe her discovery would provide the final key needed.

Molly pulled Diarmuid after her, leading him down to the library, where the journals rested on the reading table, ribbons sticking out from pages they'd marked. A wooden box approximately four inches in every direction sat beside the two books.

"Our treasure," she announced, taking her customary seat at the table, and turning up the lamp.

Diarmuid slid into the seat beside her. "What is—" He gasped, then slowly traced a finger over the image carved in the center of the box. The inch-wide convex circle had been painted an iridescent green, bordered by a thin gilded ring. "The amulet," he breathed. "This must be the box it came from."

Molly bounced in her chair, her pulse leaping in excitement and trepidation. Could this truly be what Diarmuid needed to be free of his curse? And if so, what did that mean for her? For them?

Keep calm. One thing at a time.

"I couldn't determine how to open the box, but I think the symbols on the sides match what we found in the journals," she said. She opened the closest journal and flipped through the bookmarked pages until she found the one she wanted.

With shaking hands, Diarmuid lifted the box up for comparison. "They're identical. But what do they mean?" He turned the box over to view it from different angles.

Molly stared at the neat line of symbols inked on the page. Four different shapes, repeated in no obvious pattern, some written sideways or upside-down. The shape Diarmuid was examining matched the third shape in the row, and also the fifth, and…

"Oh! It's a puzzle box! These must be the directions for opening it!"

Diarmuid fumbled the box, his gaze darting to the journal. "Of course! Darling, you're brilliant!"

He gave her a quick kiss on the cheek. The cool brush of his lips sent a surge of heat through her. Midnight couldn't come soon enough. And maybe, with a bit of May Day luck, they would have an important discovery to celebrate.

Diarmuid set the box on the table, then tipped it over so the first symbol written in the journal was facing up. He made several false starts, as he learned the symbols and how to place them correctly.

Molly leaned closer, until her shoulder bumped his. "You'll have it this time. I can feel it."

He squared his shoulders and began again. One, two, three, four…

With every turn of the cube, her muscles tightened. Diarmuid worked methodically, his brow furrowed in concentration. Molly moved a finger across the page in time with his progress, helping him keep his place.

Almost there. Almost there.

Two turns left. One.

The box clicked, and the top popped open. Molly and Diarmuid both flinched, his elbow ramming into the fleshiest part of her upper arm.

After a moment's startled silence, she burst out laughing. "I think that would have hurt if you were any more corporeal."

He grinned. "You do always help me find the good in this ghost business." He dragged the box closer and peered inside. "Empty. Obviously. Keane walked off with the amulet. But there's writing on the inside."

Molly scooted so close she nearly ended up in Diarmuid's lap. The image brought a blush to her cheeks. Maybe if this inscription held good news, she'd do it. Sit in his lap and kiss him. Straddle him like the Lusty Shepherdess did in some of the illustrations she was not supposed to be looking at.

She shivered.

"I think this says, 'Beware.'" Diarmuid adjusted the lamp. "Something about light and the Otherworld. It's a bit worn, but I think it's warning against what Keane did to me."

Molly stiffened. "I would certainly hope so!"

"'Separate the essence from the body.' Well, there it is. I'm an essence." He turned the box to read the other side and a tremor ran through him. "Here," he whispered. "It says, 'A crack in the stone will…' something… 'the cycle.'"

"Break?" Molly suggested. "End?"

"It must be." He frowned at the box. "I don't understand this last part. I *think* it says a 'ship will sail beyond without an anchor'? What does that mean? Is the amulet the anchor? If I break it am I alive? Or… or dead?"

Diarmuid dropped the box and put his head in his hands. "I… I don't even know if this helps. I don't have the amulet, and if I did… What would you do? Isn't some life better than none? Or am I a fool for trying to cling to a world that isn't mine? God, why am I burdening you with this?"

His anguished tone caused an ache in her chest. Her poor, sweet Diarmuid. Molly wrapped an arm around him.

"This is progress. We know more. We will find a way to save you." Maybe she was lying, but right now she didn't care. He needed reassurance, and she was going to give it to him. He'd helped her so much, and now it was her turn.

Molly hopped up from her seat and tugged at Diarmuid's arm. "Come. Let's go upstairs. We can read together or play a game. When you've had time to adjust, we'll examine the box again. Maybe there's more in the journals that will make sense now. But first you need a distraction."

"Yes." He heaved a sigh. "I suppose I do."

Molly led Diarmuid up the stairs and set to work soothing him. She acted out scenes from a few of his favorite books, adding exaggerated character voices and mannerisms. When that drew nothing but a few short-lived smiles, she dragged him into the bathroom and put him to work testing stain removal with half-a-dozen new soap samples. She had enough quality product to start putting notices in the paper and taking orders by mail. Diarmuid had praised both the new scents and her first attempt at an advertisement, but his mood remained somber.

"Oh, for pity's sake!"

Diarmuid jumped. "Pardon?"

Molly stabbed a finger toward the bedroom. "Go sit on the bed. It's clear you're still brooding, and none of the usual sorts of pursuits will be of any help. I won't let you waste all our kissing time being melancholy. Which gives me only one option."

"Which is?"

She strode into the bedroom and over to the bookshelf, pointing again at the bed. "Sit."

As he settled himself on his usual side, Molly snatched

up the book she wanted and climbed onto the bed to kneel beside him.

With shaking hands, she opened the book to the first page. Heaven help her, did she even have the skills to make this work? And what would happen if she did? She sucked in a fortifying breath and took the plunge.

"The first time I tupped Fanny Cumming was in Farmer Ben's hayloft," she read.

Diarmuid jerked to attention. "Molly!"

"She'd become a woman since I'd seen her last," Molly continued, "with big, bouncy titties and a lush arse that every man in the village pictured when stroking his prick at night."

Her cheeks burned as hot as they ever had, but for once in her life, she didn't feel awkward because of it. She actually felt almost giddy, especially because Diarmuid's gaze was finally, *finally*, focused on her.

"There's a picture of Fanny's 'lush arse.' Do you want to see it? Or I could skip ahead to the hayloft where her skirts are pushed up and he's 'diddling her pearl' and 'frigging her quim.'"

The wicked words rolled off her tongue with surprising ease, a little jolt of pleasure spearing through her with each one. She—odd, scared Molly Hanover—had grown bold enough to say such things aloud. To say them in front of a man she admired. And to imagine herself in the place of the Lusty Shepherdess.

"Molly." This time, Diarmuid spoke her name in a low, harsh breath. "Molly, what are you doing?"

"Distracting you." She flipped ahead a few pages. "Ahem. So, 'I sucked her love juice from my fingers while I buried my cock inside her. My sweet little fuck-bird moaned as I—'"

"Enough," Diarmuid gasped. "Good God, Molly, you'll kill me if you keep this up."

She lowered the book. A pink flush covered his face and neck, making his translucent body appear almost fully human.

"Do you have any idea how you look when you say those things? It makes me want to…"

She followed his gaze down to where his trousers bulged in a fashion she'd never seen before, but knew well from reading about Fanny and her beau.

"So ghosts can do that." A new pulse of arousal shuddered through her, adding to the gathering wetness between her legs.

"I appear however I imagine myself," Diarmuid admitted.

"So if you imagine yourself naked—"

The instant she spoke the word, his clothing vanished, as if it had never existed. He sat fully nude before her, flushed down to his chest, his erection standing out proudly from a thatch of dark curls.

He grabbed for a pillow to hide himself, but she swatted it away. "Don't you dare. I want this. I want *you*."

Molly yanked at the buttons of her shirtwaist, thankful she preferred simple fashions. Even this modest outfit had too many layers for her liking. She stripped them away, one-by-one, while Diarmuid watched in open-mouthed admiration.

No brooding now. He's only thinking of me. Nothing but me.

Never had she felt so powerful, so wholly in control of herself and her life. She would have no shame in her nakedness, no shame in her behavior. Tonight was hers for the taking. Diarmuid was hers.

When the last of her clothing slid to the floor, she flipped through *The Lusty Shepherdess* to her favorite illustration and turned it toward Diarmuid. In the drawing, Fanny sat naked astride her lover, an expression of bliss on her face.

"I want this. Can we do this?"

Diarmuid barely glanced at the book before turning his attention on Molly, looking her over from head to toe and back again.

"Christ, Mol, you're so beautiful. I don't know if I can do it or not, but I'm damned well going to try."

Molly scrambled atop him, straddling his thighs and kissing him as hungrily as she ever had. They'd learned one another well over the last few months. She knew precisely how hard to nip his lower lip to make him groan. He knew she liked it when he threaded his fingers through her hair and sent pins flying everywhere.

Tonight, though, her body had new sensations to learn. New places that ached for Diarmuid's touch. His chest was hard against her soft breasts, his skin several degrees colder than her own. Molly rubbed her taut nipples against him, sighing her pleasure at the gentle abrasion.

Diarmuid smothered the sound with his mouth and dragged her closer still, until she could feel his cock, cool and hard as steel.

"Oh, fuck, Molly," he moaned, his fingers tightening on her hips until it pinched. "You feel like paradise."

She rocked atop him, adjusting her position until the friction against her clit made her gasp. His cock pulsed, growing harder while the rest of his body turned more transparent.

"Yes, more." She increased her tempo, pushing herself closer to release, reveling in every new experience.

Yes. Yes.

Heavens, how she loved this. She loved that he was cold

where she was hot. She loved the way his caresses alternated between a ghostly breeze and a firm, human stroke. Most of all, she loved that he seemed unable to control the solidity of his body. She was driving him wild, and her entire being gloried in it.

"Inside me," she gasped. "Please. I want you."

"Molly." He flexed his hips. "God, Molly."

"Diarmuid. Please."

She lifted up, then sank slowly down as he guided himself into her. The fit was tight, his thick length stretching her, sending bursts of both pleasure and pain straight up her spine. Diarmuid let out an incoherent groan, his grip tightening.

Molly began to ride him, slowly at first, as she experimented with angle and pressure. Soon she found a rhythm, driving the tension inside her higher and higher. She placed both hands on Diarmuid's chest to brace herself, moving faster, harder, pressing down into each of his upward thrusts.

"Mol," he choked. His face had gone nearly transparent, and her hands began to sink into his chest, but his fingers on her hips and his cock inside her were as corporeal as she was.

The mantel clock began to chime midnight.

Close. So close. Faster, faster, harder, harder. Please, please, ple—

The world trembled. Waves of bliss cascaded over her, wringing noises from her throat she hadn't known possible. Diarmuid thrust again and again, every movement prolonging the torrent. He cried out, joining her shuddering climax until they both collapsed in a tangled heap.

Molly pulled a blanket up over them. She snuggled close to him, brushing her hands gently over his body as it slowly evened out into its usual semi-corporeal state.

"That," he gasped, "was the most incredible thing I've ever felt. I will remember this night forever."

"So will I," she vowed. "It was perfect. Absolutely perfect."

He kissed her and stroked her hair. "My sweet Molly. My sweet, beautiful, brave, glorious Molly. I love you more than anything in the world. More than life."

She returned his kiss with one of her own. Soft and sweet. "I love you too. So very much."

And I promise, I will do everything in my power to give you back the life you deserve. Whatever it takes.

6

Lughnasadh, August 1

Diarmuid raced down the stairs, the delightful thuds of his footsteps ringing in his ears. What a perfect way to begin his night. Lugh had designated this a day of athletic competition, after all. Honoring him with a run down to the Great Hall was only proper.

Of course, the gods probably knew Diarmuid's true reason for rushing. He was eager to see Molly, who hadn't yet returned from breaking her fast. Lugh wouldn't mind. Today was also a day for oaths and contracts. A good day to propose marriage.

If he were human, he'd already be on one knee, begging for the honor of her hand. Since he wasn't, he planned to offer her another night of rapturous lovemaking.

You shouldn't. She deserves better. She deserves more.

For three long months, he'd been reciting those words— trying to make himself remember all the reasons she wasn't meant to be his. He couldn't make love to her every night.

He couldn't give her children or grow old with her. Hell, he couldn't even leave the bloody castle!

Molly deserved someone who could give her a full, human life. He needed to let her go.

Someday he would. But not tonight. Tonight he would hold her and kiss her and feel the glorious heat of her body. He would watch her surrender to passion and he would find himself when he lost control inside her.

Diarmuid bounded down the last flight of stairs and jogged over to where Molly sat at the new—and much less ostentatious—dining table. She looked up when he approached, but without her usual smile. Instead, she looked uncertain, almost anxious. The day's mail sat in a tidy pile beside her empty plate, with the exception of a single sheet of paper she held clutched in her hand.

"Bad news?" He brushed a finger along her arm, but she didn't lean into his touch the way she usually did.

"I'm not sure."

Not sure? Diarmuid rubbed his temple. Probably not a notice of a death in the family, then. Perhaps some news of strife or unrest elsewhere. What, he couldn't imagine. The wide world seemed almost a dream.

Molly smoothed her paper out on the table. "It's a letter from my father. He writes that he is most pleased with the restoration work I have done to the castle." She made a soft noise of displeasure. "He doesn't say how he knows, but he uses phrases like, 'the reports I received,' which make it clear he has someone spying on me. I suppose I should have replaced the cook. She's a terror, but her food is good."

Diarmuid grabbed a chair and took a seat beside her. "So your father is a bit of a twat. But he is proud of your accomplishments."

"There's more. He says now that the castle is usable, he

wishes to host an event. In particular, he means to hold a full night of festivities beginning on All Hallow's Eve."

Diarmuid flinched so hard his chair banged against the table leg. "He means to fill this house with strangers? On Samhain?"

No. Absolutely not. Not during Samhain. That was his night. The one time a year he had from dusk 'til dawn to feel alive. The night he would have the most time with Molly.

Let her go. Do it now. Then she can attend this party and find herself a nice human *man.*

"Ow!" He glanced down to see that he'd clenched his fists so hard his nails had dug into his palms. And all of his body except his hands had faded.

"I'm angry too," Molly sighed. "It'll be the anniversary of the day we met and should be our night."

Diarmuid's chest tightened. How the devil was he supposed to give her up when she had plans to do things like celebrate anniversaries?

"But there's even more," she continued. She began to read from the paper. "Not only is All Hallow's Night a traditional festive occasion, but the final plans for the new railroad will be complete by then, and the castle will provide the perfect location to celebrate the new deal. To that end, I will be inviting my partner in this venture, Mr. Keane, to join us."

Diarmuid's chair went flying as he sprang to his feet. "Keane?"

"I'm certain he will be pleased with what you have done with his former property," Molly finished. She set the letter down and rose. "There can be no doubt he's speaking of your villainous cousin." She thumped a fist on the table. "I hope Mr. Keane does come here. I want to thrash him."

"Keane?" Diarmuid could hardly get the name out. "Here?"

"I know." Molly rubbed her temple, much the way he'd done not long ago. Gods, were they picking up each other's mannerisms now? "I'm furious. And hopeful. What if he brings the amulet? We can confront him. Maybe this is the chance you've been waiting for."

"Or maybe this will be the end of me." He groped for his chair, remembered he'd upended it, and half-slumped against the table instead.

Keane. The money-grubbing backstabber. If he came within ten yards of Molly, Diarmuid would rip the bastard's heart out.

Once again, his fingers began to solidify as they curled.

Molly's hand on his cheek brought his body back under control. "Forget him for tonight, my love. We have time. We can prepare. We will get you that amulet. Don't let him take tonight from us. We deserve to enjoy every moment we have together."

Diarmuid wrapped her in his arms, despite the warnings clanging in his mind. Later, he could determine how to do the proper thing. Right now he needed her. He needed them, together.

Their lovemaking was hard and fast and desperate, as if their souls knew time was running short. Afterward, Diarmuid lay clinging to his beloved, drawing in heaving breaths he didn't need. He wasn't letting go.

He would have held her for the entirety of the next three months, if such a thing were possible. Because he knew in his soul that when the clock tolled midnight on November the first, the life he'd known for eighteen years would end—one way or another.

7

Samhain

"There are so many people."

Molly's stomach churned as she stared down into the Great Hall from the shadows at the top of the staircase. So many people, so close together. The quiet life of the past year had pushed this particular fear into a distant memory. She'd nearly forgotten how strong the discomfort could be.

Diarmuid's lips brushed her neck. "You can do this. It's no different than the dirty rooms. Better, perhaps. You don't need to touch any of these interlopers."

She leaned back into his embrace. No matter what she faced, she would do it with a stalwart companion. And she *would* do it. For him.

She'd had no choice but to allow the event. The property had been bought in her name, using her dowry, but with her father as the party legally responsible for all decisions. If he wanted to build a railroad with Mr. Keane, he could. The only way out Molly could see was to expose Keane for the murderous bastard he was. And in doing so, to free Diarmuid from his spectral curse.

She squared her shoulders. "Let's do it, then."

Diarmuid kissed her again. "Whenever you're ready. Unless you decide you prefer to return to bed and make love for the rest of the night."

Tempting. Highly tempting. "If you make love to me any longer or any more thoroughly, I'll hardly be able to walk, let alone dance. I'm already a bit unsteady."

He chuckled. "Then I suppose we'd best dance while we can."

"Exactly." Molly's gaze swept over the boisterous crowd

below. Couples spun together to an old Irish tune. Laughter and merry voices wove around and through the strains of music, lifting to the high ceiling. Around the massive stone hearth, guests raised glasses and snacked on toasted fruit and nuts. "Besides, I won't let a group of strangers deprive me of a Samhain festival. I deserve a bonfire and apples and a hearty drink."

Diarmuid released her and stepped away. "Yes. You deserve that and more."

His voice had become grim. Molly gave him her best smile. It couldn't be easy for him, knowing his cousin was here somewhere. She would be his strength, as he was hers.

"Come. Let's dance."

They linked arms and descended toward the throng as if approaching a pit of poisonous vipers. Diarmuid's posture was rigid, his mouth pinched in a tight line. Molly's grip on his arm grew tighter with every step.

"Breathe," she whispered.

"I don't expect it to have much effect, but I'll try."

She let out a nervous giggle. "Not you, silly."

"Silly is preferable to anxious."

Molly glanced at him, and his mouth hitched up into a smile. It was all the encouragement she needed. She hurried him down the last few stairs and into the group of dancers set to begin a waltz. Their hands clasped and their bodies came together in the now-familiar position.

Molly's feet moved automatically in time to the lilt of the tune, easing away her apprehension. The hall faded to a background blur. Nothing mattered but the comforting sway of their bodies and the gleam of love in Diarmuid's eyes. Here on a Samhain night, they sparkled as blue as they must have been in his corporeal life.

I will set you free. I won't let this castle be your eternal prison. Even if it sends you to the Otherworld where I can't follow.

She could feel that Otherworld tonight. It seeped in with the cold wind through the chinks in the stone walls. It danced in the crackles of the fire and lingered in the scent of apples and spices. Revelers in costume wafted through the room, touched by the spirits they meant to ward off. This dark, magical November morn would be her time.

Molly surveyed the room as the dance continued. She didn't know what Mr. Keane looked like, but she could find her father. He could make the introduction and bring her to the amulet. It was here. Somewhere.

As her gaze meandered past face after face, Molly began to notice frowns, stares, and even a lone finger pointing. Her ears pricked up to catch murmurs above the music.

"…Mad?"

"Faerie magic?"

"Who are you…?"

"…Dancing alone…"

"…Don't see…"

Molly pressed closer to Diarmuid. "I don't think everyone can see you," she whispered.

The murmurs were growing louder, and some of the dancers had slowed or moved away from them.

"She's off her head!" a man declared, loud enough for dozens to hear.

"I beg your pardon!"

Molly stumbled at the sound of her father's voice, and might have fallen if Diarmuid hadn't clutched her to his chest.

"That's my daughter you speak so rudely of," her father went on. "And you've clearly had one too many. She's dancing with that tall, dark-haired fellow."

"What dark-haired fellow?" the rude man demanded.

Molly tugged Diarmuid toward her father. "Papa can see you, even if not everyone can. This is our chance. We can find Keane. If he can't see you, snatching the amulet will be easy."

Diarmuid held back. "Wait, Molly, I'm not certain…"

Whatever his objection, it was rendered irrelevant when her father came striding toward them. "Molly, what a nice surprise to see you dancing." His tone was jovial, but a deep furrow in his brow suggested confusion. "You must introduce me to your friend."

"O-of course," Molly stammered. The music had stopped and suddenly it felt as if the whole room were watching her, the crowd pressing closer and closer. "Papa, this is… Mr. Burke. He, um… lives in the area."

"Burke, eh? I think Keane said he had Burke cousins." Her father turned around. "Keane! Come over and meet…"

Diarmuid's grip tightened on Molly's hand, and all color drained from his face. Molly caught a flash of the people behind him as he went partially transparent.

"I'm here. I have you."

"Molly." A shudder ran through him. "I can't. I can't let him see you. If he knows that you know…" He pulled on her hand, trying to flee, but the crowd was too thick, and he bumped into a woman, sending her mug flying and spraying hot spiced cider over half-a-dozen onlookers.

Shouts rose up, some calling out Diarmuid's clumsiness, others blaming the woman. Eyes everywhere had turned from the crackling fire and the fortune-tellers to stare. Molly's heart hammered. They were the center of attention and there was no escape. She glanced back at her father. Was that balding man behind him Keane?

The crowd grew thicker, bodies moving in for a better

look. This was it. Her confrontation. Could she do it in the center of this mass of humanity, with her palms sweating and her throat tightening?

Breathe. Breathe.

"Molly, please." Diarmuid tried to pull her toward the stairs. "Forget him. Forget this. Leave me as I am."

"No." Her voice trembled, but she didn't care. She would not let him condemn himself to a hopeless eternity out of concern for her. "Mr. Keane!" she called out. "I believe you may be acquainted with my friend, Mr. Diarmuid Burke?"

Diarmuid stepped in front of her, adopting a protective stance. The dear, foolish man. He was certainly determined. But then, so was she. She slipped around to stand at his side.

Keane approached slowly, his gaze darting between her and Diarmuid. "W-who are you? What is this?"

Diarmuid took a single menacing step forward. "Don't you recognize me, cousin?"

Keane's eyes locked on Molly, and he pointed an unsteady finger at Diarmuid. "What *is* that thing?"

"Keane?" Molly's father clapped a hand on the other man's shoulder. "Is there some trouble?"

"T-that shadow thing..." Keane forced out, still gesturing at Diarmuid.

Her father frowned. "I see my daughter and a young man. What was in that cider this evening? I swear, all this talk about faeries and spirits is making me think I should have picked a different holiday for this party."

Diarmuid took another step. Molly moved with him, and he gave her a grim nod.

Together.

"I believe you have something that belongs to me, cousin." Diarmuid's voice was as hollow and ghostly as Molly had ever heard.

"You're dead." Keane turned a glare on Molly. "This is a trick. Get away from me, you witch!"

"That is my daughter!" Her father grabbed Keane by the arm, and Molly saw her chance.

She lunged at Keane, grabbing for his shirt collar and yanking. The studs popped, and the starched linen came off in her hand, exposing the neckline of his shirt and a thin gold chain. Molly's other hand was already moving, scrabbling to pull the amulet free.

Keane jerked away just as she worked the amulet loose from his shirt. The chain snapped, and the pendant tumbled to the floor.

Molly and Keane both dove for it, but before either of them could snatch it up, a booted foot stomped down atop it.

Diarmuid.

He dragged the amulet out of Keane's reach, then bent to retrieve it. The moment his hand closed over the stone, his entire body lit up with an eerie green light.

The crowd gave a collective gasp.

Molly scrambled to her feet. She grasped Diarmuid's arm, finding him as solid as before. "Break it, Diarmuid. Break the amulet. Free yourself."

He stared down at the glowing talisman, then snapped his head up to look at Molly. "I can't. I can't leave you. I'm sorry. I'm so, so selfish."

"You vile wraith!" Keane, who had regained his footing, made a grab for the amulet, but Diarmuid retained the reflexes of a younger man and easily sidestepped his cousin. "That is mine!"

"The amulet belongs to me," Diarmuid retorted. "This castle belongs to me. You stole it."

"Begone evil spirit!" Keane glanced around, looking to the others in the room for support. "Return to the land of the dead from whence you came! Remove your unholy presence from our sight!"

Diarmuid sniffed. He turned the amulet over in his hands. "If I'm dead, then you're a not only a thief, but a murderer. Don't expect any help from the people here. They can all see what a slimy coward you are."

Keane's face turned scarlet. "I'll kill you for good this time, you bastard!"

As Keane lunged for Diarmuid's throat, Molly went for the amulet. The instant she freed it from Diarmuid's hand, the green glow disappeared. Keane toppled straight through Diarmuid into a stunned onlooker.

Clutching her prize, Molly tore through the room, shoving people aside. Tingles of discomfort pricked her hands, growing stronger with every stranger she touched. She bit her lip and kept going, fighting through the throng until she reached the hearth.

"You foolish girl!" Keane shouted. "You don't know what you're doing!"

Molly squeezed the amulet, then hurled it into the blazing fire. "Yes. I do."

For several seconds, nothing happened. The entire room stood silent. Not a movement. Not a breath.

Pop!

Molly sprang back when a green spark burst from the flames.

Pop! Pop! Pop!

Sparks flew, this way and that, until, with an earsplitting crack, the amulet shattered into a thousand tiny pieces.

Diarmuid screamed.

Molly ran to him, the crowd now parting to make way for her. He lay crumpled on the ground, his body twitching and pulsing with green light. Nearby, Keane had fallen to his knees, gasping and clutching his chest where the amulet had once hung.

"I'm here." Molly dropped to Diarmuid's side. She lay her head on his chest and wrapped an arm around him, squeezing him tight. "I have you, dearest."

"Love. You," he gritted out between tremors. "Always. Love…"

"Shh." Her fingers trailed up and down his body, soft and soothing. "I'm here. I love you. I won't let go."

Molly stroked the cool skin of his neck. Caressed his cheek, brushing away a dry tear. Traced the lips she so loved to kiss.

The flashes of green began to fade, each shudder of Diarmuid's body becoming less violent. Molly held him through it all, whispering her love, blinking back tears.

The trembling stopped. Diarmuid lay still beneath her. Deathly still. Deathly quiet.

The world blurred. Sounds filtered in as if her ears were covered. Were those voices murmuring in the background? The swish of a skirt or the squeak of a shoe? Everything was so distant, so muffled.

Everything but a rhythmic *ba-bump, ba-bump* beneath her ear.

Ba-bump. Ba-bump. Ba-bump.

A heartbeat. A real, steady, strong, *human* heartbeat.

"Diarmuid!"

Molly sat up abruptly. His pale cheeks glowed with a warmth she'd never seen before. His chest rose and fell in even breaths. His eyelids began to flutter, and when she gasped his name again, eyes blue as the sky opened to gaze lovingly up at her.

"You're alive." She fell back atop him, hugging him and letting her tears flow. "Thank the spirits, you're alive."

"Alive." He shifted beneath her, and lifted a hand to stroke her hair. "You. You were my anchor. My bond to this world. My life. My heart. My love."

Molly helped him to a seated position and pressed a quick kiss to his lips, not caring how many people were watching, or even what her father might think. Diarmuid was alive, and nothing could take away her joy.

"You won't win," a raspy voice insisted.

Molly looked at Keane, who still knelt on the floor nearby. His face was ashen, his brow sweaty, and she feared he might cast up his accounts at any second.

"You can't stop me," he wheezed. "My railroad will go through this land, no matter what you do."

"I'm sorry, Mr. Keane." Molly gave him a pitying smile. "This property belongs to me. It's my dowry. My father does have charge of it, but I believe when I marry that right will fall to my husband. Is that correct, Papa?"

Her father came to stand beside her. "Yes, Molly, that was a part of the arrangement, but I didn't think you would ever…"

Molly linked her arm through Diarmuid's. "Papa, please meet my fiancé, Mr. Diarmuid Burke. We intend to marry as soon as possible."

"Your daughter is a treasure, sir," Diarmuid added without hesitation. "I am overjoyed she has consented to be my wife. I'm sorry we must discontinue your project with Mr. Keane, but we have other plans for my family's ancestral lands." He rose to his feet and gave Molly a hand up.

"You bastard! You can't do this to me!" Keane shouted, then doubled over in a fit of coughing.

"I'm afraid, Mr. Keane," her father said, "your deplorable behavior tonight has me rethinking our agreement. As I have a family wedding to plan, I will not have time to discuss the matter. My solicitor will send you the termination papers. I suggest you accept my escort off the premises and do not return." He turned to address the party guests. "The bonfire is still going and the drinks are flowing. Let us feast and welcome a prosperous winter!"

The revelers blinked back at him for a moment, until one brave soul lifted a glass and cried, "Huzzah!"

The festival roared to life. Musicians struck up a tune, men and women flocked to have their fortunes told, and servants hurried in with more food and drink.

Diarmuid led Molly to the stairs, tipping his head close to whisper. "Thank you, my love. You did what I was too weak to do. What I feared to do. And it saved me. It gave us the chance for a life together. I can never thank you enough."

Molly gave him a playful nudge. "Yes you can. And you can start by taking me away from this horrible party so I might relax with a nice, hot bath."

"May I join you?"

"I would like nothing better."

✦

When Brid the High One peeked through the window to mark the Samhain dawn, she spied the lovers snuggled together, heartbeat-to-heartbeat. Aengus had done well by these two. No coming darkness or bleak winter would dampen the blazing warmth of such a love.

Brid smiled at her fae-touched brethren, and slipped away in the warmth of the rising sun.

My Heiress, 'Tis of Thee

My Heiress, 'Tis of Thee

A 1904 World's Fair Romance

Sometimes all love needs is a different perspective.

Three months have passed since magazine owner Graham Ward received a letter from the love of his life, telling him everything was over. Desperate to take his mind off his heartbreak, he travels to St. Louis for the 1904 World's Fair, only to discover he's not the only one intent on getting away.

Knickerbocker heiress Lillian Belmont can't understand why Graham never responded to her coded message asking him to elope. To ease her aching heart, she's thrown herself into her photography, hoping to sell her World's Fair images and make a name for herself.

When Lillian and Graham cross paths, they discover the spark between them is as hot as ever. The fair is in full swing, a rival photographer is making mischief, and high-flying adventure awaits. But none of it can quash the passion between them, or prevent their yearning for a second chance at love.

One - Framing the Scene

St. Louis, Missouri
June 30, 1904

Graham Ward hadn't thought about Lillian Belmont all day. He hadn't thought of her at breakfast when he'd spied a woman in the dining car with her exact shade of sandy-brown hair. He hadn't thought of her that afternoon, when he'd watched the countryside roll by and recalled the plans they'd once made to see the entire U. S. of A. by train. And he certainly wasn't thinking of her now, as he walked the bustling streets of the Louisiana Purchase Exposition, surrounded by lights and music and a world that sparkled with all the gaiety of her exuberant spirit.

Graham flashed his press credentials and passed through the massive decorative archway into the Old St. Louis exhibit. This recreation of the early days of the city suited his purposes perfectly. Nothing here to remind him of home. No skyscrapers towering above him, no opulent mansions flaunting obscene wealth, no winding park paths clogged with bicycle riders and strolling families. Nothing of New York. Nothing of her.

He wandered into the exhibit and entered one of the smaller buildings. The wooden construction with low doors and ceiling was exactly what he would have imagined for a fur-trading town from one hundred forty years ago. This particular structure was a candle shop, the air heavy with the scent of molten wax. Flickering lanterns illuminated the modern fairgoers, who admired the tapers hanging from the ceiling and mulled over the purchase of yet another souvenir. Graham wasn't buying. He was here for research and nothing else.

He pulled out a notepad and pencil. The history of St. Louis might make a good article for the magazine. Give people a bit of context. How the city came to be could lead into how the Exposition came to be. It would also be equally interesting to those who had already been to the fair and those who would attend in the months to come. He'd wire Jeannie about the idea in the morning. Ultimately, those sorts of decisions were up to her.

"Are these colors true to the period, or are you using modern dyes?" a cheery, feminine voice inquired.

Graham's pencil poked clear through the paper. *No.* No, it wasn't possible.

"It's not important for the photographs, of course," the voice continued. "But I *am* curious."

Of course she was curious. Lil lived for adventure and discovery. It was one of the reasons he'd fallen for her in the first place. And the reason he wasn't good enough.

It's not her. You're tired from travel. Running on too little sleep. You should've gone to bed instead of wandering the fair.

Graham forced himself to turn around and face the too-familiar voice. One good look and he'd see he was mistaken—that it was an entirely different woman with a melodious voice and an interest in photography.

And then he could go back to not thinking about Lillian Belmont.

He came fully around and their eyes met. The perfect, sparkling, golden-brown eyes he'd gazed dreamily into not so very long ago were large and round with surprise. A fraction of a second later, they narrowed, shutting him out. The way she'd shut him out of her life three months prior.

Why? he wanted to scream.

Why had she cast him aside so easily? Had he really been nothing more than a lark to her? An adventure? He'd thought she'd felt as he did. But what did he know? He had a head for numbers and organization. Not for emotions.

"I'd like to take the photographs in the morning," Lillian continued her conversation. "That's when we will have the best sunlight coming through the window."

The candle shop woman nodded. "Miss Tieg will have the morning shift. I'll leave a note for her, so she'll be expecting you."

"Thank you." Lillian bid the woman good evening and headed for the door.

Graham followed. The magnetic pull she had on him hadn't diminished one iota in the time they'd been apart. She compelled him, and he obeyed. Reasons not to give in flittered somewhere nearby, but he couldn't grasp them.

"Lillian," he called, as she rushed away from him toward the exhibit exit. "Miss Belmont," he corrected. He had to talk to her. Had to know why she'd cast him out.

She slowed, stopped, then finally turned to face him. "Mr. Ward," she replied coolly.

"What are you doing here?" The question—already not the best of openings—came out in his usual gruff tone. There'd been a time when she would have teased him about that, but now she only glared. Glared with those perfect eyes, the mouth he'd once kissed so fervently compressed into a tight frown.

"What am *I* doing here?" she retorted. "I am embarking on my career as a photojournalist. As you ought to have known if you'd ever paid attention to my desires. The proper question is, what are *you* doing here?"

For a time, Graham remained stuck on her comment

about desires. He'd known her desires. He'd thrown himself wholeheartedly into fulfilling all her deepest desires.

"Well?" she demanded.

"I'm… researching," he managed. "For the magazine."

"You don't write for the magazine," Lillian pointed out.

"True."

"Nor do you make editorial decisions for the magazine."

Also true. "Yes, but I…" Graham composed himself. "We're putting out a special edition about the fair. We've never done a special edition before. It's important for the company and therefore important that I know what's going into it."

"You're a rotten liar, Graham." Even indignant as her tone was, the use of his given name sent a rush of heat through his veins. "Tell me why you're really here."

To get away from you.

He couldn't say that. To admit it would be to admit how deeply she'd wedged herself into his heart, and he wouldn't give her any more weapons to hurt him with.

"I told you," he grumbled.

Lil sniffed, the tiny, superior noise of disdain a stabbing reminder of her lofty upbringing. He would never belong in her world. Best to remember that.

"I suppose your reason hardly matters," she said. "The fairgrounds are quite large, are they not?"

"One thousand two hundred seventy-two acres," Graham replied, only belatedly realizing she had probably meant the question to be rhetorical.

"Precisely. With such an expanse and with thousands of visitors every day, I highly doubt we'll see one another again. Good evening." She pivoted smartly about and strode away.

Graham stared after her until she disappeared, then cursed under his breath.

Two - A Developing Situation

July 1

"I never should have said anything," Lily muttered. She adjusted her tripod and rechecked the angles.

What had Graham said? One thousand two hundred something acres? Plenty of space. So, naturally, she would repeatedly stumble into someone from home.

She resolutely turned her gaze away from where Mr. Ward stood chatting with a fashionably-dressed woman. He could chat with whomever he liked. Lily had moved on. She wouldn't let a little thing like heartbreak keep her from her dreams. She was here to enjoy the fair, take hundreds of photographs, and publish them in a major newspaper. No one would stop her. No pretty, dark eyes would sway her.

"Would you like any assistance focusing your camera?"

The condescending voice snapped Lily out of her reverie. She turned a pinched smile on the man who had spoken.

"No, thank you." She returned to her work. This location beside the Grand Basin offered the perfect view of the sunlight glinting off the Cascades fountains. The columns of Festival Hall behind made a majestic backdrop to the scene. Lily already had plans to return at night to capture the electric lights.

"Photography is such a lovely hobby," the man rambled on.

Lily captured the shot she wanted before answering him. "I'm a professional."

"Are you? So am I. I wonder if perhaps you might want a shot from the opposite side of that lamppost. I think it might make for a better composition."

Holding her smile made Lily's face hurt. This obnoxious

man wanted her spot. She'd found the best location and he knew it.

"No, thank you."

Lily carried on, ignoring the man's continued attempts to explain things she already knew, and probably better than he did. Between his arrogance and the fact that Graham Ward was standing not twenty feet away, happily chatting with another woman, Lily was having a terrible day. At least she had her photography.

And why was Graham waving his hands in such an animated fashion, anyway? He wasn't usually so demonstrative.

Maybe you never knew him the way you thought you did.

"Miss Lillian Belmont?"

Lily swung around, prepared to tell this new voice that he and Mr. Photography could both go to the devil, but any retort stuck in her throat when she beheld a familiar-looking face. She'd seen that curling gray moustache and those ice blue eyes at events in New York.

"Oliver Mainsbridge, New York Globe," he said, extending his hand.

Lily shook hands. "Mr. Mainsbridge, how lovely to see you."

"Likewise. I'm glad to find you here." He took a card from his pocket and scrawled something on it before handing it to her. "That's my direction while I'm here at the fair. I'd love to see those photos of yours after they're developed."

"Oh, are you looking for a photographer?" the obnoxious man cut in. "I'm Howard Strathmore of Strathmore Portraits."

Lily had had enough. "Mr. Strathmore, there are representatives from national publications all over this fair. Just there, for instance, is Mr. Ward, owner of Modern

Ladies' Monthly." She waved a hand in Graham's direction. "I'm sure you can find someone else to speak to instead of intruding on conversations to which you have not been invited. Good day."

"A woman's magazine?" Strathmore exclaimed. "I think not." He snatched up his camera and wandered away in a huff. Thank the Lord.

"Ah, that *is* young Ward, isn't it?" Mr. Mainsbridge observed. "I would wager he has a fine sum of money waiting to be spent on your photographs. Has he requested an exclusive contract?" He started toward Graham. "Ward! Good to see you. Oliver Mainsbridge, New York Globe."

Graham nodded a farewell to the woman he'd been speaking with and walked toward them. Lily bit her lip. Damn and blast. She did not want to talk to him. She didn't even want to *see* him. Looking at him brought back memories of all the things she'd sworn to forget. The way his brusque demeanor would give way to soft smiles when they were alone. His enthusiasm when she'd spoken of her career goals. The taste of his full lips. The heat of his skin.

The way he wooed another woman in our special place not two days after Uncle refused to let him marry me, she reminded herself.

Graham Ward was a liar and a mercenary.

Lily picked up her camera and joined the men, determined not to be rude. She would show him he no longer mattered to her.

"How are you, Mr. Mainsbridge?" Graham greeted the older man. He held himself in his customary stiff manner, his hands clasped behind him, as if he didn't know where else to put them.

"Fine, fine. Just asking Miss Belmont about her photographs. When I heard from old Belmont that she'd gone off to St. Louis, I knew I had to seek her out. I'm still impressed by those photos of the ice skaters in Central Park, you know? But I bet you got to her first, didn't you?" He dug his elbow playfully into Graham's ribs and chuckled. "Offering her an exclusive?"

Graham took a step backward. "Miss Belmont is free to sell her photographs where she wishes. Modern Ladies' Monthly would be happy to purchase some if she cares to submit them."

If she cared? What was that supposed to mean? He didn't honestly think she'd want anything to do with him and his magazine after the way he'd spurned her, did he? Or was he, too, playing at politeness for propriety's sake?

"Thank you, Mr. Ward," she replied. "I will consider all my offers, naturally."

"Planning to shoot the Independence Day festivities?" Mainsbridge asked. "Lots of music and parades, I hear."

"Absolutely," Lily answered. She had plans for the 4th. Grand plans that would elevate her above all the other fair photographers. Literally. And Graham Ward and his magazine weren't going to make a penny off her. "Now, if you gentlemen will excuse me, I need to continue to my next location while the lighting is still correct."

Lily turned away, determined not to dwell on the unpleasantness. She had a beautiful day for photography, Mr. Mainbridge's card in her pocket, and her Grand Plan.

Clutching her camera tight, she walked away, a true smile forming on her lips. No one could keep Lillian Belmont down for long.

Three - A Brief Exposure

July 2

Graham had given up. Since he couldn't actually stop thinking about Lillian, his new plan was to wander the fair thinking about her and being grumpy. He excelled at that. If he was grumpy enough, perhaps no one would speak to him again. Then he could mope as long as needed to get over her.

And if he didn't get over her… well, that was a problem for another day.

He'd selected the Palace of Transportation for today's excursion. The building was a marvel in itself, a gargantuan open space, with sixty-foot archways to allow trains to drive directly in. Acres of floor showcased historical vehicles and innovative technologies.

Lil would love this.

The thought caused an ache in his chest as he envisioned her smile of delight. She would bounce down the aisles, a buzzing counterpoint to his measured gait.

Graham gazed solemnly at one train car after another. He paused near a booth with stenciled letters proclaiming, "American Car Co." Made to look like a small private train compartment, the booth welcomed visitors inside for an up-close look. Photographs of the company's offerings hung on the back wall.

His heart lurched. It wasn't all that long ago that he'd been flipping eagerly through railroad advertisements, trying to find the perfect setting for a honeymoon.

Graham turned away from the painful reminder, only to be speared in the chest by the sight of a camera mounted on a tripod. Blue skirts fluttered behind it, and a head of light-brown hair bent over it.

He skittered backward. No, no, no. What had he been thinking? She loved trains. Of course she would come to photograph them. He should have chosen any other location. Lil was going to think he was following her, when in truth he simply seemed fated to stumble into her. He was drawn to the same things she was. Drawn to her, no matter what he did.

Graham took another step back. A second camera stood not far from Lillian's. Was that the same man he'd seen talking to her yesterday? Was the photographer following her? Or was he a friend? A lover?

God, please no.

Graham continued to back away, desperate to disappear into the crowd before Lillian caught sight of him. Something hard smacked against his legs. For an instant he hung in the air, on the cusp of regaining his balance. Then he toppled backward, right through the open window of the American Car Co. booth.

Something crunched beneath him. Several people cried out in alarm. His head smacked the floor.

"Graham!"

Lillian?

Graham stared up into the startled face of the American Car Co. representative. "Sir?" the man inquired, blinking owlishly from behind a large pair of spectacles.

"My head thanks you for the carpeted floor," Graham replied. Whatever he'd fallen on was jabbing him in the back. He hoped it wasn't anything irreplaceable.

"Graham!" Lillian's voice cut through the general clamor once again, this time bringing the rest of her with it. She forced her way into the booth to hover over him. "Are you hurt? Did you hit your head?"

Bits of murmured conversation began to filter through to Graham's brain.

"Is he ill?"

"Is he drunk?"

"I'm fine," Graham bit out. "Fine." He sat up, waving off an offer of help from the American Car Co. man. Graham climbed to his feet. A battered model train lay on the ground where he'd been. "I'll pay for that."

His eyes caught Lillian's. She stretched out a hand toward him, then snatched it back.

"You're certain you're not injured?" she asked.

"I'm fine," he repeated.

Fine except for the ache in his heart.

Why are you here? he wanted to demand. *Why are you acting as though you care?*

Did she care? Her nearness was fuel to a spark of hope he'd thought extinguished. She wasn't running. She wasn't leaving him.

Why, then? Why, if she cared, had she left him with that soul-crushing note, telling him it was over? He almost hadn't believed it was true, until she'd failed to arrive at their special bridge at the usual time. Day after day until he'd given up.

"Good," Lil said, her gaze breaking away from his. "Do try to be careful, Mr. Ward." She turned and left the booth.

"Lillian!" Graham reached into his pocket, grabbed whatever coins were there, and thrust them into the hands of the railroad company man. "Here."

He rushed from the booth after Lil. He had to know why. He had to understand why she'd left him. And if she wouldn't talk, at least he could explain that he hadn't been following her and had never intended to disrupt her photography.

Fate, once again, had different plans than his own.

Lillian's camera stood where she'd left it, but that other photographer had his hands all over it, fiddling with mechanisms Graham knew nothing about.

"I beg your pardon!" she exclaimed, but the expression of horror on her face spoke far harsher words. Ones she would not utter in public.

Rage exploded through Graham. He stalked toward the other man. "Get your filthy hands off of her property," he snarled.

The man took a step back before Graham could unleash a volley of less polite words. "I was merely making a few helpful adjustments," he argued, lifting his hands in feigned innocence.

"You were violating her personal property with no regard for her feelings or for common decency."

"I was being helpful," the man shot back. "And who are you to speak for her?"

I'm someone who knows what that camera means to her. Who's seen the care she takes with it and the pride she has in her work. I'm someone who once meant enough to her that she abandoned her beloved camera in order to make sure I wasn't hurt.

"A friend," Graham growled. "Get lost."

Lillian's hands went right to the camera, moving over every part, checking and rechecking. Graham glared at the other photographer until he departed.

"Horrible man," she muttered. "Thank goodness he didn't damage anything."

"Who is he?" Graham asked. "I saw him with you yesterday."

"Strathmore, he said his name was," she replied.

Her fingers ran over her equipment with loving strokes.

Graham's whole body tensed. She'd touched him that way once. Many times, in fact. He wanted to squash the memory, but it was lodged too deep in his mind. He'd never be free of her. Standing here beside her, he wondered why he'd ever wanted to be.

"He's jealous, I believe," Lillian went on. "I had the best location yesterday, and he tried to talk me out of it. Then Mr. Mainsbridge came to inquire about my photographs. I'm certain Strathmore was angry to see that I had interest from a major publication when he did not."

And she would only be receiving more interest. While Mainsbridge had been talking to her, Graham had been praising her work to Mrs. Paulson, a representative of another popular women's magazine. Papers around the country would follow when they saw what a talented eye Lil had.

"Do you think he's dangerous?" Graham asked.

Lillian's eyebrows rose. "Strathmore? I don't think so. But he's certainly a nuisance."

"Perhaps you might consider the company of an old friend? At least until you can be certain he's gone for good?" The words were out of Graham's mouth before he could reconsider.

She shook her head. "I don't need you to follow me."

"I'm worried he might mean you harm."

"Worried?" she scoffed. "You don't get to be worried about me. You lost that privilege when you left me."

Left her? What was she talking about? *She'd* done the leaving. He had the letter nestled in his pocket to prove it.

"You can't tell me not to worry, Lil. It doesn't work that way. I worry whether you like it or not."

Lillian lifted her chin and looked defiantly into his eyes. "Worrying is for people who actually care."

Why in hell was she acting like the wounded party? It made no sense. She was probably right that he shouldn't stay with her. Already her presence was muddling his head.

"Look," he sighed, "I don't want to be around you any more than you want to be around me."

Lies. He wanted to be near her. Closer than near. He wanted her in his arms, where he could feel the soft curves of her body and taste her sweet mouth. If he could, he would wrap himself all around her, bury himself within her, and never let her go.

"But I can't in good conscience walk away when someone is harassing you," he insisted. "Please. I promise to leave you to your work. I won't even speak, if you prefer. But allow me to see to your safety. For old time's sake."

She gazed at him a long time, her brow furrowed. "Very well," she acquiesced. "But this is temporary."

Graham nodded. He could handle temporary. As long as he had enough time to discover why she'd changed her mind about him. Once he knew that, surely, *surely*, he could put her behind him.

He wondered how long he could keep lying to himself.

Four - Maintaining Focus

July 3

Lily mopped her brow with her handkerchief. Even with her wide-brimmed hat, hours of photographing the people of the fair beneath the blazing summer sun was a hot, sticky business. She moved her camera back for a wider shot that would capture the entirety of the Great Floral Clock in front of the Palace of Agriculture. Graham picked up the heavy cases of photography equipment and moved them along with her.

He'd proven useful that way. It was nice to have someone

to help carry her nearly fifty pounds of equipment instead of hiring a local boy to do it, or towing it around herself on a little wagon.

Lily arranged the camera and focused on the scene before her. When a woman standing beside the clock stretched out a hand to point, Lily took the photo. Excellent. Candid, not posed. That was what she wanted. The real people of the real fair.

A new bead of sweat ran down the side of her face. "Let's head inside," she suggested. "We've been out here for an age."

"Forty-seven minutes, according to the giant clock," Graham specified.

Lillian nodded. She didn't think she'd ever met anyone quite as literal-minded as Graham Ward. Hyperbole was not in his nature.

Which made her wonder yet again how he'd managed to be so effusive in his declarations of love if he hadn't meant them. She'd been wondering all day, to be honest. His insistence on seeing to her safety and the way he'd taken to being her camera-toting servant with zero complaints were like the Graham she'd thought she'd known. It was not the behavior of the money-and-power-hungry man who had thrown her over for Rose Preston the moment he'd discovered he wouldn't get any money or connections from marrying Lily.

It didn't make sense. *He* didn't make sense. But Lily knew what she'd seen and heard. For three months she'd hardened her heart and prepared to get on with her life. Only to discover now that her heart wasn't nearly as icy as she'd believed.

Ask him. Ask him why he did that.

Maybe he had a reason. Maybe he'd misunderstood her

note—entirely possible—and had been lashing out due to a perceived betrayal. But revenge didn't seem like him, either.

Why did you leave me?

The words hovered on the tip of her tongue. But this wasn't the time. She had a job to do. The World's Fair would be the making of her career, and she could not neglect that. Her time here was limited. Her uncle didn't like her "gallivanting all over the country like a hoyden." And since he had control of her inheritance, she risked being cut off if she defied him too much for too long. The bulk of her photos needed to be complete before her big finale on July 4th.

Talking could come later. After sunset.

They lugged the equipment into the Palace of Agriculture, where Lily studied the light coming in through the windows.

"We'll start here in the dairy section," she decided. "Then hopefully I can get some photos of the Corn Palace."

"Can we visit the California exhibit?" Graham asked. "I hear there's a Wine Temple with 300 varieties, and I'm parched."

Lillian waved a hand. "That's a working dairy right there. Have a glass of milk." She set down her tripod and positioned her camera to capture the dairy. With the angle of the light slowly changing, it would hit exactly right in a few more minutes. All she needed to do was have her equipment set up in time.

Some minor adjustments, recheck the lighting, check the focus. There. Perfect. Lily took the shot, then removed the plate holder. She'd swap in another plate and get a second shot here.

As she was storing her exposed negative carefully in the box, a sudden commotion made her look up. Several nearby people sprang back in alarm.

"Watch out!" someone cried.

A wheel of cheese at least two feet in diameter rolled across the floor directly toward Lily. No, not her. Her camera. The massive round was headed straight for her tripod.

Letting out a cry of anguish, she leapt toward her equipment, knowing it would be too late to stop the collision. The tripod's wooden leg buckled on impact, sending splinters flying and the camera tumbling. Lily reacted on instinct. She dove to catch the precious apparatus, sheltering it with her own body, bracing for a crash.

She never hit the ground. Strong arms caught her, spinning her up into a protective embrace.

"Lillian," Graham gasped. "Are you all right? Is the camera—"

"Fine. We're fine."

She clutched the camera, heart racing. Graham's arms held her tight to his chest, the wool fabric of his vest pressing into her cheek. She caught a whiff of starch and soap. Dark, fathomless eyes stared down at her face, fixing on her mouth in the way she knew meant he wanted to kiss her.

"Lil," he breathed.

He was the only person who called her that. To others she was Lillian or Lily, but only Graham had ever called her Lil. It had been—still was—special. For him alone.

Kiss me. Kiss me, please.

His head lowered a mere fraction of an inch. Lily lifted her chin.

Yes. Kiss me.

"No!"

Her sudden exclamation startled Graham, and his grip on her faltered. She clung to the camera as she began to slip.

"Whoa." Graham recovered quickly, steadying Lily, then helping her to an upright position. "All right?" He released her, but hovered close, hands outstretched in case he needed to catch her again.

"Y-yes." Lily took a deep breath to compose herself. She was unhurt. Her camera was safe, though the remains of the tripod dangling from it were now only so much firewood. "Yes. Everything is fine."

Everything except for the desire raging unchecked throughout her body. Her skin prickled from the loss of his touch.

She forced herself to take a step back. No more touching. Certainly no kissing. They were in public. And he was... not the enemy, precisely. He'd hurt her badly, though, and she would take care not to be burned again.

"I'm sorry about your tripod," Graham said. "We'll find you a new one. For the rest of today, we'll have to find places where you can rest the camera atop something. I assume you want to keep going, despite the accident?" The slight edge to the word "accident" suggested he wasn't convinced it really was one.

"Yes, I do."

"I thought so." He set about gathering up the pieces of the ruined tripod, then latched and picked up her two equipment boxes. "Lead on, Miss Belmont."

Back to work. Lily led the way to her next planned shooting location, keeping a tight grip on the camera and an eye out for anything amiss. Focusing on her work and her surroundings almost kept her mind off Graham, off the feel of his arms and the eager kisses she so missed. But the longer she worked, the more she ached for him. Because this was the Graham she remembered. The man who was kind and helpful. Who loved to see her thrive. Who'd once promised they'd be partners in life, in exactly this way.

"We're nearing your golden hour," he said, hours later. "Where are we going for your final photographs of the day?"

Lily opened her mouth to reply, but the plans she'd made slipped from her mind as she gazed up at him. His expression was so open, so artless. So genuinely focused on her wants and needs. How could she ever have believed him capable of lies and deceit?

"Why did you leave me?" she asked.

Five - A Calculated Composition

Graham rubbed his temple. Sadly, the movement did nothing to relieve his confusion. Lillian blinked up at him, eyes wide. Christ, she looked so vulnerable. What on earth had he done to cause that? Because she clearly believed he'd done something. Damned if he knew what.

"I didn't leave you," he stated tersely. Best to be as straightforward as possible. Lay out all the facts and arrange them sensibly, the way he would do with company finances. "You left me. I have the note to prove it."

Lillian's shoulders slumped. "So it *was* the note. I tried my best, but Uncle took to opening every message I sent and received. I had to write in code."

Graham's fists clenched. "Code? You wrote a damned code? And expected me to... what? Just understand it?"

He blew out a long breath, then glanced around him. People streamed in and out of the Palace of Agriculture, but fortunately none of them appeared to have heard his outburst. This was not the place for this conversation.

"'Everything is over,' doesn't sound like a code to me," he said, his voice lower. The flash of anger he'd felt subsided into melancholy. "It sounds like a rejection."

"I tried to be as obvious as possible," Lillian replied. "I'm sorry. So sorry. I should have known it wouldn't work." Her wide-eyed, sorrowful look returned and her gaze turned from him. "But you couldn't have been so terribly upset, to be wooing *her* two days later."

"What? Who? I haven't courted anyone. I…" Once again, Graham scanned his surroundings. "Lil, we can't talk about this in public. Let's—"

"Miss Belmont?" a woman's voice called. "Oh, it is you. Thank goodness. I've been wandering that enormous building forever, it seems! Hello!"

Graham turned around. Mrs. Paulson came swishing in their direction, the feathers on her large hat waving as she walked.

"Good evening, Miss Belmont, I'm Mrs. Paulson, from the New York Women's Reader magazine. Do you have a moment to talk?" She waved a small card. "We can arrange another time if you're busy with Mr. Ward."

"No," Graham said at once. He stepped away from Lillian. "We were only chatting. Please, feel free to talk." He caught Lil's surprised expression and gave her a quick nod. "You're here to work and I know you have limited time. I don't want to interrupt that. Other matters can wait."

"But you and I will talk later?" Lil asked.

"I promise," he vowed.

Once again, Lillian's expression changed, this time into a smile so radiant Graham's breath caught in his throat. The intensity of her golden-eyed gaze set his heart to racing.

"Thank you." Her words were soft, but warmer than the July sun. And maybe even—dare he hope—suffused with love.

A new determination flared inside him. They would fix this problem between them. Settle whatever miscommunication had torn them apart. He would hold her again.

Graham tagged along while Lillian took a few final photographs of fairgoers enjoying George Ferris's Observation Wheel, then carted her equipment off to her hotel while the ladies went to dinner. He hoped the meeting would bring Lillian all the success she deserved.

Back in his own room, he finally took a moment to retrieve the note he'd been carrying tucked in his vest pocket. The paper was beginning to tear along the fold lines, but the words remained clear as day, in her neat handwriting.

Mr. Ward:

Let me be frank. Everything is over. This will be my final letter to you. So sorry if I hurt you, but you must understand. Even if you love me, it is not enough. Love is a fleeting, silly emotion. One we all grow out of in time. Please do not write me again. Especially not to beg me to run away with you.

-L

She'd called it some kind of code, but he couldn't see anything but what was on the page. The words stung, even now that he knew she hadn't meant them.

What *had* she meant?

He couldn't deny that the letter didn't sound like her. It was terse and awkward. And strange, especially the last line. He'd even thought it odd at the time he'd received it. He certainly hadn't wanted to believe it was the truth. So he'd continued going to their usual meeting place, hoping for an explanation. She'd never shown up.

"Why?" he asked aloud. "Why did you stay away? And who did you think I was wooing? Why would you think I wanted anyone but you?"

Tomorrow was the 4th. Lil would be busy all day with

work, and Graham was going to make damned sure neither Strathmore nor anyone else ruined that. But he *would* find an appropriate time to talk with her in private. Their separation was all a misunderstanding. One conversation, and they could clear everything up.

Graham tossed the note onto the dresser and flopped onto the bed. Closing his eyes, he relived the brief moment that afternoon when he'd had her in his arms. She'd been soft and warm. Her hair had smelled of flowers. And then her lips had parted. The way they always did when she wanted to be kissed. How many times had he seen that? Seen the hunger in her eyes to match his own? If they hadn't been in public, he might have had a taste of those lips again.

Graham unfastened his trousers to free his stiffening cock. He wrapped a hand around himself and stroked, picturing Lillian's glorious, naked body. Ever since he'd received that damned note, he hadn't allowed himself to think of her when he did this. Now, though, things were different. She still wanted him. Still loved him. They would be together again. Whatever it took.

His hand moved faster, and he thought about Lil in her favorite position: straddling him, her breasts bouncing as she slid up and down on his cock. Finding her own pleasure. Bringing herself to climax and carrying him along for the ride. Perfect, fun, feisty Lillian, making her life her own.

The orgasm came swiftly. Afterward, Graham lay gasping, staring up at the ceiling, wondering what the odds were that somewhere else in this very hotel tonight, she would be doing the same thing.

Six - Being Candid

July 4

Independence Day was in full swing at the Louisiana Purchase Exposition. All throughout the fairgrounds, marching bands and orchestras struck up patriotic tunes. Visitors waved tiny US flags. And the merchandisers had turned out all their best red, white, and blue products.

Lillian had chosen a bright blue dress with a red sash around her waist for the occasion. Equipment in tow, she moved through the fair snapping photos of adults and children laughing, smiling, and enjoying the sights. Today would be her big day. Her Grand Plan that would bring her photos national attention. Her own personal Independence Day.

With her career established, she could move out of her uncle's house. She could ignore his high-society associates and his elitist snobbery. She'd been born Lillian Belmont, Knickerbocker Princess. Today, she was proclaiming herself Lillian Belmont, Photojournalist.

And maybe, if Graham could explain himself satisfactorily, she could also stake claim to the title of loving wife to a man who would support her goals and dreams.

Thinking of such things made her pulse quicken and her palms sweat, so Lily fended off any fantasies by concentrating on work. If she allowed herself to grow too excited, she risked being hurt again, and she wouldn't stand for that on her day of triumph.

Graham was once again kind, helpful, and genuinely interested in her work. He toted her equipment here and there, helping whenever she asked. Occasionally, he jotted notes for his magazine. He didn't say much, but he listened, he watched, and he smiled.

Oh, how he smiled. When his mouth curved up at the corners and his eyes locked on her, desire coiled tight within her. She felt seen, admired, adored. This was the smile he'd given her in the days when she'd been certain they were meant to be.

Before she'd bungled everything with the note he hadn't understood. Prompting him to romance someone else. Maybe. Unless he had a twin brother she somehow hadn't known about.

"That's enough for now," she declared, closing up her case. "The rest of the plates are for the balloon race. We can ride the intramural railway to get to the Aeronautic Concourse."

"I expect there will be many photographers at the balloon race," Graham said. "What's your plan for upstaging them all?"

Lily grinned. "I can't tell you yet, but you'll see when we arrive on the concourse. It will be spectacular."

"I don't doubt it."

"Perhaps someone will be impressed enough to sponsor me for a longer stay. Right now I'm scheduled to leave on the sixth, but I would dearly love to extend my time here. There's so much more I want to cover."

Graham nodded, but said nothing. They both knew he could hire her to stay and photograph for his magazine. But it wouldn't be right, given the uncertainty between them. His restraint was another point in his favor.

"Tomorrow I will make certain to shoot the Philippine exhibit," Lily continued. "It bothers me, the way the people there were brought from a foreign land to be gawked at. It's not right. I don't want to photograph the exhibits as they're presented, but instead to show the people as they really are. So that others can understand. If I had my way, I would shoot the entire fair this way, showing the visitors, the workers, and all parts both good and bad. I want people to know it all, and to question it. That's how we'll learn and make the next fair even better for everyone."

Graham's adoring smile grew even wider, and Lily's knees went weak. "You've been sneaking out to meetings of that progressive society again, haven't you?" he teased.

Her cheeks heated, but she held her spine straight. "As often as I can."

He winked at her. "That's the Lil I know."

Lily swayed toward him, yearning for a kiss. Craving his strong embrace.

"We're going to talk soon, you and I," she declared. "Very soon. We'll talk about us, about everything. Clear the air once and for all."

And then I'll have that kiss.

She fidgeted the entire train ride, the restless energy inside her growing with every clack of the wheels. When the train at last arrived at the station, she bounded to the ground, camera held tight in her arms. The lush green grass of the Aeronautic Concourse spread out before her, dotted with colorful balloons that swayed in the slight breeze. Only her equipment stopped her from racing ahead.

"This way," she instructed Graham, bouncing as she walked. "My location is up ahead, at the east end of the concourse. Oh, Graham, I'm so excited! I can't wait to fly!"

"Fly?" His brows knit together. "You're going to fly?" His frown lessened. "Oh. Did you mean that in a metaphorical sense? Am I misunderstanding you again?"

"No, I'm truly flying. There." Lily pointed at a simple balloon about twenty yards ahead. "That's my ride. Everyone else will be photographing the balloon race from the ground. I will be photographing it from the air."

He gaped at her.

"And you're coming with me. We will have absolute privacy up in the balloon. We can have our talk while I take my photographs. Then tonight, we can go out to celebrate my triumph."

And maybe to celebrate the rekindling of our romance.

Graham continued to look puzzled. "But who will be piloting the balloon?"

"Oh, no one. We'll be tethered to the ground the entire time. Let's get started so I can get a good photograph of the competitors from above before the race begins."

A man with a tall hat and a prodigious moustache strode toward them. "Miss Belmont, I presume? We have your balloon all prepared. Right this way."

"Thank you. Mr. Ward will be assisting me today, if it's not too much trouble?"

"Not at all. The balloon is large enough for you both."

"Excellent."

Lily saw her equipment loaded carefully into the basket, then allowed the gentlemen to assist her in boarding. She was perfectly capable of clambering on board herself, of course, but the professional situation called for decorum. The fact that she enjoyed Graham's steadying hand against the small of her back was merely coincidental.

One of the balloon wranglers checked over the aircraft's burner, adjusting the flame to ensure the craft would remain safely in the air. He hopped out, loosened the ropes, and the airship began to rise.

When Graham offered Lily a hand, she took it, giving him a squeeze. Up they rose, higher and higher until she had the sort of view she'd only ever seen from a Manhattan skyscraper. And never with a camera in hand.

The tethers caught, holding the balloon securely in place. Lily prepared her equipment and set to work photographing the fairgrounds in every direction.

"We're alone now," she said, positioning the camera to capture the racers when they began to float up into the skies. "Let's finish our talk."

Graham stepped closer to her, though no one would hear them up here. "It's as good a place as any, I suppose. Could you please explain your code? I looked over the note and I still don't see it." He reached into a pocket and removed a folded piece of paper.

Lily flinched. He'd been carrying her note? All this time?

"Look at the first letter of every sentence," she explained. "I made them all larger than the others."

"Well, sentences begin with uppercase letters," Graham replied. "That's not so odd."

Lily sighed. "Read only those letters."

He peered at the paper. "'Let me be frank.' So, L. 'Everything.' E. T. S." He fumbled the paper. "Let's elope?" The words squeaked out. "You were asking me to run away with you?"

A pistol shot announced the beginning of the balloon race.

Lily raised a hand. "Hold that thought." She took her first photo, then slid the plate holder out.

Graham handed her an unused plate without prompting. "That's why you said not to ask to run away with you at the end of the note. You were trying to put the idea in my head. And I still missed it. I'm sorry."

Lily caught the racing balloons in mid air, directly in front of her. She swapped out the plate again.

"I'm sorry for not finding a way to be more clear," she said. "Now explain about the bridge."

"The bridge?" Graham asked.

"Our bridge. I couldn't get away the first day after I sent the note. You know that happens when my uncle is in one of his moods. But I went the next day. Only to find you there with Rose Preston."

"Rose?" Graham sounded thoughtful. "Oh. Oh! You saw us talking?"

Lily took her third photograph before replying. "Yes, I saw you. And heard. You said to her, in an impassioned voice—"

"Bridges are places of transition," Graham cut in, his voice soft but no less passionate than that day three months prior. "Touching the earth and above it at the same time. Magical places. That's what makes them romantic. Because anything can happen there. Even love."

Lily blinked tears from suddenly moist eyes. Her words. Words she'd said to him the very first time she'd taken him to that little rustic bridge in Central Park.

"How could you?" she whispered.

Defiantly, she returned to her work. She would capture every moment of the beauty of this event, despite the stabbing pain of the memory. Graham continued handing her new plates, saying nothing in his defense while she worked.

Only when she finally paused did he speak. "I wasn't saying that to Miss Preston. I was saying it to you."

Lily squinted up at him. "Me?"

"Or *for* you, more accurately. My sister Jeannie hired Miss Preston in early spring to write an article for the magazine's May Day issue. About New York's best romantic locations. She wanted a man's perspective for comparison, and I'm the only man in the company. So I showed her my most romantic place."

Lily stood with her hands frozen on the camera as she processed his words. She'd known Modern Ladies' Monthly was a collaborative business between Graham and his older sister—Jeannie working as Editor-in-Chief while Graham was the figurehead and finance man. She'd known they hired women from all walks of life. And yet she'd never considered that Graham's meeting with Rose Preston might be business-related.

"I never thought a debutante like Rose might be a working girl," Lily admitted, her head drooping in shame. "She's a girl like me. And I assumed the worst. About both of you."

"Sometimes we fall victim to the things society tells us, even when we're fighting against them," Graham replied. "For example, I never imagined you here, photographing the fair. But of course you're here. It's where all the best photographers are. Even knowing your ambitions, I underestimated you."

Lily lifted her chin and straightened up. "I suppose we will simply have to do better in the future," she vowed.

"Yes."

"Starting right now. I'd like to take one final photograph, and then—"

The balloon wobbled and Lily stumbled, nearly knocking into her camera. She grabbed hold of the basket with one hand, protecting her equipment with the other.

"What's happening?"

Graham peered over the edge. "A tether snapped. Hold tight. They'll likely reel us in and—"

"What?" Lily stretched to look over the side of the

basket. A man stood beside the one remaining tether rope, but he didn't appear to be pulling them down or encouraging anyone else to. Something metallic gleamed in his hand.

"That bastard Strathmore," Graham snarled. "Stop that man!" he shouted down.

Whether anyone heard him or not, Lily couldn't tell. Strathmore hacked at the rope and it snapped in two.

The balloon drifted up and away.

Seven - Aerial Shots

All the color had drained from Graham's face. Lily launched herself at him, and he caught her in a fierce embrace.

"How do we make it stop?" he fretted.

"I don't know. I don't know." She clung to him, willing her brain to function. This wasn't the end. She only needed to think. "It's… it's the heat. It makes the balloon rise."

"Heat." Graham looked up. "This burner thing, yes? If we turn it off, we'll go back down?"

"Yes. In theory. When the air inside cools off, we go down."

"Right. I can do that." He released Lily, then reached up to fiddle with the burner. "We won't crash if I shut it all the way off, will we?"

"I don't know," she admitted.

He bit his lip, frowning at the apparatus above him. "I'm turning it down now. I'll leave a small flame in case we need to turn it on again. Any idea how long until we start descending?"

"No. How fast does air cool off?"

"I haven't the foggiest idea."

Lily picked up her camera. "Let me secure my equipment, and then we can sit, and, uh, keep an eye on the balloon."

She checked that the exposed plates were safely covered and packed, then closed and latched everything. Work was complete. Now, though, she had no distraction from her predicament. She lowered herself to the floor of the basket, settling beside Graham.

The balloon swayed in the steady breeze, and Lily's stomach churned. Had they made the right decision? Would they fall, would they crash? Would they float for hours, at the mercy of the air currents? They were trapped, lost, helpless. The lack of control gnawed at her insides until she wanted to scream or cry.

"I think maybe we've stopped rising," Graham observed. "I hope that means we did the right thing. We're floating sideways with the wind, though. Who knows where we'll end up?"

"Splashing down in the Mississippi, perhaps. Or on the other side, somewhere in Illinois." She forced a smile. Lillian Belmont was a professional, and she would not fall apart. "It'll be an adventure."

Graham turned his head to look into her eyes. "If I had to have an unexpected adventure, I'm glad it's with you."

Her gaze dropped to his mouth. Him. He would be her distraction. If anyone could keep her from impotent worry, it was this man.

"Lil," he murmured.

Lily pushed up off the floor, straddled Graham's legs, and kissed him soundly. His arms wrapped around her, pulling her flush against him.

Her whole body came alive. How she'd missed this searing passion between them. Missed giving herself over to the hunger.

Graham was hungry too. He licked into her mouth, thrusting deep, reclaiming territory too long deserted.

Lillian met him stroke for stroke, relearning the taste of his lips, the caress of his hands across her back, and the tiny sounds of pleasure she coaxed from him.

She dragged her hands across his chest, tugging at the buttons of his vest, needing to be closer.

"Lil," he gasped. He nipped at her lower lip while his hands skimmed over her torso, finally settling on her breasts. "Lil, maybe we shouldn't…" He trailed off and went right back to kissing her.

"Need. Distraction," she mumbled between kisses. Why did she have so many layers? Her nipples were aching beneath her corset, her bare skin so far from his. "Need. You."

Graham's lips moved over her cheek, her chin, and down to her neck. "Oh, God, Lil," he moaned against her skin. "I need you too. But…" He pulled away and looked around. "Are we going down now?"

Lillian slid a hand inside his partially open shirt. Warm skin. Firm muscle. Steady heartbeat. All hers. She gave him a coy smile.

"Is that an offer?"

Graham blinked at her several times before he comprehended her innuendo. "Yes, it is. If we're safe."

She eased off of him. "Let's check."

They rose to look out over the rim of the basket. Already they were putting the fair behind them, heading across the city toward the river. The racing balloons, whose pilots understood the air currents far better than Lily ever would, had passed them by and were pulling steadily away. Her own balloon had begun a slow descent toward the rooftops below.

Lily gripped Graham's arm. "We can't land in the city," she blurted. "We'll crash into a building."

He turned the burner back up. "Not to worry. We have fuel. Let's take our time."

The tension eased from her muscles. "We seem to be caught in a nice air stream. If we stay aloft, we can drift until we're over fields."

Graham's smile was pure wickedness. "And enjoy the ride in the meantime."

They dropped to the floor, reaching for one another again. Graham grasped Lily's hem and tugged it toward her waist.

"I believe you had a request."

His fingers crept over her stockings and up to her thighs. Lily leaned back against the side of the basket and spread her legs to give him room. He found the seam in her combinations, parted the fabric, and bent to press his mouth to her sex.

Her eyes slid closed. *Yes.* Graham's lips and tongue were perfect. Warm and wet, stroking her flesh and teasing her clitoris with licks and sucks. How many times had she imagined this while they were apart, thinking she'd never feel it again?

Already her climax was nearing, bolstered by her burning desire for him and the months apart. Lily threaded her fingers through his hair and let him take her higher and higher, until she peaked and began to float gently to earth.

She opened her eyes to find him gazing at her in rapt adoration.

"You're so damn beautiful," he vowed.

Lily smiled at him, her heart swelling with love. If that Mr. Strathmore ruined her career with this stunt, she would press criminal charges and sue him for damages. But she also might write him a thank you note for giving her this opportunity to reconnect with Graham. Giving them the time they'd needed to resolve everything between them.

She let her gaze fall to the bulge in his trousers. "More."

Graham arched an eyebrow. "Whatever you desire, love." He climbed to his feet, then offered her a hand up. "Although, I'd hate for you to miss the view any longer."

Lily took his hand and he pulled her to a standing position. He turned her around and pressed her up against the side of the basket, kissing the back of her neck. Fabric rustled and she felt a cool breeze against the back of her legs. A moment later, the hardness of Graham's cock nudged at her entrance.

"Lillian, love." He pushed slowly into her, groaning. "I adore you."

Lily braced herself against the basket and pressed backward to meet his thrusts. Ahead of her, the wide world stretched out invitingly. A lifetime of adventure with this glorious man.

High above the treetops, Lillian reveled in the pleasure, letting every moan escape her throat, feeling each of his strokes deep inside. Every rock of her hips urged him to move faster, harder. With each new spear of pleasure, Lily rejoiced in herself and in him, and in this place where they could soar free.

Graham clutched her tight when the climax trembled through her, clinging to her until his own shuddering release had subsided.

Slowly, she turned to face him, wrapping her arms around his neck and kissing him, gently this time.

"I love you," she murmured.

"I love you too." He pressed his forehead to hers and gazed into her eyes. "Let's never be apart like that again."

"Agreed. All misunderstandings will require an immediate conversation until the matter has been settled."

Graham laughed. "Do we need to put that in our vows?"

"Yes. Assuming we can manage to land this balloon."

"I'll do my best. Now that I understand your note, I'm eager to follow its instructions."

They sprang into action. By turning the flame up and down, they managed a lurching descent, aiming to put down in a patch of farmland across the Mississippi.

"Watch for the—"

The balloon jostled as the basket grazed the top of a tree at the edge of a small grove.

"Sorry," Graham cried. "I think we're out of fuel."

The balloon swiped another tree, twisting and tangling among the branches. Lily and Graham crouched on the floor, holding one another close as twigs snapped and the basket bounced this way and that.

"I have you," Lily murmured, her face buried against Graham's shirt.

"I have you too, love," he whispered into her hair. "I have you too."

A terrifying minute later, the snapping and tumbling subsided. The balloon stuck fast and the basket swayed to a standstill.

When her breathing and pulse had returned to normal, Lily eased herself out of Graham's arms and peered over the side. "Well, we're mostly down."

He joined her at the rail. "What now?"

"I have one unused plate among my equipment," Lily replied. "We climb down and take a photograph, of course."

Graham's hearty laugh was music to her ears. "Have I mentioned that I adore you?"

Lily grinned. "Yes. But you may say it again."

He bent to kiss her. "Every day. For as long as we both shall live."

Epilogue - Finished Prints

August 4, 1904
St. Louis, Missouri

Graham spread the finished postcards out on the desk in his hotel suite. Perfect. Lillian would be returning from her latest photo shoot any minute now. He couldn't wait to surprise her with this.

The postcard project had been fun, but it hadn't given Graham any further ambitions beyond running his one magazine. True, they would never be Fifth-Avenue-mansion rich, but they would be comfortable-home-with-a-beautiful-photo-studio rich. After a month at the fair, he was ready for New York and that new life together. It was up to Lil, however, to determine when their combination business trip and honeymoon would be over.

The door opened and she walked in, towing her equipment behind her in a little wooden wagon.

"I missed you today." She gave him a broad smile. "I got a number of excellent shots. I'm looking forward to developing them."

Graham walked over to give her a kiss. "Before you do that, let me show you why I was working all day today. These came in from the printer." He held out a postcard.

Lillian gasped as she took hold of the printed piece of cardstock. "Oh, Graham, it's beautiful!" She ran her fingers reverently over the colorized version of her most popular photograph. "Balloon Race as seen from the air," she read. "St. Louis, 1904." Her thumb skimmed over the photo credit in the bottom right-hand corner. "Lillian Belmont Ward."

Tears glistened in her eyes, and Graham had to blink to clear his own vision. Not only was the photograph a memory of her greatest career triumph and the adventure that had brought the two of them back together, but it was a nod to their wedding. *Securely* tethered this time, they had exchanged their vows up in a balloon, both above the earth and tied to it. A place of magic.

"The postcards will be sold all over the fair," Graham said proudly. "And the same photo will be the cover for our Exposition Special Edition when it releases in a few weeks."

"I love it!" Lil grinned and waved the postcard. "Should I send one to Mr. Strathmore in jail, or is that too mean?"

"Seeing as how he could have killed us…" Graham shrugged. Strathmore had fled after setting their balloon aloft, but the police had tracked him down a few days later. Eventually, he had confessed.

"I'll definitely send one to my uncle," Lillian declared. "He'll probably scowl and throw it in the fireplace, but maybe if we keep reminding him how happy we are with our careers and with each other, he'll come to accept what we've done." She took Graham's arm and led him to the sofa. "Now, tell me all about your Special Edition. We'll have to get you back to New York in time for publication. I'm sure you're tired of doing all your work over the phone."

He chuckled. "You might be surprised how much of my work is done over the phone back home. But, yes, I'd like to return soon."

"Good. I'm nearly done here, and I miss New York. There's this one little bridge, in particular, in the Ramble in Central Park. I believe you had something to say to me there."

Graham slid an arm around her and brushed his lips

to hers. "I have many things to say to you there. And all of them end with 'I love you.'"

Historical Note

Lillian was inspired by Jessie Tarbox Beals, a pioneering photojournalist who used her determination and skill to become an official photographer of the 1904 World's Fair. During her time at the Exposition, Beals produced more than 3,500 photographs. Her often candid images of the Philippine exhibit and other indigenous people at the fair were notable for portraying the people as they truly were in their daily lives, rather than attempting to conform to the racist pseudoscience pushed by the exhibit creators. Beals was known to go to whatever lengths necessary to get the shots she desired, often climbing ladders in her long skirts, and, yes, even taking aerial photos from a hot air balloon.

Mishaps & Mistletoe

Mishaps & Mistletoe

The magic of Christmas may have been mishandled.

All Lady Mabel Fairweather wants for Christmas is to experience one night of dancing and freedom from her horrible nickname. Her family assures her that a simple magic potion will do the trick. But when something goes awry, Mabel finds herself with a mob of amorous men descending upon her.

Andrew Holbrooke has loved his friend Mabel for years. Now that he has the means to marry, he's come home intending to seek her hand. What Drew didn't expect was to find other men eager to do the same. When strange magic puts Mabel in danger, however, he vows to protect her, even if she wants someone else.

Hiding from the mayhem, Drew and Mabel rekindle their friendship, uncover old memories, and discover new passions. With snow falling and mistletoe hung, these two friends might just find a magic of their own and unwrap a love for the ages.

Prologue

December 17, 1883
London, England

1 week before The Dowager Duchess of Winstead's Annual Christmas Ball

"It's not that my granddaughter needs *help* finding a husband…" the dowager began.

Yes. Yes it was. Of the six daughters of the Duke of Winstead, five were happily settled in successful, well-received marriages. Marriages combining affection and society's approval. Marriages that had happened swiftly, easily, as if the duke and duchess had conceived all their children under a matrimonial star.

All except Mabel. The youngest daughter would be twenty-five come the New Year and she had no suitors, no prospects, and no expectation of anything more than a long spinsterhood.

"We simply must give her the little boost she needs to draw attention," the duchess continued. "Once eyes are on her, the rest will happen. And what better venue for it than my Christmas party?"

The potion maker nodded, although it wasn't certain whether she agreed or was merely being polite.

"I should like you to mix up something special for her, along with the other potions I have requested for the party. I have no doubt you will make her shine. Everyone knows you are the best. Cost is no concern."

The potion maker nodded again. "I'll send you a contract," she said in her lilting French accent.

"Excellent. And you must attend as well. I will send an invitation." The duchess lifted her chin and swished away in a swirl of silk.

*

December 23
1 day before the ball

"I've got the potion!" Henrietta held aloft a tiny bottle of orange liquid. "Fresh from Mr. Allen the chemist. We'll add it to Mabel's champagne and she'll dance the night away."

Georgia frowned at her younger sister. "Are you sure about this? I know it's what Mabel *said* she wanted, but…"

"It's only a simple allure potion," Hen argued. "Harmless."

Georgia worried her lip between her teeth. "I'm a bit concerned that it's not what Mabel wants but what she pretended to want to soothe Grandmother."

"It will be good for her. It will draw enough attention that men will ask her to dance and she will finally be able to escape that horrid nickname."

Three other heads nodded.

"One night for her to shine the way we know she deserves."

Georgia hesitated only a moment more, then clasped hands with her sisters in solidarity.

I - Mishaps

The Dowager Duchess of Winstead's Annual Christmas Ball
December 24

"Ah, yes. The magic of Christmas," Lady Mabel Fairweather sighed. "When everyone gets drunk on silly potions and pretends a cluster of leaves and berries is a rational excuse for kissing someone you oughtn't."

Mabel waved a hand at the kissing ball hung from the ceiling. All across the room, potion lamps made to look like candles cast light and shadow over a multitude of ribbons and garlands, their flickering too regular to be truly mistaken for flame. But at least they wouldn't cause any of the dozens of wreaths to catch fire like had happened when Mabel was ten years old.

Susan gave an exasperated sigh. "Why must you be such a spoilsport?"

Mabel had attended enough events with her cousin to expect such a reaction to her cynicism. "I'm always a spoilsport. You know that." She had to be. Disdain and sarcasm were what had gotten her through years of pitying looks. They had carried her beyond the horrid snub that at nineteen had made her "Maybe Mabel" for life.

The cruel nickname still circulated in tittered whispers, but Mabel had risen above it. She'd made a career for herself with her piano lessons for girls. Spinsterhood would neither change nor destroy her.

"Oh, I suppose," Susan said. "But wouldn't it be fun for one night to escape from real life and be the belle of the ball?"

Yes, Mabel had to admit. *It would.* Just once to dance with a man who wasn't married to one of her sisters…

Susan plucked a small vial filled with a thin, orange liquid from a beaded purse at her hip. "You said it was what you wanted."

"I know, I know." And she did want it. She only wished she could have it without the aid of some ridiculous potion. "Very well. I'll try your tonic. But once it wears off, that will be the end of it. A brief moment of fun and then back to reality."

Mabel allowed Susan to steer her to the refreshments.

"Champagne, Lady Mabel?" asked the round-faced footman manning the table. "I have a glass here all for you." He offered her a flute and she accepted with a nod of thanks.

"Here." Susan handed Mabel the vial. "Pour it into your drink. All it will do is heighten your natural charms."

Mabel poured the potion into her champagne, watching it disappear into the bubbles. She took a sip. The liquid burned her throat, and her mouth puckered at the bitter, almost caustic sensation.

"Ugh. It tastes terrible." She tossed back half the glass, wanting to get this done with. The momentary unpleasantness would earn her a few dances.

Susan frowned. "It shouldn't. Not unless it was so potent—"

"Lady Mabel!" exclaimed an eager male voice. "How lovely you look tonight."

Mabel turned slowly. She knew that voice. She detested that voice. It was seared into her memory.

My sister Mabel would love to dance, Lord Edgewood. Don't you think she'd make a fine partner?"

The reply, so haughty, bored, uninterested: "Maybe."

Lord Edgewood had never thought Mabel anything more than barely adequate. Yet now he stood staring at her, his coldly handsome face alight with admiration. Clearly, the potion was working.

"Lady Mabel," he breathed, his voice low and reverent. "Would you care to dance?"

A smile crept over Mabel's face. She let it grow into a wide grin, then gave a careless shrug and replied, "Maybe."

She whisked away, leaving him gaping like a fool. Six years late, but she had repaid the snub.

"This potion was a brilliant idea," Mabel said to Susan. "Let's see who else wants to dance."

Susan hurried after her. "Yes, but it shouldn't have worked so quickly and it seems rather strong. I'm a bit concerned."

A flurry of voices intruded on the conversation.

"Lady Mabel! You look sublime!"

"Is that beauty the duke's youngest?"

"She's magnificent!"

"Where have you been hiding, gorgeous?"

Before Mabel could even think what she might say to the sudden influx of compliments, a stampede of eager men pounded across the parquet floor in her direction.

"Might I claim a waltz?" asked a fresh-faced lad.

"Would you care to take a turn about the garden?" The very married man gave her a salacious wink.

"Would you do me the honor of becoming my wife?" asked a man old enough to be her grandfather.

Mabel tried to back away, turning a worried gaze on her cousin. "What's happening?"

More men crowded in. From across the room they abandoned wives and companions, pushing and shoving, calling her name.

"Susan!" Mabel called in desperation, but they'd been cut off. The men pressed closer.

✦

Tonight was the night. Professor Andrew Holbrooke—
"noted Egyptologist" to the papers, but simply "Drew" to
his friends—spied his Belle the instant he walked into the
room.

Not that this surprised him. He'd always been hyper-
aware of her. Ever since the day seventeen years ago, when her
eldest sister had married his eldest brother. He'd remember
it forever. Little Mabel, in a frilly green dress, flinging white
rose petals into the air as she danced beneath them on a hot
July afternoon, shouting, "It's snowing! Merry Christmas!"

Drew had fallen in love, right there and then, and his
affections had never wavered.

But a fourth son of a financially inept father had no
money and nothing to offer a duke's daughter. Drew had
been away for years, making a name for himself. And now
that he had the means to support a wife, he was here, ready
to declare to his long-time friend and correspondent just
how far beyond friendship his feelings extended.

God, but she was gorgeous. In the intervening years,
she'd only become more so, growing into her curves, carrying
herself with greater confidence. Unruly wisps of dark hair
had escaped her updo, as they always did. He wanted to
wrap those curls around his fingers while he kissed the
gentle curve of her lips. Pressed their bodies so close they
became one.

Hell. He dismissed the prurient thought before he could
embarrass himself.

Drew watched as Mabel lifted her glass to her lips,
tossing back a long swallow of champagne. He let his eyes
drift from her mouth down the column of her throat to
the daring neckline of her holly-green gown. The gown he

would strip from her body the moment she said, "Yes." He started across the room.

A hot rush of fury went through him when he spied Edgewood rushing to speak with her. *That bastard…*

Drew never completed the thought. Whatever Belle said left the man flabbergasted. Damn, but she was everything and more. Drew quickened his pace.

A sudden flood of men cut him off. Pushing, shouting, as though they were in a gaming hell rather than a ballroom, they blocked both his path and his line of sight. Confused and irritated, Drew used muscles honed and strengthened by digging and outdoor living to force his way through the throng, desperate to protect his beloved from the unnaturally rowdy crowd.

He'd only just spied a hint of her green dress when a cultured voice said, in passionate tones, "Lady Mabel, will you marry me?"

Drew froze. No. His knees trembled, barely supporting his weight. He was too late. He'd misconstrued the affection in her letters. Been too hesitant to disclose his own feelings. Of course she would have other suitors, especially with the way she'd flourished into womanhood. Edgewood's snub was surely ancient history. It was a miracle she'd been unattached even this long.

Drew staggered back, freeing himself from the crowd. He'd leave her to the celebration. He wouldn't interfere with her happiness. Maybe someday he'd be able to offer her congratulations and sincerely mean it. For tonight, he fled.

*

Drew?

Mabel tried to push her way through the mad crush of admirers toward the space where the familiar face had momentarily appeared. Could he truly be here? She hadn't seen him in four years. Perhaps she'd been mistaken.

"Lady Mabel, might I have the honor—"

"No," she blurted, done attempting any semblance of civility. "I do not want to dance, I will not join you for an illicit tryst, and I will absolutely not marry you. *Any* of you."

What had she done? What was in that potion? She slapped at a groping hand and shoved a reedy young man hard enough to clear a small path. A flash of nut-brown hair on a tall man caught her eye. He was hurrying away from her, unlike every other man in the room.

Could it really be Drew? He didn't look lanky enough. She rushed ahead, regardless. Andrew Holbrooke was the friend she needed. One who could help her out of this mess. He could hold off the other men while she escaped to the ladies' retiring room or another safe location.

Mabel burst through the wall of men, only to collide with a muscular chest. The startled man staggered backward.

"Beg pardon," he said, then stared at her in confusion. "Damn. I want to kiss you more than just about anything." He took another step backward. "Something is very wrong. Excuse me, I must find my wife."

He ran off, clearing a path as he went. Mabel followed, a bit of her faith in humanity restored. Drew—if it had been him—had vanished, but she'd reached the relative safety of a group of women, including an ashen-faced Susan.

"Mabel! I'm so sorry. I don't know what went wrong. Let's get you out of here. The drawing room?"

Mabel shook her head, glancing back at the horde of potion-crazed suitors. "No. I must go." She broke into a run. "Somewhere no one will think to find me."

II - Folly

"I suppose if one is going to choose a foolish location to flee to, a garden folly is rather apt," Drew said aloud.

He shivered. The folly was dark, the winter air frigid, and of course he hadn't thought to grab an overcoat before tearing from the house. After so long away, the cold and damp of an English winter had become a strange, foreign thing.

Drew flicked on his pocket torch. He'd only had the brilliant new device for about six months, but now he carried it everywhere. Already it was revolutionizing his work. He adjusted the beam to a wide setting, the steady, potion-fueled light illuminating familiar walls.

The small stone building, made to look like a half-burnt ruin, had been a favorite hideaway for himself and Mabel during their childhood. Which was both what had drawn him here and another reason it was a poor choice. Why run away from someone to a place that will only make you think of her? God, he was an idiot.

Drew lifted a finger to brush the spine of a crumbling, old tome set into a niche in the wall. "A priceless text," Belle had dubbed it. They had named the folly The Great Library, and stuffed it full of discarded books and papers. They'd spent hours upon hours here, creating their own pretend artifacts and decrypting secret codes and ancient writing. It was here his career had truly begun.

The crunch of footsteps on gravel made him swing around and shine his torch at the folly's entrance. The footsteps came to a sudden halt.

"Who's there?" a woman's voice demanded.

Drew moved toward the doorway. "Belle?" Damn, he shouldn't call her that. He always thought of her by the long-ago nickname, but it was too intimate. She was Lady Mabel to him now. He had to accept that.

"Drew?" She stepped into the entrance, her green dress shimmering in the soft light. This close, she was even more beautiful than she'd appeared in the ballroom. Her silver-gray eyes sparkled like moonlight, and wisps of raven hair tumbled about her face. A rosy tint stained her cheeks, and her ample bosom rose and fell in heavy breaths. Had she been running? "Is it really you?"

Drew set the pocket torch into one of the wall niches, casting light throughout the room and allowing her to see him. "Yes, it's me. Merry Christmas." He beckoned to her. "Come in out of the wind. It's freezing out there."

Mabel clutched at her shawl, pulling it tighter around her shoulders. The thin fabric must have been next to useless against the winter air. "You won't… do anything crazy, will you?"

Crazy? What could be crazier than running into the garden without proper outerwear?

"I, uh, wasn't planning to."

She took one step closer. "No wild raving about my beauty? No marriage proposals?"

Ouch. He rubbed his chest, but it did nothing to relieve the stabbing pain of her invisible knife.

"What are you doing here, Lady Mabel?" he asked, unable to answer her questions and keep his composure. "Shouldn't you be inside celebrating?"

She took another step forward. "I could say the same for you. Why aren't *you* inside celebrating?"

"I have nothing to celebrate," he growled. Dammit, he actually growled the words. He *never* did that. He had a reputation for a cool head and cheerful disposition.

Mabel stepped all the way into the folly at last, her rosy

lips pinching in a tight frown. "Christmas?" she suggested. "Your homecoming?" Her whole body trembled, and she tugged on the shawl again.

"Dammit, Belle, you shouldn't be out here in the cold." And now he was cursing in front of her. God, but he was an emotional wreck. It was why he'd come here in the first place: to have time alone to recover from the blow of losing her.

He shrugged out of his jacket. He might not be talking like a gentleman just now, but he could still behave like one. He closed the distance between himself and Mabel and draped the garment around her shoulders.

"You don't need—"

"Take it," he insisted. "You're freezing." And now he was, but he probably deserved it for behaving like such a dolt.

She pulled the coat around herself, hiding her dress and the lovely body it displayed. "Thank you." She turned a slow circle, taking in their old playplace, much the way he had. Her fingers traced the faded spine of the book exactly where his had been minutes before. "It hasn't changed at all, has it?"

"Not really, no."

A small smile touched her lips as she turned back to him. Her gaze roved up and down his body and he felt his skin heat in response. Perhaps he wouldn't freeze after all. "But you have."

His eyebrows shot up. "Have I?"

"Yes. You're so…"

His shoulders tensed, anticipating more painful observations. *Sullen? Melancholy? Heartbroken?*

"Tan."

"Oh." He wasn't sure that was what she had initially

intended to say, but it was better than anything he'd been expecting. "I spend a great deal of time outdoors. It happens."

"It suits you. And the sun brings out the blond highlights in your hair."

He had blond highlights? He had blond highlights and she had noticed them? The intensity in her stare made his blood boil.

Two steps. Two steps and he could press her up against the wall of the folly and kiss those ruby lips and bring their bodies together in a way that would leave no doubt how wild she made him.

He staggered back. Was he out of his mind? He was misinterpreting things. Again. She couldn't possibly be thinking the sorts of things he was thinking. She had just been proposed to. By someone a good sight richer and more polished than he was.

So what was she doing here? With him?

"Drew, are you all right? You have a peculiar expression on your face, and you still haven't explained why you're out here."

"Nor have you."

"I had to get away from the party," she said, giving the tiny shrug of her shoulders he remembered from years ago. All her body language was like that. Small. Subtle.

"As did I." He fought a rising shiver. Bloody hell it was cold out here. His toes were beginning to go numb inside his dancing shoes, and without his jacket the rest of his heat was rapidly leaving his body. "You should go back inside."

I should go back inside.

"I can't."

"Of course you can. I know parties haven't always been easy for you, but doesn't everyone want to celebrate with you tonight?" His teeth chattered a bit on the last few words.

"You're cold." She stepped toward him, pulling the jacket from around her shoulders.

"I'm perfectly well."

"You're freezing." She reached to wrap the garment around him. The moment her hand met his body, all the breath rushed from his lungs.

"Belle." He grasped her arm, not sure if he meant to push her away or tug her closer. "Belle, we shouldn't be here, alone like this. What… what would your fiancé think?"

She went still, her hands still touching him, the jacket slung halfway around his back. "My *what*?"

✳

Mabel reeled. Was he drunk? Crazy? It was strange enough that the potion didn't seem to be affecting him the way it had every other man. He'd made no amorous advances, no comments about her appearance, and now he was talking nonsense.

He trembled beneath her hands. Good heavens, the poor man was freezing to death and she was standing here gaping like a fool. If his body temperature had dropped too low it could be affecting his mind. She had to warm him. She pressed the full length of her body into him, sharing her heat, wrapping his jacket around shoulders that had grown broad and muscular since she'd last seen him.

Drew gasped and stiffened at the contact. "Mabel," he moaned.

His voice sent an entirely different sort of shiver down her spine. He had changed so much from the skinny, bookish boy she remembered. He was bigger. Stronger. Rugged. Tanned and muscled like a laborer. Things that ought not to have appealed to her. But here, with no space between them, her body was begging to differ.

"I'll warm you," she promised. "Let's get you inside."

"I'm fine." He jerked away from her, knocking the jacket from her grip. It fell to the floor, and he scooped it up and draped it around her once again. It smelled like him. An understated scent that mixed a touch of sweet with a more earthy base. Sandalwood? Some soap or lotion he'd picked up in a foreign land. She wanted to wrap herself in it, in the hopes she might absorb all of his travels and adventures and make them her own.

Mabel dragged herself back to reality. First she had to get the stubborn man out of the cold and then hopefully ascertain why he was behaving so strangely. She seized his hand and dragged him toward the exit.

He flinched, but he didn't pull away again. He grabbed his odd little lantern from the niche and pointed it at the ground to light their path.

"Let's get you inside and warm, and then we can talk," he said.

Fine. Let him think he was the one helping her. As long as he followed her into the house.

"We can't go through the front door," Mabel thought aloud. "But if we enter through the kitchens—"

"Why not?"

"Pardon?"

"Why can't we go through the front door?"

"Um. I'd rather no one sees me." Mabel hefted a sigh. "The party was, er, more rowdy than I expected and I drew quite a bit of undesired attention."

His fingers clenched around hers. "Did someone try to hurt you?" His voice was tight with anger. "I swear, Mabel, if anyone did anything to hurt you…" He trailed off.

"No, no. There was simply some confusion over who

was to dance with me, and I didn't want to be the center of an argument."

"Shouldn't your fiancé have priority?"

"Why do you keep saying that? I don't have a fiancé. Where would you get such a ridiculous idea?"

Except now that she'd said the words, she knew. He'd overheard one of the five different marriage proposals she'd received during those mad minutes after she'd drunk the potion. Which was better, she supposed, than his having heard one of nearly a dozen indecent proposals she'd also received. He may have turned into some sort of virile outdoorsman, but he was still the Drew she had exchanged letters with. The Drew who insisted she wear his jacket while his teeth chattered. He was a gentleman through and through, and she didn't doubt he would jump to defend her honor.

"I heard a man propose to you shortly before I left the party," he confirmed. He slowed, and she had to yank on his hand to keep him walking toward the house. "Are you saying you refused him?"

"Of course I refused him!"

His feet stopped moving. He flicked off the lantern and stuffed it into a pocket. "Thank God. Then I won't feel so guilty when I do this."

"Do—" She gasped when he wrapped both arms around her, crushing her against his solid chest. "What?"

"Kiss you."

III - Heating Up

Mabel had fantasized a time or two about what it might be like if Drew kissed her. How could she not, when they'd written letters back and forth for years? Occasionally she'd thought she sensed affection in his concise prose that went beyond friendship. He never ran on or became poetic, but she could read the excitement in his discoveries and his eagerness to share them with someone who cared. Once in a while, when he asked after her or mentioned missing home, she'd imagined herself sparking that same sort of excitement. And then she'd imagined kissing him.

Her imagination, apparently, was lacking.

A little tilt of the head was all it had taken. A tiny lift of her chin, and then his mouth had crashed down on hers, driving away the cold and the dark and the rest of the world and leaving only this sensation of craving and being craved in return.

His lips sipped at hers, savoring every part, from the plump middle to the corners and then back again. When his tongue darted out, Mabel didn't hesitate to open for him. She had five married sisters. She knew what proper kissing entailed.

Oh. Her little gasp was smothered beneath his questing mouth. No wonder he had done so well in his career. Andrew Holbrooke knew how to explore.

His hands burrowed beneath the jacket draped around her, stroking up and down her back in slow, but deliberate caresses that matched the movements of his tongue and lips. He left nothing undiscovered, his every motion methodical and adoring. Eager, but unwilling to miss any part of what she offered.

Mabel felt his hunger in the tension of his muscles under her hands, in the insistent press of his lips. When her own tongue slicked across his, he pressed deeper, tightening his embrace and angling his mouth to give them both better access.

He devoured her, fully, completely, leaving no part of her untouched by his desire. Tingles flew up and down her skin.

Delicious yearning blossomed deep beneath her clothing. She burned for him, the heat of the embrace melting her even as soft flakes of snow began to flutter around them. She clutched at him, rubbing herself against him in a helpless attempt to ease the ache of her suddenly sensitive breasts. When the thick, rigid length of his arousal met her belly, she let out a squeak, whether of alarm or excitement, she wasn't sure.

The sound was enough to startle him, and he withdrew, leaving her suddenly aware of the cold she'd meant them to escape. The cold. The house. The party.

"Oh, no!" she gasped. The potion. Oh, goodness, the potion. He must have been fighting it all this time, and then she'd given in and he'd forgotten himself. He wasn't ravenous for her. He only thought he was.

"Belle?" He sounded dazed. "What's wrong? Did I go too far? Push you too fast?"

She grabbed him by the wrist and propelled him toward the house. "Inside."

"Oh, God. I'm so sorry. I should never have... Please don't hate me."

"Don't be ridiculous. It wasn't your fault."

Mabel flew through the garden with furious strides. How could she have been so foolish? What would happen once the potion wore off? Now that she knew what it was to kiss him, she could never go back. How could she see him look at her with nothing more than friendship and not remember that desperate desire?

And how would *he* feel? As a gentleman, the guilt would plague him. He would continue to blame himself, whatever the circumstances. What had she done?

Drew's long legs easily matched her pace. "It was absolutely my fault. I started it."

"You're confused. It's only the potion."

"What potion?"

She pushed through the small servant's entrance into the warmth of the house. The kitchens buzzed with activity, the dedicated staff working feverishly to keep the large party flush with food and drink. Mabel pulled Drew's jacket up to cover her head as she rushed through, not wanting to risk any of the male servants seeing her face and causing another uproar. Drew followed close behind, compelled, no doubt, by the blasted potion.

"I should never have drunk Susan's silly concoction," she muttered under her breath.

"Lady Mabel, shouldn't you sit and warm up?" Drew asked, concern and confusion mingling in his voice. "Have some tea, perhaps? Or a brandy to settle your nerves?"

Mabel whirled around and they collided, the contact sparking a new wave of desire. "My nerves are perfectly fine," she snapped, stepping back to look up into his face. It didn't help. The ring of gold in the center of his brown eyes blazed like the sun. His lips were reddened from their kisses and still moist. She inhaled sharply. "Now be quiet," she scolded. "We must find a place where we can be alone." She spun away and began to walk again, knowing he would follow.

"I don't know whether 'alone' is a good idea," he replied.

It probably wasn't. She'd already demonstrated how easily she could lose all common sense. But she didn't dare go anywhere near other men, and she needed at least a moment to explain the situation to him. She couldn't let him go on thinking he'd somehow taken advantage of her.

She led him straight to the breakfast room. No one would be using it until morning, but even so she wedged a chair beneath the door handle to prevent anyone entering behind them. Confident she was safe from prying eyes, she turned up the lights and gestured at the table.

"Please, sit. We need to talk. Are you warm enough, now?" She removed his jacket and held it out to him. "Here, this will help."

"I'm fine." He slipped the jacket back on, but didn't sit, staring her down with arms crossed over his chest. "Now tell me what is going on and why I can't take you back to the party."

"My cousin Susan—"

A fist hammering on the door interrupted. "Lady Mabel!" a man's voice shouted.

"Dammit," she grumbled, shocking herself with the curse. "Someone recognized me."

Thud. Thud. "Lady Mabel, we know you're in there!"

"Come out, my love!" another voice called.

The door trembled as someone rammed into it from the outside. The chair beneath the knob shifted.

"Who's in there with you?" a third voice demanded.

Drew's eyes flicked back and forth from the door to Mabel. "Dash it, Belle, what the devil is happening?"

Before she could answer, the door burst open with a reverberating crack, sending splinters flying and the chair tumbling. Men poured into the room, half trampling one another, calling her name.

Her heart pounded. Panic swelled within her. She had only one recourse. She grabbed hold of Drew's arm with both hands and cried, "Protect me!"

IV - Sanctuary

Drew swept Mabel up into his arms and barreled his way through the frenzied crowd, kicking and jabbing with his elbows. The men were out of their minds, grabbing for Mabel's skirts, beating on him, trying to tear her from his grasp. Drew lowered his shoulder and rammed it straight into the chest of the Duke of Thurston, praying the man wouldn't remember him in the morning.

He tore down the hall, the mob at his heels. Even with Mabel in his arms, Drew had the advantage. He'd explored every inch of this house, knew every hall and staircase. They were burned into his memory, and he could navigate them even in the dark. He spun and swerved, racing down corridors and through rooms—some occupied, some not—moving higher and higher until the last of his pursuers fell away.

Gasping for breath, his muscles burning, he pushed through one final doorway, set Mabel on her feet, and sagged against the wall. A musty scent tickled his nose and he sneezed. He fumbled in his pocket for the torch, flicking it on to illuminate the cluttered attic space.

Like the folly, it was exactly how he remembered: unused furniture, trunks and boxes packed with odds and ends, the terrifying taxidermied fox with its beady eyes and unnatural posture.

Mabel hurried over to a chest of drawers and put her shoulder against it, trying to push it. It groaned and screeched as it scraped across the floor, inch by tiny inch. Drew moved to help her, his arms and legs still aching, but having caught his breath again.

Together, they maneuvered the bureau in front of the door, barring anyone who might track them here. Drew set the torch atop it, lighting up most of the room. He didn't trust any of the old chairs to hold his weight, so he settled on the sturdiest-looking trunk, motioning to Mabel to take a seat atop another box opposite him.

Instead she plopped down right beside him, seizing his hand in both of hers. "Thank you. I don't know what I would have done without you."

As his body recovered, his brain at last began to process everything that had happened during the last few minutes. "Bloody fucking hell," he cursed, his language causing Mabel to emit a shocked gasp. "What was that?"

Her gaze dropped to the floor, her forehead pressing against his shoulder. "I'm so sorry. I've made a terrible mess of everything."

"You?" He put an arm around her, relieved when she didn't pull away. "Those men made the mess. They were insane! What have they been drinking?"

She shook her head, still refusing to look up at him. "It's not them. It was me. I drank an allure potion. It was supposed to draw attention. Make men notice me so they would ask me to dance." She heaved a sigh, then straightened up. "Well, they did. They wanted to dance, they wanted to marry me, they wanted… other things. Dozens of them, fighting for my attention, grabbing at me. That's why I fled to the folly. Any man who looked at me wanted me. And it seems to only have gotten worse."

"Fucking hell," he repeated.

This time she didn't flinch, merely nodded. "So now you understand."

"No. I don't understand. I've seen allure potions. They're common enough. Even in Egypt I'm occasionally invited to English-style parties, and such potions are used by both men and women. They compel you to look, spark your interest, but they don't do *that*." Drew had danced with plenty of women who had drunk such potions and never once had he lost control the way the men at tonight's ball seemed to have.

"That's what I thought, too. I thought it was harmless.

All I wanted was to make enough people notice me that I could dance. And Susan's been studying potions. She would know better than to give me something harmful."

Drew drummed his fingers on his thigh, thinking. "How much of it did you drink?"

"One tiny vial. Exactly what Susan gave me. She seemed surprised at how suddenly and strongly it worked, but the crush of men separated us and I wasn't able to speak to her about it."

"Well, the good news is that potions wear off. By tomorrow all those men will want nothing to do with you anymore." And thank God for that. Fighting off drug-crazed suitors hadn't been part of his proposal plan.

Mabel turned away. "I know." She pushed herself up from the trunk and paced to the window, staring out at the snow, now falling steadily. Melancholy hung over her like a shroud, hunching her shoulders, muffling her voice. Why? Would she regret the loss of someone's attention?

Drew's gut twisted sharply. Just because she didn't have a fiancé didn't mean she didn't want one. And he'd gone and kissed her.

An involuntary shudder shook him. Good Lord, that kiss. He'd wanted to stand there forever, kissing her, soaking up the sweetness of her lips, inhaling the piney fragrance of her skin cream—she hadn't given up her teenage habit of matching her scents to the seasons, and he adored that about her. A hint of it lingered on his jacket, sharpening the memory, making him yearn for the press of her body to his own.

He forced his gaze away from her. Being here alone with her was a terrible idea. He didn't want to tempt her into any unwanted kisses. He didn't want her reputation ruined if anyone found them together. Yet he couldn't leave her. Not until the potion had worn off. Some of the men would resist the magic and remove themselves from her presence. Others would beg but do her no harm. Too many, though, would take advantage of the circumstances, in whatever way they could. Even if Mabel didn't want him, Drew would put her safety above all other concerns. He wasn't leaving her side for an instant.

He rose from his seat. They may have been in a cluttered attic, but that was no excuse for ungentlemanly behavior. "Mabel, is something wrong? I think we're safe here, but you still seem unhappy. This wasn't your fault, you know. The potion was tainted, or it reacted badly with your drink or… or something." He didn't know enough about potions to guess. They fueled his lanterns and healed sickness and injuries at his dig sites, and he didn't usually think much more on it.

She turned to face him at last. "I'm fine. Everything will be fine. I will rest here, and by morning it will all have passed."

She shivered, just for an instant, but Drew caught it. The attic was chilly and would only grow colder as the night went on. They'd need to wrap up to remain here. He lifted the lid of a trunk, hoping to find a blanket inside. Instead he found a pile of old clothing. Familiar clothing. They'd played kings and queens, knights, warriors, fairies, and more with these. The memory brought a smile to his face.

"I think we will want a few more layers if we're to stay in the attic all night. Would you like to help me dig through these boxes?" He plopped a ridiculous, floppy hat on his head. It fit better now but probably looked even worse on him than it had when he was a boy. "For old times' sake?"

Mabel stared at him for several seconds, then burst out

laughing. "That would be an excellent way to pass the time, thank you."

V - Devotion

"I didn't have any weapons at hand, but we did have a chamber pot in the tent. So I improvised."

Mabel giggled. "Eew."

"Clonked the bastard over the head with it. Turned out, he was a known tomb robber and had been wanted by the local authorities for some time. And that is by far my most exciting Egypt story."

Mabel snuggled closer to him, using the temperature as an excuse to touch him. "I like all your stories. I wish I could have seen some of those things with my own eyes."

"I'd be happy to take you along next time."

Mabel's heart leapt in her chest, but she quickly tamped the excitement down. That was only the potion talking. Even friendly as they were, he wouldn't want her tagging along.

"I'm teaching here in England for all of next term, of course, but I had assumed that when I led another dig, I would naturally..."

He halted mid sentence, looking away abruptly.

"Drew?" Was he regretting the words he'd just spoken? It had been mere hours. Had the potion's effects begun to falter?

"I would be happy to extend the invitation," he said at last. "To you and any... companions you wished to bring along."

What companion could be better than you? she wanted to say. Already he'd turned her night from an utter disaster to one of the happiest in recent memory. She plucked the pocket watch from his waistcoat and checked the time again.

Four hours, they'd been here now, all of it chatting and laughing, making jokes and sharing stories. In some ways, their time in the attic was exactly as it had been when they were children. And in others…

Mabel twisted the quilt in her fingers. This raging desire to kiss him was eating her alive. She knew he felt it too. She'd seen his fists clenching as he stopped himself reaching for her. The golden centers of his eyes burned when he looked at her. He wanted. But he held himself back, because he knew as well as she did that those feelings were temporary.

A sudden need to escape from it all crashed down on her. It was late. She'd grown weary. Maybe tomorrow with a clear head and no more potion she could see him and not crave so much more.

"Do you think it's late enough to retire to bed?" she asked.

"To *what*?" His eyes grew rounder, then narrowed into a smoldering stare, his tongue snaking out to moisten his lips. Then he jerked. "Oh. Are you tired? It is rather late." He shook off the quilt and rose, backing away as if he could no longer bear her presence.

Mabel's jaw tightened. Poor Drew. Fighting an unwanted attraction hour after hour to keep her safe and give her a friend to talk to. If circumstances were different, if his desire for her was real, she wouldn't hesitate to offer all she had. He deserved it and more.

"Yes." She clambered to her feet, shook out the quilt, and folded it. "I would like to try to go to my room, if possible."

He nodded. "I'll escort you there. People may still be looking for you. I'll stay by your side until we're certain you can retire unmolested."

"Thank you. And thank you for spending the evening with me. I had a lovely time."

His worried expression faded into a smile. "As did I."

They moved the chest of drawers away from the door and started for her room. Drew kept his pocket lantern off and stashed away, and they took back staircases to avoid detection. Mabel's skin crawled as they walked the dark, silent corridors, expecting randy men to leap out at her from behind every corner. She reached for Drew's hand, and he laced his fingers through hers.

The murmur of voices reached her ears when she stepped into the corridor with her bedchamber. She looked quickly around, but saw no one. Light spilled from the cracks under a nearby door. Her sister Henrietta's room. Hen always abandoned parties early, not to go to bed but to chat in private with her sisters or her husband. Mabel's clenched muscles relaxed. She would be safe with family nearby.

She opened her own door and stepped inside, not relinquishing her grip on Drew's hand. "Don't leave yet. I want to be sure no one is hiding here." *I'm not ready for you to leave.*

Mabel checked inside the wardrobe, behind curtains, under the bed, and gave the room a long look before declaring it safe.

"Will you be able to sleep?" Drew asked. "I won't leave you if you're afraid. I can station myself outside your door, scowling at anyone who passes by."

"It will never work. You are a terrible scowler. A smile looks so much better on you."

Her words brought one to his lips, those wonderful, kissable lips. She swayed toward him, yearning for one last taste.

"Thank you for tonight," she breathed. "I may not have gotten the dance I wanted, but you made the night special, nonetheless."

"You want to dance?" He strode toward her dresser. Her cherished music box rested atop it, and he picked it up and wound it. When he flipped the lid open, the tinkle of a waltz began to play. Drew turned back and bowed to her. "Lady Mabel Fairweather, might I have the honor?"

Mabel took his hand, he swept her into his embrace, and they began to dance. Around and around she spun in his arms, their bodies pressed scandalously close. The music swirled around her like magic. His strong arms and searing gaze set fire to her body, dragging gasps of pleasure from deep within her.

"Belle," he murmured, resting his head against hers, their steps coming to a halt as the music began to wind down. "Belle, I love you so much."

His words swept Mabel away into a swirling maelstrom of emotions. Shock. Joy. Horror. Heartbreak. Her head dropped to his chest as she clung to him—her doom and her salvation twisted terribly together.

"No," she whispered. "You're saying that because of the potion."

He stiffened and pulled back to stare into her eyes. "It's not the blasted potion. What effect could an allure potion have on me? I already loved you. You were already the most beautiful, the most special, the most magnificent. I have loved you forever. No one and nothing can change that."

Her foolish heart beat a hopeful staccato beneath her breast. The desire to believe him burned through her, as bright and powerful as the insistent, humming yearning in her body. A simple word, a slight movement, and she could have him in her bed, pleasuring her as he whispered promises of the future.

Yes. Yes. Take it. He's here. This is your chance.

She stepped from his arms. "I'm sorry. I-I can't respond

to that in any way while the potion remains inside me. In the morning we can talk, if you still feel the same way."

He wouldn't and her heart broke for it. But she had no other option. If she allowed him into her bed, as a gentleman he would feel obligated to marry her. And she couldn't bear to let him wed her out of duty. He deserved a choice. She deserved a husband who chose her unreservedly.

Drew released a long, shuddering sigh, his eyes squeezing momentarily closed. "Until morning, then."

*

Mabel slept fitfully, dreams of Drew mingling with nightmares of potion-fueled mobs. When her door opened, she bolted upright, her hand shooting out to grab her bedside lamp, prepared to defend herself by any means necessary.

"Sorry to wake you, my lady," the young maid murmured, rushing to tend the fireplace.

Mabel relaxed, her fingers uncurling.

"I should tell you, though, um… there's, er, a gentleman sleeping outside your door. Shall I call for a footman to haul him away?"

Mabel slid from the bed. "What does this gentleman look like?"

"Not like the usual gentleman, my lady. Very tan and muscular. I worry he might be a ruffian."

"No. He's a friend. He thought to protect me from unwanted advances. Thank you."

Mabel washed up and brushed out her hair, and by the time she had finished, the maid had departed. Heart hammering, Mabel cracked the door and peeked into the hall. Drew sat on the floor, his back against the wall, head slumped to one side. She nudged him with her toe. He jerked and his head snapped up.

"Belle?" he murmured sleepily. He blinked several times, then looked her up and down. Passion flared in his eyes and her body warmed in response. "Dash it, Belle, you're in your nightgown!" He scrambled to his feet and backed her into the room. She closed the door behind them, turning the key.

Drew stared down at her, his lips parted, his body angled toward hers. Beautiful, aching desire swelled within her, drawing her nipples to tight points and starting a rush of liquid heat between her legs. He wanted her. He wanted her and she wanted desperately in return.

"Do you still love me?" Her words were a breathless plea.

Drew caught her by the waist and hauled her against him. "More than anything. I've spent my whole life loving you and I've spent all night wanting to ravish you. No, more than all night. Years. I've been waiting years. May I touch you? Please?"

Mabel lifted her eyes to stare into his as her fingers dropped to catch the waistband of his trousers. "Yes," she replied.

Their mouths came together in a raw, urgent, desperate kiss. Hands tore at clothing as they stumbled toward the bed, unwilling to part even for a moment. He cupped her breasts, strong fingers massaging and tweaking. She moaned into his mouth, reveling in every tiny stroke as he mapped her body.

Refusing to be outdone, she freed his shaft from his drawers and wrapped her fingers around it, stroking up and down the length of him. Her whole body thrilled to his helpless, strangled groan. He cursed, but here the profanity only excited her more.

"I like your naughty words," she said.

"Good. Because they tend to come out when I'm feeling strong emotions."

Drew scooped her up and laid her on the bed, pausing long enough to shuck the remainder of his clothing. He was magnificent. Tanned from the waist up, giving her an image of him shirtless in the sun, his muscles rippling as he worked.

He stared down at her as she wriggled free of her drawers and offered herself to him, fully naked and willing.

"Damned strong emotions," he breathed, his eyes dark with desire. He curled his fingers around his jutting erection. "Look what you do to me, Belle. You make me want you. Need you. You're my other half. Make me whole and I'll make you wild with pleasure."

She held out her arms to him. "Yes, please."

He was on her in an instant, spreading her wide, the crown of his cock pressing at her wet core while his fingers slicked over the needy bud at the apex of her sex. She gasped, knees bending in instinctive invitation. He drove into her, filling her in a shocking but not unpleasant invasion.

"God, Belle," he moaned, withdrawing then thrusting deep again. "You're bloody perfect."

Tension spiraled within her, higher and higher as he stroked her and thrust again and again. She copied his desperate curses, matched his every motion, loving the freedom of letting go of rules and boundaries and everything in the world except him. Nothing else mattered. Only their bodies. Only their love.

When the climax took her, she cried his name, her back arching, giving him the opportunity for a final, trembling thrust that sent them both tumbling into a haze of mad pleasure. Sweat-slicked and gasping, they clung to one another until the spasms subsided, then curled up side-by-side, exchanging soft, tender kisses.

"I love you," she sighed.

His lips caressed hers. "Forever," he vowed.

VI - Mistletoe

Drew propped himself up on one elbow and watched Mabel dress. She'd chosen green again, for Christmas, this time with white pearl trim. "You look like a kissing ball."

She smiled and twirled for him, her unbound curls waving as she turned. "Do you like it?"

"I love it. I want to crawl beneath and kiss you until you scream my name again."

Her silver eyes grew saucer-wide as she slowly comprehended his meaning. "Do it."

Sweet and naughty all at once. His perfect partner. She settled into the armchair where she liked to read, arranging her skirts to give him plenty of room. Drew scrambled from the bed, dropped to his knees, and burrowed beneath her layers. He sated himself on the musky scent of their lovemaking, the taste of her desire, and the eager rocking of her hips against his mouth, until she came again in a long, glorious orgasm.

"From now on, your nickname is Mistletoe Mabel," he declared, wiping himself clean with a handkerchief, then reaching for his scattered clothing. "And only you and I will ever know what it really means."

"I don't know," she replied, her lips twitching as she fought a smile. "I might accidentally call you Amorous Andrew in return and then everyone would figure it out."

He grinned. "Honestly, I don't mind in the slightest if people know I like to pleasure my..." *Wife. Dammit.*

"Your wife?" Mabel echoed his thoughts.

Drew rubbed his temple. "I'm a cad. I'd promised myself

I wouldn't do all this," he waved at the tangled bedsheets, "until you'd said yes."

"I did say yes."

"Not to the question I meant to ask."

She laughed, hopping up to embrace him. "Yes, Drew, I will marry you."

"You might let a fellow ask first."

Mabel gave him a quick peck on the cheek. "Go to your room and dress while I finish readying for the day. Then we can head downstairs for what will surely be a very late breakfast and you can ask me properly."

He returned her kiss, but on the lips. "You always did have a good head for planning."

Twenty minutes later, they descended the stairs arm-in-arm, ready to celebrate the merriest of Christmases with a proposal and announcement to their families. Drew fingered the ring in his pocket. The gold band with a single rectangular emerald was a reproduction of a ring he'd seen in Egypt, and he knew she would love it. If he could manage not to lose it in all his nervous excitement.

As they neared the breakfast room—its door still damaged from the previous night's insanity—Drew's eldest brother stepped through the door. Drew raised a hand in greeting.

"John! Merry Christmas!"

"Merry Chr-Christmas," John stammered, coming to a sudden halt. He stared at Mabel, a hungry look washing over his features. He muttered an oath and fled down the hall, not looking back.

All color had drained from Mabel's face. "It hasn't worn off," she whispered. "It h-hasn't worn off."

Drew put an arm around her. "Don't worry, love. We

can go away until it does or find you an antidote. We'll solve this."

She slipped from his embrace, her eyes clouding with tears. "No. Don't you see? It *hasn't worn off.* You… you think you love me, but it's all a lie."

"It's not. Belle…"

She ran from him, into the breakfast room. Drew followed in time to see half-a-dozen men leap from their seats to hurry toward her. Her cousin Susan reached her first.

"Mabel, I've been waiting for you." Susan grabbed her cousin's arm and dragged her right past Drew and back out the door. "We have a cure for you. Come quickly."

"Belle," he called again. "Please, hear me out."

"I'm sorry," she sobbed, letting Susan rush her down the hall. "I'm so, so sorry. I'll always be your friend. I promise."

Drew let her go, watching her vanish down the hall and fingering the ring in his pocket. He could wait until she'd had her cure. When this potion nonsense was over, then he would convince her that his love was genuine. Even if it took 'til next Christmas.

✶

Mabel blinked away her tears, determined not to succumb to her devastation. She would accept the cure, she would refuse the proposal Drew would certainly make out of gentlemanly obligation, and then she would return to her spinsterly way of life. When she had recovered, she would be able to look back and fondly remember the one beautiful Christmas morning of love and passion.

Susan ushered her into the drawing room, where her sisters, her mother, her grandmother, and one unfamiliar woman all stood in a tight circle, quietly talking. They fell silent when Susan and Mabel entered, and the unknown woman stepped forward.

"Lady Mabel?" the woman asked.

"Yes," Mabel replied, managing not to sniff.

"I'm Elle Ainsworth, master potion maker. I have an explanation for you, and a cure."

"*We* have an explanation," Georgia added. "We, uh, put an allure potion into your champagne.

"As did I," the dowager chimed in. "Susan's potion made three."

Mabel gaped at them. "You…" She clasped a hand to her chest. "Did you never even think to *talk* to one another? Or to simply give me a potion?"

Guilty faces stared at the floor.

"We didn't want you to worry about it," Georgia sighed.

"And thought this would be better than letting you get nervous and back down at the last minute," Hen added.

Their grandmother shook her head. "I'm so sorry, dear. We all only meant to give you a pleasant evening, but I'm afraid we made everything so much worse. Please forgive us."

Imploring eyes lifted to meet Mabel's gaze. Her dear, sweet family, who loved her. And who had acted with appalling foolishness.

"I do forgive you," she said, sincerely. But would Drew forgive *her*? Would she ever forgive herself for what she'd done to him?

"Now, about the potions," Mrs. Ainsworth explained. "I make my own allure potions sight-focused. It allows the drinker to slip away when they no longer desire attention. Other allure potions rely more heavily on scents and tend to linger in the minds of the affected. The combination of the two types in an already dangerously high dosage addled the brains of most of the men and some of the women at the party last night." She produced a small vial full of liquid thicker than Susan's allure potion, dark red in color with swirls of green throughout. "Drink this. No need to mix it with anything."

Mabel took the vial, uncorked it, and downed the contents, trembling a little as she did. Cure or not, drinking another potion made her stomach churn with dread. The liquid had a slightly minty taste, and didn't burn the way the allure potion had. Instead it felt cool, soothing.

The contents gone, she took stock of herself. Nothing felt different. Nothing looked different. "What now?"

"Give it a quarter hour or so, to be absolutely certain, and then all should be normal," Mrs. Ainsworth assured her.

Mabel took a seat, spreading her skirts carefully around her. The dress sported a few wrinkles from Drew's amorous attentions this morning.

Poor, sweet Drew. He would be distraught at having taken her innocence while under the spell of the potion. Mabel swore to do all she could to reassure him. And then try to woo him. He would be in England all next term. Could she make him love her, all on her own? She vowed to try.

Christmas services in the chapel hardly registered through her fretting. All the men had returned to their usual state of ignoring her, but even that did little to ease her mind.

"The cure looks to have been a success," Susan said, taking Mabel's arm as the party gathered in the ballroom once again for celebratory drinks and caroling. "Yet you seem distracted. I hope you're not worried about what the gossip rags might report."

Gossip rags? Such a thing hadn't even entered Mabel's mind. She couldn't have cared less what people called her.

"No. Nothing like that. It's only that Drew…" What could she say? She couldn't very well confess what they'd done together that morning.

"Has been staring at you since the moment we left the drawing room," Susan finished. "I hear he slept outside your room all night in case you needed a champion to defend your honor. That's very gallant. Here." She paused in the middle of the room. "Stay right here and talk to him."

"What? Susan, I—" But her cousin had already dashed off and Drew was striding across the room with all the determination of a warrior heading into battle. Mabel's heart began to thump.

"Lady Mabel," Drew called, in a voice loud enough for the entire room to hear. "You are standing under the mistletoe."

Mabel's gaze shot upward to the kissing ball hanging above her, and she darted out of the way before anyone could think to take advantage.

Drew stopped directly in front of her, close enough that she could smell his freshly used sandalwood soap and see the fiery rings in the center of his irises. He raked her with his searing gaze, his whole body taut with anticipation. Either her cure had made no difference to him, or he was the greatest actor she had ever seen, because this was not a man looking to wed her to ease a guilty conscience. This was a lover who had slept with her outside of wedlock and didn't regret it for one instant. Who would do it again and again and not care if their first child was born suspiciously soon after the wedding.

"Mabel Fairweather," he said, his voice ringing through the room that had fallen mostly silent. "I have loved you since the day we met. You are my greatest friend, my closest confidant, my dearest companion. I loved you when I was too young and too poor to even consider an offer. When I was selfishly thrilled you were a wallflower because no one would steal you away from me. I loved you from afar when I was away at school and again while I built my career so I might offer you a home. I've never met anyone more beautiful, more charming, more interesting and fun to talk to. I will never, ever understand how you evaded the notice of so many other men. You were all I ever saw. You are my heart and my soul." He produced a ring from his pocket. "I commissioned this ring three years ago, using every scrap of money I had, because I knew from our letters you would love it. I am finally at a place in my life where I can offer it to you, unreservedly, and beg you for the honor of your hand. Marry me, my Belle. You are my everything. Let me be yours."

Mabel grasped his jacket by the lapels, and pulled him beneath the kissing ball. "You already are," she vowed, and gave him a long, hard, scandalous kiss in front of the entire assembly of the Dowager Duchess of Winstead's Christmas Ball.

When at last they parted, Drew cupped her cheek, his eyes bright with tears of joy. "You are absolutely Mistletoe Mabel from now on," he teased.

"Yes," she whispered. "But only you and I know what that really means."

His eyebrows arched and he favored her with a salacious grin. "Indeed. Merry Christmas, my love. You were my favorite gift this year."

Mabel took his arm and they began to stroll the room to accept congratulations—and the censure of the people who disapproved of their zealous kissing display. As they walked, she leaned close, savoring his presence with all her heart and all her body.

"You can unwrap me anytime you'd like," she promised.

Epilogue

Egypt, December 25, 1884

White flower petals rained down on Drew. He plucked one from his teacup and glanced up at his wife. Mabel twirled in her mistletoe green dress and tossed another handful of petals.

"It's snowing! Merry Christmas!"

"Missing England, love?"

"A bit. But you know I always enjoy getting into the spirit of the season."

"True." Drew caught her arm and pulled her into his lap. "I love how the little girl who first stole my heart is still there inside the woman who owns it now."

"She'll never go away. You're her best friend and best friends have adventures *together*."

He nuzzled her neck. "That they do. Are you still enjoying this one, or is it time I took you home?" Four months seemed nothing to him, when he'd spent years away in the past, but this was Mabel's first foray outside of England. He'd take her back and spend the next few terms teaching if she wanted.

"And miss the digging in the tomb we only just discovered?" she cried. "Never!"

Lightness filled Drew's chest. He'd been hoping she'd say as much.

"I don't need to go home, because I am home," Mabel continued. "Wherever you are, that's where home is."

His arms tightened around her waist. "I absolutely concur." He glanced up at the ceiling. "Now, where's that mistletoe?"

What Are You Doing New Year's Eve?

What Are You Doing New Year's Eve?

A Sass and Steam Novella

**One thousand ladies want his attention.
He only wants one.
Too bad he doesn't know her name.**

Eschewing his privileged life as heir to an automaton empire, William Ashton, Jr. spends his days diving into research and pining for the young woman who frequents his branch of the NYPL. Until one careless word from his mother leaves him with every Knickerbocker princess and penniless chambermaid eager to become his date for the biggest New Year's Gala in Manhattan.

Maddie Peters has long admired sweet and shy librarian Will Ashton, but his family's position in high society means anything more than friendship is a fantasy. When a letter arrives to say that Will has invited her to his mother's exclusive party, Maddie is flabbergasted. She's sure it's a mistake, but she's not one to waste the opportunity to woo him.

Angry neighbors, meddling guardians, and rampaging mechanical dragons all threaten Will and Maddie's chance at holiday romance. But when the clock strikes midnight, these two lovers might find they have what it takes to wind up in each other's arms.

1

New York City
December 27, 1904

"Nine hundred ninety-nine, one thousand." The last two letters fluttered down atop the pile scattered at the feet of William James Ashton, Junior. "Don't tell me there's not one woman in there you'd take to Mother's party."

Will glared at his younger brother. Sam was barely one-and-twenty to Will's twenty-seven, but in these matters Sam was far more sophisticated. Eager and friendly, he threw himself into the social whirl with the glee of a child in a candy store. Will didn't like sweets. And he didn't like parties.

Will hated parties, in fact. Loathed them. Went into a cold sweat just thinking about them. He spent the holidays in a state of perpetual panic, always searching for exits, counting the minutes until the guests would be drunk enough that he could run away and they wouldn't remember. And Mrs. William Ashton's New Year's Gala was the worst.

Will laid a hand atop the desk to steady himself. The polished oak surface was cool and smooth beneath his fingers. Usually the library comforted him, with its floor-to-ceiling bookcases, plush armchairs, and the gentle glow emanating from the crackling fire. Today, his cherished space was marred by the offensive heap of unwanted mail. He glanced out the window. The cold, gray drizzle only heightened his discomfort.

"I'm not going," he declared.

He said the same thing every year, but it was always a lie. During the inaugural gala in 1893, sixteen-year-old Will had been so nervous he'd vomited all over the dance floor. And yet, there he was at the next party come the end of 1894.

Sam folded his arms across his chest, every one of his six-foot-two, football-playing inches looming over Will's terribly average frame. "Mother wants you married."

And there it was. The reason for this absurd pile of correspondence. Mother had informed her friends—and through them, the world—that Will needed a bride.

Will could imagine exactly how his mother must have sounded. She had probably waved her hand in that particular way of hers as she had said to the assembly of women, "It's the modern age. Interested young ladies should simply send him an invitation."

Her outrageous words had spread like wildfire. They'd even been printed in the Times, for God's sake. Now every Knickerbocker princess and penniless chambermaid had sent him a letter, begging for the chance to attend a party on the arm of New York's most elusive bachelor and heir to the Ashton Automata fortune.

"I don't want to get married."

Another lie. Will liked the idea of a wife. One single companion in an otherwise quiet home. It sounded like paradise. If only his skills at wooing women weren't... well, nonexistent.

"That doesn't matter," Sam insisted. "Today all you need to do is pick a woman to bring to Mother's gala. Any woman. You don't truly have to marry her."

"Fine. Then you pick." Will gestured at the letters with an impatient swipe of his arm.

Sam grabbed a letter and tore it open. "'My dear

Mr. Ashton,'" he read. "'I did so admire your speed and coordination when I watched Columbia playing…' Er, seems this young lady has mistaken me for you." He chucked the letter into the fire and picked up another. "'Dear, sweet Willie—'"

"Burn it."

"Oh, no. This one is too good." Sam cleared his throat. "'Dear, sweet Willie. My heart aches for you. It's been so long since we touched.'" Will tried to snatch the letter away, but Sam lifted it out of reach. "'The handkerchief you gave me nestles between my breasts…'"

"I've never given a woman a handkerchief in my life. Who the hell is that?"

Sam scanned the paper. "Um, a Miss Veronica Frost."

"Never heard of her."

"Too bad. She seems eager. I bet she'd give you a New Year's kiss. Any place you wanted it."

"She called me Willie. Burn it."

Sam's blue eyes danced with mischief. "Nah. You told me to pick for you. I like her."

"Goddammit." Will thrust a hand deep into the pile of letters and pulled out a fistful. He spread them on the desk and looked them over. One, from a Miss Madeline Peters, had a small pencil sketch of a book in the corner of the envelope. "That one. I'll take her." He spun around and strode from the library.

Sam raced after him. "You didn't even read it."

"I don't care. She likes books. If I can spend even a quarter of an hour showing her the library instead of mingling, I'll count it as a win. I choose her."

"She could be a lunatic."

"Even better. She'll maim me and I will have an excuse to stay in my room past Twelfth Night."

"Will…"

"It's done. I chose." The clock on the wall spun and whirred, the tinkle of chimes announcing quarter-to nine. "Excuse me, I have to go to work."

"Why? You don't need a job."

Yes, he did. The public library was the only place in the world he felt he belonged. "Miss Madeline Peters. Have someone send her a reply. And I'm taking the steam car."

Will marched to the front hall, took his coat and hat from the revolving mechanical rack, and walked out the door without looking back.

2

Maddie ran her fingers slowly over the envelope, soaking in the smooth texture of the paper as she read the address of the sender over and over: 647 Fifth Avenue. The Ashton mansion.

Her initial surprise at receiving the missive had worn off after a few stupefied minutes. The writing wasn't his, so surely this was a generic reply sent off by the family secretary. Still, Maddie lingered, feeling the fine fibers of the envelope and imagining dinner and dancing and whatever else one did at a high society gala. Anything at all would be magical on the arm of Will Ashton.

"For goodness' sake, child, put your gloves back on."

Maddie spun around in her chair to see her godmother wafting into the dining room, one reproachful hand waving in Maddie's direction.

"Do you want anyone to see you like that?"

Maddie dropped the letter onto the dining room table and flexed her right hand. The metal and flesh moved together, as smoothly as if Maddie had been born that way.

Yes. I do want people to see it.

She swallowed the words she would never say. Mrs. Hastings meant well. She had done her best raising the child who had been unexpectedly dumped on her. She was set in her ways and would never see the world as Maddie did, but Maddie loved her nonetheless.

"It's easier to read my correspondence bare-handed, and we are quite alone," Maddie replied, trying to keep her voice casual. She hated the gloves that usually covered her biomechanical hand. The fabric was hot and diminished her sense of touch. After the accident two years ago, Maddie had learned to treasure each tiny sensation in her fingertips, knowing how close she'd come to losing her hand forever. The memory still gave her chills. The tumble into the street. The carriage barreling toward her.

But it also brought a remembrance of the kindness of strangers: the people who had rushed to her aid and the remarkable medicinal and engineering skill of the biomechanologist who had saved her hand.

Maddie rose from her seat and picked up her letter again, watching the mechanical joints as they flexed. She believed herself a true marvel. Her fingertips were her own, but her hand had been crushed so badly that half the bones had been replaced, and two-thirds of the joints. The brass and steel prosthesis melded with her skin in an astounding display of modern technology.

This was the twentieth century. Such a wonder should be celebrated, not hidden beneath hideous, itchy fabric.

"Madeline!"

Maddie tucked the letter into a pocket and reached for her gloves. "Yes, yes. Someone could come along any minute, I'm sure." She stuffed her hands into the stiff leather, vowing to remove the gloves again the minute she was alone.

"It's not only that, dear. You must accustom yourself to wearing them at all times, even in the home. When you marry, your husband will not wish to see your irregularity."

Maddie gritted her teeth. She would never, *never* marry a man who would treat her that way. Not for all the money in New York.

Mrs. Hastings would disagree, of course. Her chief goal in life was to see Maddie married to someone of higher social standing. And the higher and wealthier the better. An old-money family. An aristocrat from overseas. One of those madly rich, self-made men of questionable morals. She wasn't picky. When all the recent papers had splashed stories on the front page about how multi-millionaire Evan Tagget had left the country amid scandal, Maddie's godmother had sighed—actually sighed!—and said, "Pity. One less option for you, Madeline."

Thank God for small mercies. This was why Maddie would say nothing regarding the letter that now rested in her hip pocket. Mrs. Hastings would assume it was from one of Maddie's school friends, and Maddie wouldn't dare disabuse her of that notion. If Mrs. Hastings even suspected that Maddie was corresponding with William Ashton, she would get *ideas*.

And ideas of that nature could ruin everything. If Mr. Ashton thought her a scheming gold digger, he would never speak to her again. Not that he ever spoke much. But he listened. She liked that about him. And when he *did* speak, it never failed to make Maddie's belly flip-flop in excitement. A quiver ran through her, just remembering the first day he'd truly initiated a conversation.

"You have to see this!"

Maddie almost jumped out of her skin. She'd developed a sort of friendship with Will Ashton since she'd begun frequenting the library, but in all that time he'd never spoken first, except to ask, "May I be of assistance?" Today, however, he rushed out from behind the desk, blue eyes shining, his usually calm body bouncing with excitement.

"Uh... okay." A ridiculous reply, but her brain simply wouldn't form anything more coherent. Had he truly grown so comfortable with her that he'd overcome his natural reserve? Perhaps they'd become something more than "sort of" friends after all.

His posture grew stiff and he looked away from her. "Er, if you want to, of course." Drat. There was that shyness again.

Maddie gave him a smile. "How can I not want to see it when you're so excited about it?"

He shrugged, but his own lips began to curve as his gaze returned to her. "Well, it might be the librarian in me overreacting. But you'd been doing all that reading on astronomy, and then I stumbled upon this and I thought... Never mind. I'll just show you. Follow me."

As they walked through the stacks, Maddie hovered so close their shoulders nearly touched. It couldn't be helped. The aisles were narrow and she didn't want to bump the shelves. It had nothing to do with the fact that she was drawn to him, and particularly drawn to his rare moments of unguarded enthusiasm.

She studied his profile, nervousness and excitement battling for supremacy on his handsome face. His pale cheeks had a slight pink tinge today, and at this distance she could see each individual freckle dotting his nose. Cute. Those people who said redheads weren't attractive were spewing nonsense.

"Our collection of rare books here at this branch is small," Mr. Ashton began, waving Maddie into a little side room she'd never entered before. "But yesterday I was shelving one that had been borrowed by a professor at New York University, and what was right next to it but an antique sky map atlas! Please, sit." He gestured at a desk, atop which sat a large tome with a cracked and faded spine.

Maddie took one of the chairs, and Mr. Ashton sat beside her, donning a pair of gloves before gently opening the book.

"Since you'd been reading all about astronomy, I felt compelled to pull it out for a look," he went on. This may well have been the most words he'd ever spoken to her at one time. "And when I began to flip through, I knew—I just knew—I had to share the discovery with you."

The passion in his voice caused Maddie's heart to skip a beat. She leaned in, pretending not to notice the way they both trembled a bit when their arms bumped. Mr. Ashton turned the page and Maddie drew in an astonished breath.

"Isn't it amazing?" Mr. Ashton ran a gloved finger gently over the exquisite hand-inked illustration of the night sky before turning another page. "Each drawing is scientifically accurate to the listed time and place. I checked against a modern star chart."

Of course he had. He was a researcher. Another little shiver raced through Maddie's body. How could any one man be so adorable?

She carefully turned the brittle pages to the next illustration, for once glad of the gloves she reluctantly wore. Each page had been inked with the deepest blues and the most vivid purples, the constellations glimmering with delicate slivers of gold and silver leaf. "They're so beautiful."

"I know."

Maddie's gaze jerked from the book to Mr. Ashton's face. He was staring not at the drawings but at her. Her skin went hot. Her pulse quickened. "Thank you for showing me," she whispered.

He leaned closer. "You're—"

A knock shattered the moment. A bespectacled librarian peered at them through the open door.

"Mr. Ashton, I'm sorry to interrupt your studies," she said in a prim tone that implied she wasn't sorry at all, "but we have a patron with an urgent request."

Will rose abruptly. "Please excuse me. Feel free to continue to peruse the book. I will return it to the shelf when you have finished." He nodded to Maddie and hurried from the room.

Maddie sighed and gently turned another page. She'd be returning to this book again in the future. And contemplating other ways to coax Will Ashton out of his shell.

*

Maddie's godmother would scold her if she disappeared into her room in the middle of the day, or assume she was ill and make her drink some awful tonic, so Maddie retreated to the tiny rooftop garden to read her letter. All the potted plants sat dormant in the brisk winter air, bare branches swaying gently in the breeze. Maddie liked it here, even without the bright greens and pinks that came in the spring and summer.

She tore the hated gloves from her hands and opened the letter. She'd been so silly to write to him in the first place. Some fit of insanity had overtaken her, clearly. Or perhaps a fit of jealousy, thinking of all the ladies who surely would be begging for Will's escort to a New Year's event.

"Dear Miss Peters," it began. They'd acknowledged her by name. That was much more than she expected from a polite rejection.

Dear Miss Peters,

Thank you for your letter. Mr. William Ashton, Junior would like to extend you an invitation to join him for Mrs. William Ashton's New Year's Gala, to be held at her home beginning at 8:00 p.m. on the 31st of

December. A car will be sent for you at 7:30 p.m. Please reply to confirm your acceptance.

Maddie nearly dropped the paper. Impossible. She read the note again, and then a third time. Good heavens. William Ashton had invited her to the biggest New Year's party in town. But how? Why? When she wrote that letter she'd been certain she stood no chance. Or perhaps only a very little one.

Shivering from both the cold and a strange, nervous anticipation, Maddie gathered her gloves, folded the letter, and hurried back into the house. Questions raced through her mind. What could she tell her godmother that would allow her to attend without causing a giant fuss? Why had Mr. Ashton chosen her? She couldn't remember ever giving him her name. A bad oversight on her part. Yet he must have learned it somehow and singled her out. Would this alter their peculiar friendship?

She hoped not. Maddie cherished those moments together, and though she fantasized about something more, she had never expected it. Nor did she want it, if it would mean the end of their amiable interactions.

As she wandered back down the stairs, turning over possibilities in her mind, a final, equally urgent question sprang to mind: What in the world could she possibly wear?

3

December 28

Will stared at the book he had just shelved, his brain taking far too long to process the error he'd made. He sighed, pulled it back out and moved it to the correct location. He was too distracted today. The upcoming party was making him anxious, naturally, as were his mother's more-persistent-than-usual pleas to attend other events.

He shelved the last of the books and returned to his desk, skimming through the small pile of questions patrons wanted answered. Nothing complicated. He could have these done in no time.

The fun and challenging questions always came from patrons who came to the research desk themselves, but he'd had few of those yesterday and none thus far today. Ordinarily, Will preferred quiet. Part of why he loved his job was that the research desk was far less busy than the circulation desk where the patrons checked out their books. Rarely did he need to worry about anything but one-on-one interactions. Today he'd had no interactions whatsoever. With so many people spending the holidays with family, the usually bustling library branch had only a trickle of visitors.

Which is exactly why you should stop expecting to see her here.

The Library Co-ed. Will didn't know what else to call her, since he didn't know her name. She came to the library nearly every day and pored through books, taking notes and asking many, many questions. He'd learned early in their acquaintance that her guardian had deemed it inappropriate for a young lady to attend college. Defying this blatant inequity, the determined young woman had made it her mission to educate herself. Will scoured the shelves to help her find reading material, brought in books from other branches of the NYPL, and had twice even used his brother to borrow books from the university collection at Columbia.

In the past six months, a friendship had grown between them—and something far more on Will's side. At times he thought he might stand a chance at wooing her. Which was ridiculous, since he'd hardly said a word to her that wasn't related to her research.

She was friendly, certainly, but that was just her way. Reading any more into it was a mere fantasy. Will told himself this every damn day...

"I will be professional," Will murmured, snapping the cap of his pen off and on again, as if the movement would somehow calm his nerves. So far it never had. "I will not gawk at her. I will not touch her. I will absolutely not kiss her."

He repeated the words again, steeling himself for that moment when she would come dancing into the library, blond wisps escaping her updo, cheeks rosy from running or skipping all the way here. Will imagined she ran or skipped everywhere, as full of life and energy as she was.

"Will!"

Her eager cry destroyed any hope of him keeping his cool, especially given the intimate way she had addressed him. And he didn't even know her name. Blast.

She skittered to a halt in front of the research desk, a piece of paper clutched in her hand. "Oh, Mr. Ashton. Please excuse me." Her smile was so broad, Will thought his knees might give out when he rose. But he couldn't be rude, so he forced himself to stand anyway, gripping the desk, just in case.

"What can I do for you?" he asked.

"Nothing!" she exclaimed. She bounced up and down. "You've already done it! I've been admitted to a correspondence class at the University of Chicago! Look!" She set the paper on his desk and lowered her voice. "I can't tell my godmother about it, because you know how she feels about women attending college, but I know you will understand." She clasped both her hands together over her heart. "All the studying and researching we've done these past five months. Everything you've helped me with. Your suggestion ages ago about looking into correspondence classes. Oh, Mr. Ashton, I could just kiss you!"

Will wobbled and fell back into his seat. He picked up the letter, pretending he'd meant to sit and read it, but he couldn't take his eyes off her radiant face.

"Congratulations," he choked out. "You deserve it."

Her entire face glowed. "I can't stay for research today, I'm afraid, but I wanted you to be the first to hear my news. I can't thank you enough. You've been such a good friend."

He nodded, still staring at her. Can I be something more? Is there any hope?

Her head cocked to one side as she gave him an affectionate smile. "I'll see you here tomorrow, I hope?"

"Yes." There it was. Hope. "I'll be here."

"Excellent. Have a lovely day, Mr. Ashton."

Will handed her back the letter and she hurried off, not quite skipping, but as close as a lady could come and not be indecorous. He exhaled slowly, leaning back in his chair. They were good friends. Maybe someday he and...

His exhalation turned into a groan. The letter. Why had he not looked at the letter? It would've had her name on it.

"Well, fuck," he blurted. Sometimes even librarians needed to swear.

Will fought the urge to swear in the library once again. "I should have invited *her* to Mother's party," he sighed.

He dove into the pile of research correspondence to distract himself, but the thought continued to nag at him. It was impossible for many reasons. He could never manage to ask in the first place because every time he saw her his brain turned to mush and inane things poured from his mouth. When he spoke at all. Besides, she was too sociable. She would want to mingle and dance and talk to people.

"Mr. Ashton. Hello."

The familiar voice shattered his concentration. *She's*

here! Will's chair wobbled and he smudged the reply he was writing. He took a steadying breath, then set down the pen and rose from his seat. "How may I help you today?"

"It's an unusually fine day today, don't you think?" she asked, tipping her head slightly to one side. Her eyelashes fluttered. Beautiful, long eyelashes. A dark contrast to golden hair and eyes like a cloudless sky. That perfect, heart-shaped face and those soft, smiling lips. "For December, of course."

Will blinked dumbly at her. He would have said she was flirting with him, but she didn't do that. Never had, though she'd known from the start who he was. Hard not to when he had his mother's bright red hair and was the only man on the staff.

She tugged at the ends of her wrist-length gloves. Ah. She was nervous and overcompensating. He understood that. Now he could see how her wide smile didn't quite reach her eyes, and the way her weight shifted slightly as she stood in front of him. He didn't have any idea what she might have been nervous about. Most days she exuded confidence. And, of course, he couldn't pry.

"Shall we pull out some almanacs and compare the weather of previous late Decembers to this one?" he asked.

Her brows rose in surprise, but she laughed. "That could be interesting, but in truth I came here… to talk."

"Talk?" Did she mean in a "we need to talk" way? He could imagine that conversation. *You stare at me too much, Mr. Ashton. It is decidedly inappropriate, and I am taking my researching to another branch.*

Miss Library Co-ed nodded vigorously. "Don't you think we ought to get to know one another better? It will make things easier."

Things? What things? Was she anticipating some sort of

relationship outside of their research? What mad, wonderful, alternate universe had he walked into?

"You know all about me, after all," she continued.

Not your name. Not enough.

"But all I know about you is what the gossips say, and I can't rely on any of that."

"I was absolutely sick all over the floor at my mother's very first New Year's Gala," Will blurted. He knew that story still made the rounds, though people seemed to overlook it when the words "Heir to Fortune!" were tossed about.

"Oh." She frowned for a moment, then shrugged. "It could happen to anyone. It's cruel for people to continue to dwell on it."

"It could happen again. I hate parties. With a fiery passion."

"Why do you go, then?"

"Because I love my mother and the New Year's Gala is her prize event."

Her smile shined like the sun. "That's very sweet of you."

Will shrugged. He didn't think of it that way. He thought of it as Mother's due. She'd done so much for him. Her position as a patroness of the library was the reason he had this job. Every year he said he wouldn't go to the gala, and every year he saw the disappointment on her face and relented.

"You like parties, I'm sure," he said.

"They can be fun. I don't go to many. I'm a bit nervous, actually."

Will's brows knit together. "Nervous about a party?"

"Well, nervous about *this* party. It will be rather more lavish than I'm accustomed to."

"Oh." Will fidgeted with his cufflinks until he realized what he was doing and let his hands drop. "All the parties

I've ever attended were the height of fashion. My parents would never stand for anything else. Did you have questions about your party? I might be able to answer them. What sort of event is it? A ball? A dinner?"

Her jaw dropped open. "You… you don't know."

The utter shock in her expression made him take a step back. "Know what?"

4

He didn't know. *He did not know who she was.*

Maddie's head spun. This made no sense. Why on earth would he have invited her if he didn't know? And how was it even possible for him not to know? She'd mentioned the library in her letter. She knew she had.

Perhaps it is much too early in our acquaintance, though I do feel I have come to know and respect you from the library…

That was exactly what she had written.

He'd never read her letter. It was the only explanation. She should have known. If he had truly invited her of his own inclination, he would have responded with a note in his own hand. Someone had selected her and responded in his stead.

"Know what?" he asked again, when she continued to say nothing.

"About my complete lack of knowledge regarding parties of any sort," Maddie rambled, too embarrassed to confess the truth. He'd probably be shocked. He might even laugh. That nobody from the library, his date for New Year's Eve? What nonsense. "I've, uh, never actually been."

"To a party." Lord, did he look confused. His brows were all scrunched up and his nose twitched.

"Correct. I've never been to a party." The lie came easier

the second time. "I do not know how to behave, how to dance, or anything of the sort. I require information."

He relaxed immediately. "I would be happy to help you find some books on the subject, as well as tell you what I can from my limited experience."

"Wonderful."

They set out through the stacks, walking side-by-side as they had so often over the past six months. Maddie always felt comfortable in his presence. He didn't leer, didn't condescend, didn't treat her as fragile or too emotional, or any of the things most men of her acquaintance did. Mr. Ashton was kind and thoughtful, and he probably would never dream of forcing her to wear gloves day and night because he couldn't bear to look at her hand.

She jerked to a stop. He didn't know her name, but he knew *her*. Better than most people did. And she wanted him to know the real Maddie. Not the Maddie who hid behind gloves, but the Maddie who intended to show up at his New Year's Gala and give him the surprise of his life.

As Will turned to look at her in befuddlement, she began to remove the gloves, one finger at a time.

"I'm sorry," she said. "I lied to you."

"I beg your pardon?"

"I've been to parties. I know how to dance. I don't need books about any such thing. I simply wanted to get you alone."

Maddie glanced back and forth down the aisle. They were, indeed, entirely alone, and she heard no voices or footsteps to suggest anyone else might be approaching.

"You wanted me alone." Some other emotion mingled with his confusion. His voice had a strange, breathy quality to it that made Maddie's skin tingle.

"Yes. So I could show you this." With a final tug, she

freed her hand from the confining material and flexed it in relief. So much better. She pulled off the other glove and stuffed them both into her pocket, then held her right arm out for his examination.

"You've a biomechanical hand!" His eyes widened in amazement. "Er, as you know, obviously."

"Yes. Not many others know about it, however."

"You came here today to show me?"

"Yes," Maddie lied, although now that it had happened, it felt as though this had been the true purpose of her visit all along and she simply hadn't known it.

"It's ingenious, the way the mechanical joints fuse with your skin."

He wasn't put off. He actually sounded intrigued. Maddie's heart leapt for joy. "It is, isn't it? So many people don't understand, but I thought you would." She'd imagined he would, at least, in her crazy dreams. Her crazy dreams which seemed to be coming strangely true lately. She knew she shouldn't tempt fate, but she pushed ahead with one more of those dreams. "You may touch it, if you'd like."

He took her biomechanical hand in both of his, clasping it firmly while his fingertips roved over her half-metal fingers. She flexed for him, letting him see the way the hinges bent and turned as she moved.

"You're utterly remarkable," he breathed, his thumb gliding up and down each of her fingers in turn. "The craftsmanship is astounding. Each part must have been manufactured to the most meticulous of standards. Not a click or a creak anywhere, and each weld and rivet is perfection."

"You know engineering?"

Mr. Ashton laughed. "I may not be following my father in the running of Ashton Automata, but I've learned a thing or two over the years. This is fine work. A true marvel of technology and medicine together."

Maddie let out a long breath. "I knew it. I knew you'd understand. That you wouldn't think me a freak."

"Never." A gentle finger stroked across the center of her palm and she gasped at the sensation. Warm. Caring. Intimate.

"Do that again."

"This?" He repeated the motion, adding in a matching caress over her metallic knuckles.

Maddie stepped closer. "Yes."

"Or perhaps this?" Mr. Ashton—Will—lifted her hand and pressed a kiss to the back. His soft lips rasped over skin and brass, creeping from knuckles to fingertips.

"Yes," Maddie sighed again, sliding up to him, pressing her body to his, lifting her chin. "Kiss me."

He released her hand, bending his head to hers.

"Will!"

The rumbling voice brought them both back to earth. Good heavens, they were in the library stacks. Doing wanton things. Not nearly enough wanton things. She hadn't gotten her kiss. If only they'd been somewhere more private.

"Will, are you back there?" the voice called. Whoever he was, he sounded worried.

"That's my brother," Will said, disentangling himself from Maddie. Her left hand had clenched on his jacket during their almost-kiss. His voice was unusually deep, and his pale, freckled cheeks rosier.

"You should go. It sounds important."

Will nodded, stepping back to put more space in between them. "I'm here!" he answered. His eyes locked with Maddie's. "Will I see you again tomorrow?"

"I don't know," she admitted. She had so many things to

do. She had yet to tell her godmother about the invitation, and she desperately needed to find a dress. A dress that would dazzle. A dress that would make Will wish to kiss her at midnight in front of everyone, and not merely in secret in the stacks of the library. A decision he might already be regretting, by the look of apprehension on his face. "During the holidays everything is busy. But soon. I promise I'll see you soon." *At the party.* "Goodbye." She turned and rushed through the stacks toward the exit. Those novels she'd been meaning to check out could wait.

"Miss…" he called after her, but Maddie didn't turn back. He didn't even know her name. He didn't know she was his New Year's date. More likely than not, the entire invitation was a mistake. He'd probably arrive at the party with a proper high society woman on his arm. Maddie rushed out into the cold winter air and turned down the street toward her favorite second-hand shop. If she wanted to win him, she needed battle armor.

5

Will almost pulled the car to a halt. "What is that awful screeching?" He winced at the sound assaulting his ears, some cross between an animal's cry and an unoiled hinge. He slowed as they approached the Ashton mansion, trying to keep his focus on the road and not on the noise. A pedestrian with his hands over his ears darted into the street, and Will had to swerve to avoid hitting him. A driver headed in the opposite direction laid on his horn, adding to the cacophony.

"That's what I've been trying to explain," Sam replied, half-shouting to be heard, though he sat in the passenger seat right beside Will. "Norris claims all his dragons are defective."

Will's eyebrows arched. "Suddenly. All at once."

Ashton Automata was the largest manufacturer of personal dragons in the country. The Ashton's neighbor, Mr. Norris, was a supplier of parts for the mechanical animals and owned enough of them to make his own zoo. And Norris knew full well they didn't all spontaneously malfunction.

Sam nodded. "Exactly."

Will spied the source of the sound, Norris's enormous lupine guard dragon. The mechanical wolf sat on its haunches by the front steps of the townhouse, baying mournfully. Will had never thought guard dragons particularly effective, and this one was currently more useless than usual.

"I take it that's not the only screaming creature?" he asked.

Sam shook his head. "A whole house full. And he's got all the windows open. He's blaming Father for it."

Will pulled the car up to the curb, where he handed it off to their driver, Biggs, for cleaning and refueling. He followed Sam into their house, still cringing from the noise.

"Come into the study," Sam urged. "Father wants to talk with you about it."

"Why me?" This wasn't the first time Norris had behaved in such a fashion. He was a menace, always blaming others for his own failings, whether they be business, social, or political. But his rivalry had always been with Father, not with Will.

"Something about you snubbing his daughter Kate."

"I haven't spoken to Miss Norris in more than a year," Will replied. And God willing, it would stay that way. She was as self-centered and mean as her father. "She's a bitch."

"I know, but I hope you didn't say that to anyone else."

"Probably to Alex, but no one else."

The two brothers entered the study, where their father sat behind the large desk, tapping his pen against the wood as he stared off into space. Several moments passed before he stopped and looked up.

"Ah, William. You're here. Sit down." The noise next door made the windows vibrate, and he spoke loudly to compensate. Will and Sam took the two seats in front of the desk. "I assume your brother explained the trouble."

"Somewhat."

"Norris has turned his household into a screaming menagerie. Not sure what he did, since half those creatures didn't make any noise whatsoever, but he's set them all to howling, and is bothering the whole neighborhood. Claims it's a flaw in our products."

"Bullshit."

"Obviously. I expect it will cease in another hour or two. You know him well enough to understand his methods. It's a demonstration."

Will's fingers clenched. "He means to do it again during Mother's party unless he gets what he wants."

His father nodded. "I think so, too. I walked right over there and shouted over the noise whether he believed I'd wronged him somehow, and he yelled back something about you slighting his daughter."

"You know I don't like her," Will replied, attempting to be tactful. "I avoid any interaction with her whatsoever."

"She insults Will's friends, mocks him for avoiding social events, and starts nasty rumors," Sam added, apparently not feeling the need for the same restraint. "If she's been slighted, she deserves it."

"This is a specific case," their father explained. "It seems the young lady wrote you a letter recently?"

Will's gaze flicked toward the door, thinking of the

giant stack of letters he'd left piled in the library only yesterday. "I have no idea. I didn't read that ridiculous flood of correspondence."

"According to her father, you invited her to your mother's party, then followed up with a later note saying you'd thrown her over for someone else."

"A lie. I never invited her, nor would I have. If she sent me a letter, it went unread and unanswered."

"She thinks she has some claim on Will because we're neighbors," Sam said. "She doesn't even like him. She just likes money and notoriety."

"Obviously, the easiest thing to do would be to write the young lady a letter and invite her to the party," Will Senior mused.

"They're already invited," Will snapped. "They always are."

"But not with you."

"I invited someone else." Miss… Peters. Whoever she was. "I refuse to snub her. That would be unpardonable." Not even for his mystery library woman. Why, oh, why hadn't he simply ignored all the letters and asked *her*?

Another second alone in the library stacks and he would have been kissing her. He would have known the taste of those lips, would have discovered how perfectly their bodies could align. Damn Norris and his scheming to hell.

Father nodded his agreement. "I suspected that would be the case. I propose a compromise. You invite Miss Norris and a few other young ladies as well. Let it be known that the flood of invitations was too large to choose from, therefore you selected several at random to be as fair as possible."

"That's still unfair to Miss Peters."

"How so? Did you tell her she alone was chosen?"

Will's jaw twitched. "I don't know," he admitted. "I didn't write the response."

"Well, there you have it. I'll have my secretary send the same message to a few others and we'll be done with it."

Will shoved his chair back and stood up. "Or you could not let Norris blackmail you."

"I do not like conflict and disorder, William. There is a simple solution here, and—"

"It's blackmail," Will interrupted, not caring that he was defying his father. "I refuse to be a part of this. I will not parade around with woman after woman like I'm some sort of prize in a debutante competition. And you *know* what parties do to me. I will not become a spectacle. I will escort Miss Peters and no one else. Good day."

Will stormed out, leaving his father and brother gaping at the outburst, and headed straight for the small office where Schuler, his father's secretary, sat scratching away with a pen.

"You wrote a reply for me to a Miss Peters yesterday?" Will asked.

"Yes, sir, I did."

"Excellent. Do you still have the letter? I need her address." Will couldn't stop his father from inviting whatever young ladies he wanted, but he could give Miss Peters some sort of explanation. As the one Will had chosen, however randomly, she deserved that courtesy.

"I disposed of the letter, but I do have the address, as I made arrangements for a car to pick her up that evening. One moment and I will have it for you."

Schuler checked his books, jotted down an address, and passed the scrap of paper to Will.

"Thank you." Will took the paper and hurried out of the house, deciding to walk back to the library. The long, brisk walk would give him time to think. He could write his message to Miss Peters from work, where no one would bother him.

Once he was out of earshot of Norris's screaming guard dragon, Will pulled the paper from his pocket and read the address again. She lived not far from the library. Convenient.

Perhaps a letter wasn't the solution. Will could go to see her in person when he'd finished working for the day. A brief moment with her, one-on-one. That would be so much better than attempting to speak with a complete stranger during a party.

He'd go tonight, before dinner. Introduce himself and warn her that his family might be inviting more ladies on his behalf. Perfect.

He took a deep breath. Only a few days until this was all over. Then he could return to wooing his Library Co-ed in the stacks.

6

"You are the best." Maddie hugged her friend Victoria one final time, then gathered up the precious bundle. Finding the perfect dress had taken most of the day, scouring every article of clothing in Victoria's second-hand shop, but they'd pieced together an ensemble that would make Maddie shine like a jewel. She needed to buy a special pair of gloves and make a few minor alterations, but by New Year's the dress would be flawless. Will Ashton would never know what hit him.

Maddie hurried toward home, the bundle clutched to her chest, eager to unroll it in her room, where she could strip down completely and try on everything as it was meant to be worn. But first, dinner, where she would finally inform

Mrs. Hastings that she had been invited to a New Year's party. Maddie would probably have to confess who had extended the invitation and then endure hours of discussion about the best way to snare a rich husband. Unfortunately, such lessons would include suggestions like, "Don't act too brainy," and, "Let him assist you with even the smallest of tasks," rather than the far more interesting, "Have a near-kiss in the library."

A cold drizzle had begun to fall. Maddie ducked her head and walked faster. In her rush, she didn't see the man with the umbrella turn the corner until they had nearly collided. She staggered to a stop. He paused and tilted the umbrella back. Even in the dim glow of the streetlamps, his red hair was unmistakable.

"Mr. Ashton? What are you doing here?"

"Miss… er, I'm so sorry, but I've never learned your name. I have a brief call to pay before I return home, but perhaps I can escort you where you are going first?" He held the umbrella over her. "I'd hate for you to catch a chill."

"Thank you." Maddie stepped close to him so they could share the umbrella. Was this the time to tell him her name? Would he even recognize it, or did he have no idea whose invitation had been chosen? "My home is just up the street."

"It is?" He twitched and the umbrella wobbled.

"Yes. In the next block."

They began to walk, their steps slow both because they were crowded under the umbrella and because he was staring at her.

"Then you must know… Excuse me, might I inquire as to your name?"

Maddie hesitated a moment. If he did recognize her name, her appearance at the party would no longer be a surprise. Then again, a surprise was still a surprise, no matter when and where it happened. And she could still wow him on New Year's with her fabulous dress.

"Maddie Peters," she replied.

"Miss Madeline Peters." Will stopped walking and turned to look her in the eye. "You're her! She's you! My God." He swayed as if wanting to step away from her, but he was too much a gentleman to leave her without the umbrella. "You… I… You must think me a fool. Or crazy. Or… How did I not know your name?"

"What I want to know is, why did you invite me, when you didn't know the letter was from me? You didn't read it. If you had, you would have known who I was."

He looked at the ground, shifting uncomfortably. "I had a stack. A pile. A thousand deep. I saw the little book sketched on the envelope and chose her. Chose you."

Maddie almost reached to touch his arm, stopping herself at the last second. "Maybe part of you did know. Maybe you'd seen my name when I was checking out books." Maybe that was her own wishful thinking, wanting to be something more than random chance.

His gaze lifted back to hers. "But I never work the circulation desk."

Maddie pressed her party dress to her chest. "Maybe it was fate. Walk me home? It's not far."

He nodded and they began to walk again. The raindrops grew fatter, splattering on the pavement and dampening Maddie's skirts. She edged closer to Will. He said nothing, but she sensed a tension in his posture. He was troubled by her revelation.

Perhaps she was too far beneath him to be an appropriate party date. Or perhaps he was bothered by what had happened at the library.

When they stopped in front of her house, he finally

spoke. "I honestly don't know if this is the best news ever or the worst."

"Oh. Well, sorry to be confusing."

That got a chuckle out of him. "I should have just asked you. At the library. I feared I'd muck it up, and now I have."

Her heart thumped in her chest. He did want her. "How? You still invited me, in however roundabout a manner."

"No. I shouldn't have answered a single letter. Our neighbor is causing trouble now, and my father is insisting I invite multiple women, as if the letters were a lottery to choose finalists. If you come to the party you'll become part of the spectacle. You'll be talked about, evaluated, perhaps become the target of cruelty. You deserve better than that. I'm so sorry."

Maddie's fingers dug into her parcel. "I don't understand."

This up and down of emotions was driving her mad. He'd invited her, but he hadn't. He wanted her there, but he didn't. She didn't know whether to be happy, sad, or simply confused.

Will walked her up the stairs. "I came here expressly to explain the matter to you, Miss Peters. If you will permit me to call on you briefly, I will attempt to do so. Unless you'd prefer to speak at the library tomorrow?"

"No, tonight." The impulsive words were out of her mouth before she could think. Her godmother would interpret his presence here as tantamount to a marriage proposal. On the other hand, having Will confirm that they were merely friends could help. *If* they were merely friends. She wasn't certain.

"I should warn you that my godmother, Mrs. Hastings, is somewhat…"

The door flew open. "Madeline Rose, what is the meaning of this?"

Will nudged Maddie through the door, tipping the umbrella to reveal himself. "Mrs. Hastings?" he inquired. "I'm William Ashton, and I—"

"Ashton? *The* William Ashton? But, of course you are with that hair. Quickly, young man, come inside. You'll catch your death of a cold."

Will shook out the umbrella and stepped into the hall, only to have his outerwear all but ripped from his body by Maddie's godmother.

"Madeline, do take our guest to the parlor at once. I'll call for refreshments. What do you prefer, Mr. Ashton? Coffee? Tea? Dinner?"

"Er…" His eyes had gone round and he stood frozen in place, like a startled animal. "Nothing, please," he managed at last. "Only a moment with Miss Peters."

"Coffee," Mrs. Hastings declared. "The parlor, Madeline."

Maddie took Will's arm and hurried him into her small, austere parlor. "I do apologize for her," she sighed.

"Is she always like that?"

"Yes." Maddie took a seat on the sofa, tucking the bundle of her dress behind her like a pillow. Will took a nearby chair.

"Then let me explain everything before she returns. I selected one young lady to invite to my mother's gala: you. When my brother came to get me at the library, it was to inform me that those plans were now unacceptable. Our neighbor is a longtime business associate and rival of my father. He wants his daughter to have the distinction of becoming my date for the party and has implied he will ruin the event if that does not happen. My father's solution is for me to have multiple ladies join me for the event. I can't stop him from inviting them on my behalf. Since his secretary sent you the invitation, he can send other, identical notes. That is my fault and I apologize. But I wish you to know that I invited you and no other."

"Invited?" Mrs. Hastings' eager voice rang out. "Madeline, to what has this nice young man invited you?"

Will's posture immediately tensed. Maddie's own body did as well, though less obviously. She had more practice.

"To Mrs. Ashton's New Year's Gala, Godmother," she replied. "Mr. Ashton and I met at the library and he has invited me. As a *friend*." Maddie didn't think the emphasis would help much, but she put it into her voice nonetheless. Might as well try everything.

"Oh, Madeline! What an honor! Mr. Ashton, you are so gracious to have singled out our dear Maddie. I assure you, she is everything that is lovely in a woman. So kind, well-spoken, knowledgeable on all social graces, with a good head for household management, and such a lovely figure, with those wide hips and ample bosom, don't you think?"

Maddie's face turned as red as her new party dress. Her entire body folded in on itself. She wanted to crawl away and die of embarrassment. Will's blue eyes were wide with horror and he squirmed in his seat.

"Ah, yes, very, er, lovely," he babbled. He hopped up from his seat. "I'm so sorry, but I cannot stay. I only had a moment. I hope you understand, Miss Peters?"

Maddie only nodded. She understood. She understood that her dream night had been ruined before it began and that her godmother had just made her look a fool at best and a gold digging schemer at worst. She mumbled a goodbye as Will rushed from the room. A moment later, the front door opened and closed.

Maddie grabbed her dress and ran to her room, locking the door behind her, tears welling in her eyes.

None of this is your fault, she told herself. *You can't control Will or his father or Mrs. Hastings.*

Slowly, she unwrapped her purchases, examining the beautiful fabrics and the perfect accessories. What she could do was go to the party. She could show the world who Maddie Peters really was. And she could have a grand time, whether Will Ashton wanted her or not.

7

December 31

Will gripped the washstand with both hands, staring into the mirror, willing himself to breathe. Even done up in his holiday best, he looked like hell. He'd hardly slept the last two nights, and he'd been too queasy to eat much. His father's idea grew increasingly worse. Will now had six women to deal with, and he'd been instructed to meet each one in the atrium, escort her into the party, dance with her at least once, see she had refreshments as needed, and keep her company if others did not.

"Your mother is right. It's time you found a wife," Father had said, in a tone that indicated he would not change his mind. "You must have some interaction with the candidates in a social setting, and given your difficulties mingling at events, the best strategy is to do it all at once."

After all these years he still didn't understand. No one understood. How could anyone really know what it was like to be betrayed by his own body? To be trapped in the grip of irrational panic, unable to stop the reactions no matter how desperately he wanted to. It wasn't a discomfort, it was an actual, physical illness. Will's coping mechanisms could only slow the inevitable. Remaining in the crowd long enough to dance six dances, make small talk, and do whatever else his parents deemed necessary for "evaluating" these women would only lead to disaster. And Maddie Peters would be witness to his humiliation.

You knew nothing could come of it. She has to learn eventually, and no woman wants to be burdened with a man like you.

Which was why he would never wed. He refused to settle for a marriage of convenience, no matter how much his parents wanted grandchildren.

"Will?" Sam rapped on the door. "Are you still in there?"

Will hesitated a moment, then replied, "Yes."

Sam opened the door and stepped inside. "Ready?"

"I can't do this."

Sam crossed the room and clapped him on the shoulder. "Sure you can. You've been doing it for years. Only difference is you'll have some ladies to entertain. They'll meet friends and start to chat and you can slip away."

Will shook his head. The routine he'd crafted in previous years wouldn't work tonight. He had always kept it simple. He stayed near his parents for greetings and introductions so all the high rollers would know he was there, then spent the remainder of his time circling the edges of the room, watching for an opportune moment to slip away. Circulating undisturbed wouldn't be possible with six ladies vying for his attention and all of New York watching.

"Dammit, why didn't I just ask her?"

"Ask who what?" Sam gripped Will's arm and tugged him toward the door.

"Maddie Peters, my library mystery woman."

Sam stilled. "I thought Miss Peters was the invitation woman."

"She is. They're one and the same."

Sam stared at Will for a long moment, then broke into a window-rattling guffaw. "Oh, God, Will, that's brilliant.

Your random woman is the girl you've been pining after for months? Funniest damn thing I've ever heard."

"It's not. If I'd asked her straight up and never answered a single letter, this wouldn't have happened."

"You're underestimating the eagerness of our parents to see you settled."

"She's going to hate me, Sam. I went to her house to explain it to her, but that can't change the fact that what should have been a pleasant evening for her is now a public farce."

"She'll see she's the one who has your true attention. As will everyone else. Relax."

"I. Cannot. Relax." Even now, his heart was racing. The way his stomach was churning made him fear he might repeat the infamous dance floor illness.

Will plodded down the stairs with all the cheer of a condemned man marching to the gallows. The first of the young ladies had already arrived, a Miss Linden straight out of the schoolroom. Her face was pale, and she trembled a bit when she took Will's arm.

"Don't worry, I'm at least as terrified as you are," he whispered.

"I don't want to dance in front of all these people."

"Excellent. I will walk you to a friend or whatever corner of the room is most comfortable for you, and let you be."

She let out a long, relieved breath. "Thank you so much."

"Believe me, I understand."

Will led the nervous girl to a secluded seat—one he had occupied many times in the past—fetched her a glass of lemonade, and left her. Poor girl. He hadn't thought of it before, but they were as much victims in this as he was.

He hurried back to the foyer to wait for the next lady to escort. People filed in, but he hung in the corner, letting them pass by without a word. None were the women his father had invited.

Where is Maddie?

The lack of her presence made his anxiety spike. Had she decided not to come after all? Had his father decided she was an unsuitable bride and rescinded the invitation? Will hated to even consider the possibility, but he couldn't deny that his father was far more concerned with the family status than Will would ever be.

Guests streamed past, until Will began to wonder how they would even fit in the ballroom. This may have been the largest event this house had ever seen. And still, no sign of Maddie.

Will's worries mounted and his gut churned dangerously. He abandoned the foyer and sought out his father, who was greeting guests as they entered the ballroom. Will watched for a small break in the flow and pounced.

"Father!"

"William." Will Senior frowned down at his son. "Why are you not dancing?"

"Where is Miss Peters?"

"I arranged to have the arrival of your young ladies staggered."

"Staggered?" Will echoed. "What do you mean? When will she be here?"

"They will all be along in good time. I want you to have time to spend with each of them. Now, why are you not dancing with Miss Linden?"

The simmering fury Will had been holding inside began to boil, fueled all the more by the press of guests eager for a word with their host and hostess. An arm jostled him. Hot bodies of people he hardly knew edged closer and closer.

"Stop!" he blurted. He had to get away. He needed

space. He needed silence. "No. I won't do this. I'm done." He chose the largest gap between guests and forced his way through it, rushing across the room to the sofa where he'd left Miss Linden. "Let me sit by you," he begged.

She slid over to give him plenty of room, eyes wide with surprise. "You weren't jesting."

Will nodded. He was certain he was pale as death, and his hands trembled, even when he pressed them against his thighs. He ran through several coping techniques, counting slowly, focusing on his breathing, picturing a calm, comfortable place.

"Would you mind pretending to talk to me if anyone approaches?" he asked.

Miss Linden nodded. "You didn't force me to dance. I'm happy to return the favor."

"Thank you." Sweet girl. Will liked her already, though her presence caused none of the electric sparks Maddie Peters roused in him. And good thing, as Miss Linden's affections plainly lay elsewhere. Will watched her as he composed himself, following her gaze across the room to where Sam stood, a drink in his hand, laughing at something a friend had said. Miss Linden released a tiny sigh.

"I will ask him to introduce himself," Will said softly. "Quietly. Where others won't be watching."

Miss Linden turned pink, but she murmured, "Thank you."

Will's heart rate slowly returned to normal. Thank God for small miracles. His father appeared to be ignoring his outburst so long as he sat with one of the chosen ladies. The unpleasant churning in his stomach hadn't entirely receded, but he was no longer in danger of losing what little lunch he'd eaten.

He was almost feeling brave enough to stand up and

take a lap around the room, in case Maddie had arrived without his noticing, when a peculiar buzzing sound pricked his ears. A hum of curious voices followed. As Will rose to better assess the problem, the crowd parted in front of him. Marching toward him, in a frothy white dress resembling a meringue, with a melon-sized mechanical bee buzzing above her scowl, was a furious Kate Norris.

Oh, fuck.

The large, glass eyes of the bee-dragon flashed as Miss Norris stalked closer. Will's eyes darted back and forth, searching for a path to freedom, but people clustered all around, eager for a glimpse at the spectacle. A trickle of sweat ran down Will's back. He forced a deep breath into his lungs, trying to wrangle his respiration into a slow, steady rhythm.

The bee's eyes flashed again. What in hell was that thing?

"How dare you do this to me?" Kate snarled, invading Will's personal space until he stumbled back into the wall. Voyeuristic onlookers moved closer. The dragon's eyes flashed again, and this time Will heard the familiar click of a camera shutter.

Oh God. She's taking pictures of me.

Will's stomach heaved. He tasted bile rising in his throat. He was trapped against the wall, in front of hundreds of people, with no clear escape, and it was on display for all the world.

Kate Norris' mouth twitched in the tiniest hint of a smirk. "You all deserve it," she whispered. "For forcing my father into obscurity."

Will grasped hold of the anger her words sparked. Her family's business manufactured quality parts, but had never done anything groundbreaking. They had plenty of money. Their inability to break into the top tier of society had nothing to do with Will's family and everything to do with the insular nature of the upper class. And probably something to do with Norris's arrogance.

"Your father is a horrible person, and I beg you to stop acting like him," Will retorted. It was all he had in him. He clutched his heaving gut, trying to shoulder his way past people to an exit—any exit.

"For heaven's sake, leave him alone!" Miss Linden exclaimed, as the camera bee continued to buzz and flash, recording Will's pallid complexion and panicked expression. "Can't you see you're making him uncomfortable?"

Will gave the young woman the best smile he could manage, given his traitorous body. He was absolutely introducing her to Sam. Later.

He tried to push past another person, cringing at the contact. His eyes drifted to the main entrance. Too far. He'd be sick long before he reached it.

A flash of red caught his eye. *Maddie.* Even across the room he could see the way the dress displayed her figure. Golden curls tumbled from an intricate updo to frame her face. He fixed his gaze on her. Beauty. Happiness. He began to count, trying to match his breathing to the tempo of the numbers.

Miss Norris was still ranting, but the words no longer registered. Everything was noise and stifling heat. Will pushed along the wall, heading for the windows. With the cold weather, they weren't open to the small balconies, but they were his best hope for a quick exit. Watching Madeline all the while, he inched along the wall, feeling behind him until the subtle floral paper gave way to smooth glass. He fumbled for the latch.

Maddie had spied him. Of course she had. Everyone

in the room was staring at him and at the awful buzzing camera hovering over him. Her hands clutched her skirts, lifting them to hurry toward him. His stomach heaved again and he almost choked. He couldn't let her see him like this.

I'm sorry, Maddie.

The window opened behind him. Cold air rushed across his back and neck, icy relief to his overheated skin. Will darted out onto the balcony and swung himself over the edge, dropping to the street below.

8

The instant the window opened Maddie knew she'd never catch Will in time. She whirled, her skirt spinning around her, then raced from the ballroom. She took the stairs two or three at a time, bounding down to the ground floor and flinging herself out the front entrance while startled guests and staff hurled worried questions in her direction.

Outside, cold wind whistled down Fifth Avenue, the noise mingling with the puffs and rumbles of the fanciest steam cars whisking their wealthy owners to the grandest New Year's celebrations. The lengthy line of vehicles in front of the townhouse declared Mrs. Ashton's gala to be among the finest.

Maddie's head whipped back and forth, looking for Will, but the crowd was too dense to see much past the house. With the streets as bustling as they were and the weather bitingly cold, the outdoors couldn't have offered him much refuge. Maddie forced herself to think. Where might he have gone?

The sound of a fist pounding against wood nearby cut through the drone of arriving guests.

"Open up, dammit!"

Will.

His voice drifted up from just below her, at the bottom of the basement stairs. Maddie ran to the steps and leapt down to his side just as the servant's entrance swung open. Will's jaw dropped open in shock.

"M-Maddie?"

She propelled him through the door, into the warmth of the house.

"Is there a problem, Mr. Ashton?" asked the young maid who had opened the door.

"No, no problem," Will replied. His voice had a slight tremble to it. He hadn't yet recovered from the scene upstairs. Maddie longed to wrap her arms around his waist and hug the discomfort away. "I simply needed a less-chaotic entrance to the house. Thank you."

The girl made a little curtsy and scurried away.

Will sagged against the wall. "Maddie, you shouldn't be here," he said, not looking at her.

"Do you need time alone? Can I fetch you anything? Water? Brandy? A book to read?"

Silence descended. Maddie waited. She wouldn't press. Not after witnessing his terrified escape from the party. She didn't ever wish to be a source of distress to him.

"I think… I think I'm okay," he said at last. He had yet to look at her, but his voice had evened out, and he wasn't shaking. "Brandy would be welcome. There's some in the library cabinet." His head turned, just enough for him to glimpse her. "If you'd like to accompany me?"

"You know me, Will. I never say no to a library."

The hint of a smile on his lips warmed her insides. He was coming back to her.

"This way." He motioned down the dim hall. "We'll take the back stairs."

Maddie followed in silence through the working areas of the house, until the sounds of the party reached her ears. Will quickened his pace, leading her down a hall and through a door, closing and locking it behind them before flicking on the electric lights.

Maddie gasped.

Bookcases ran from floor to ceiling over every wall, their shelves filled to capacity, every tome arranged with loving care. Rolling ladders provided access to books well above her head. Every shelf bore an engraved plate, labeled with categories from mathematics to philosophy to the latest novels. Reading lamps with stained glass shades stood beside cozy chairs and atop a pair of beautiful oak desks. Dictionaries and references sat open on reading stands. A heap of cozy pillows lay in one corner, in front of a shelf holding children's books.

"You did this," she breathed.

"My mother started it," Will replied. "I merely added a bit of organization."

Maddie walked further into the room, taking a moment to turn in a full circle. "It's like a mini public library."

"That was the plan. My mother has been a library patroness for longer than I've been alive. She wanted to replicate that in her home. Her idea was to make a space where the entire family and entire staff could have a place to discover and cultivate the love of books. It's not unusual to find a maid perusing the shelves or a footman with his nose in a novel. A peculiar perk of working for the Ashtons. I practically grew up in this room and added more and more of my own touches over the years—the sorting system, the labels, the card catalog." He waved a hand at the cabinet full of small drawers. "The children's corner is for the grandchildren mother is urging me to give her." He turned away from Maddie once again, his shoulders hunching. A little shudder ran through him.

"I know how you feel," she said. "You heard my godmother when you visited. She couldn't have been worse unless she'd hung a sign around my neck saying, 'broodmare for sale.'"

Will spun to face her. "The way she spoke of you was repugnant." He clasped his hands behind his back, his weight shifting from one foot to the other. "I apologize for my failure to respond appropriately. I ought to have denounced her treatment of you."

"I don't blame you at all," Maddie assured him. "She was terrible to you as well. All she could see of you were dollar signs and a famous name. I admit to worrying whether you'd ever want to speak to me again."

"Of course I want to." He moved toward her, his eyes roving up and down, taking in her carefully crafted ensemble. Her hair was tumbled from running, but all else was in order.

"Oh." Maddie smoothed down her skirts, her stomach fluttering.

"You're all I've been thinking about for days," he whispered. "Not your godmother, not my family, not this awful party. Only you. And now here you are. In a dress that is beyond what I ever imagined."

The fluttering quickened. Prickles raced along her skin. "You like it then?" She spun for him, showing off a hint of her scandalous, lacy stockings as the skirt twirled up from the floor.

"Very much."

"Good. Because it has some special modifications that make it even more... exciting."

All Will's anxiety had vanished, replaced by a hunger that darkened his light blue eyes. "Show me."

Maddie unhooked the decorative clasp that closed the cute little cap-sleeved jacket topping her black corset. She wriggled a bit, and the jacket slithered over her gloved arms, falling to the floor, leaving her shoulders and upper back bare to Will's sight. Her breasts mounded over the top of her corset, exposed nearly down to the nipple. He stared, just the way she'd imagined he would.

Nothing, though, could have prepared her for the blazing intensity of that stare. He stared as if he'd never desired anything more in his life. As if he'd forgotten the entire rest of the world even existed. Maddie's head spun with the force of it.

I am powerful. I am beautiful. I am wanted.

"There's more," she said.

"More." His tongue snaked over his lips, leaving them red and moist, slightly parted, begging for a kiss.

"Yes." She bent to grip the hem of her red and black brocade skirt, feeling for the hidden ties tucked underneath.

"I think I need that brandy."

Maddie paused. She'd never tasted spirits in her life. Her godmother didn't approve of ladies drinking anything stronger than wine and had never allowed it in her house. And while one could read all about alcohol production and consumption at the library, one could not acquire a sample there.

"I'd like some brandy as well," she said, straightening up.

"Certainly," Will replied. His eyes were on her skirt now, no doubt wondering what she meant to reveal. "Though I don't know what need you have to fortify yourself. You're bolder than hell."

Maddie's mouth curved up into a bashful smile. "I was

only eight when my parents died, and many of my memories are blurry, but I do remember one thing my mother said. 'You're a very determined girl, Maddie,' she told me. 'When you want something, you go after it with all you've got.' I try to live up to that."

"And you want *me*?"

"Yes."

Will's big, blue eyes continued to stare at her. He gave a single nod. "Brandy."

He crossed the room and pulled open a section of a bookshelf to reveal a hidden liquor cabinet behind it. He picked up a bottle of amber liquid, poured two small glasses, and passed one to Maddie. He downed his own in a single gulp.

Maddie sipped hers. It was… rather terrible, to be honest. The combination of fruit and harsh alcohol made her think of medicine, so she could understand why doctors sometimes used it to dose their patients. She forced herself to drink all of it. Most likely she'd never drink it again, so she ought to do the thing right this time.

"You don't like it," Will observed. He poured himself a second glass and drained it as quickly as he had the first.

"Not at all. But I am pleased to have sampled it. Thank you."

He chuckled. "Glad to be of service." He returned the bottle to the cabinet and closed it up. "Now…"

He stepped toward her. He wasn't an especially tall man, but standing this close Maddie needed to tilt her head back to look him in the eye. Which put her mouth in a highly kissable position.

"Now?" she echoed. "Shall I show you what my skirt can do, or shall we finish what we started at the library the other day?"

"Both."

Maddie stepped just far enough away to reach for the ties beneath her skirt. A quick pull cinched it up almost to her knees. Will took a sharp breath.

"My skirt is very practical," she explained. "If I need to run, climb, jump, or… display my stockings to a man of my choosing, I need only pull these little, secret ties."

"How high does it go?"

Maddie didn't know. She pulled the strings tighter and the skirt inched up her thighs, until the ribbons holding up her lacy stockings were fully visible, a sliver of bare flesh showing above them. "That high." She tied the strings securely and straightened up.

Will coughed. "You make a compelling argument for practicality." A rosy shine touched his cheeks, and his voice was thick and hoarse. "And I notice that your stockings match your gloves."

Maddie held out her right arm. A fingerless lace glove covered her from palm to biceps, while still allowing any observer to notice the brass and steel modifications to her hand. "I couldn't possibly come to such an event with bare arms. It would be unseemly."

Will grasped her hand and raised it to his lips. "But you still wanted to show off. For me." He flipped her hand over and kissed her palm through the gauzy barrier. Heat flicked up Maddie's arm.

"Yes." She stepped closer and his free arm wrapped around her waist. "You should kiss me now."

"I am at your service."

Will's mouth dropped to hers. For an instant their lips merely brushed, a sweet, startling intimacy. Then she touched the tip of her tongue to his upper lip, as an experiment.

A low growling sound emerged from his throat and he

crushed her body against his. His mouth settled more firmly against hers and he licked at the seam of her lips until she opened wide to his plunder.

Maddie's hands clutched at his jacket, holding herself upright as her wobbling legs threatened to give out. Where did a shy man learn to kiss like this? He possessed her. Claimed her. Opened himself for her so she might barge in and claim him in return. Back and forth they went, eager lips and tongues teasing and tasting, trading control as smoothly as if they'd been practicing for years. When he moved his lips from her mouth to trail kisses across her jaw and down her neck, she surrendered. When she grabbed his hands and dragged them to her breasts, demanding his touch, he obeyed.

"Oh, Will," she groaned. She had considered the possibility of seduction tonight—planned for it, even— but everything was happening so much faster than she'd anticipated. Every time he drew near, some invisible current swept her into a stream of passion, with no notion where it might carry her. Tonight, as his fingers dipped beneath the edge of her corset to tease her nipples and his mouth sucked the exposed flesh of her shoulders, she'd lost all sense of direction. She was a rock, tumbling through the water, slipping, sliding…

Will drew back, his skin flushed, breathing heavily. "Maddie." His gaze flicked to a sofa. "I don't know if we should… how far you'd like to…"

A metallic wail prevented her from answering. A second, similar sound followed. Will's entire body jerked.

"Oh, no."

"What is that awful noise?" Maddie asked.

"Mother's party," Will gasped. "He's going to ruin it."

Maddie grasped his wrist, the strong grip of her

biomechanically-enhanced fingers preventing him from pulling away. "Who? What's going on? Will, tell me what the trouble is. Let me help."

Their eyes locked, his expression fierce. "How good are you with a screwdriver?"

9

Will hadn't thought his body could grow any more stimulated. He was wrong. When Maddie reached down between the luscious mounds of her breasts, a new burst of desire rocketed through him, tightening every muscle in his body, making his cock even harder. Not good timing.

"I carry this with me everywhere," Maddie said, pulling a small tool from beneath her corset. "It has two screwdriver tips and some small screws and nuts inside. In case anything goes wrong with the mechanics in my hand, I can make small, temporary repairs that will hold until I can contact my biomechanologist."

"And you can do those small repairs one-handed with your non-dominant hand?"

"I can."

She was a sensation. The better he knew her, the more he admired her. No wonder he'd rebelled at the idea of escorting any other woman. Who could match her?

Maddie picked up her discarded jacket, swinging it around her shoulders and clipping it in place over the black satin of her corset. Will had seen plenty of gorgeous dresses in his lifetime, many of them on gorgeous women. He'd seen scandalously short skirts and tops that left little to the imagination. But never had anyone looked as perfect to him as Maddie did tonight.

The gown hugged her figure, showing off her curves

instead of diminishing them. The red and black drew the eye, forced you to look, and Will couldn't comprehend how anyone would be able to look away. Her lacy gloves revealed smooth, pale skin and the polished metallic pieces of her biomechanical hand that gleamed in the glow of the electric lights. With her skirt hiked up, Will could see the same, creamy skin beneath her stockings, begging him to stroke her calves and maybe higher.

Even her accessories were perfect. Her jewelry was made from small machine bits: gears and springs and hinges. The fascinator in her hair held more mechanical parts, mixed with bright red roses and black lace. She was modern, brazen, unafraid to embrace an era of technological marvels and intellectual freedom. Will wanted to fall to his knees and worship her.

Only the animalistic machine cries in the distance prevented him from doing just that. He had to stop Norris before he interfered with the party. He had to protect his family. He wouldn't let them become the victims of scandal simply because he couldn't handle a crowd.

"Follow me," he said to Maddie. "I'll explain on the way."

Will briefed her on what he knew of the situation as he led her up one flight of stairs after another, trying to give her any details he might have missed in his previous, rushed explanation. They paused briefly at his bedchamber to grab a small toolkit, then continued up toward the attics.

"Do you think Mr. Norris is simply going to set his dragons to screaming all night?" Maddie asked. "It's disruptive, but the party is loud enough that it might be no more than a minor nuisance."

"I think the screaming is step one. They are loud enough to attract attention. After that, who knows? Maybe he'll let them all loose. If it happens when people are leaving the house, or if he can sneak them inside, someone could get hurt. And then he will blame my family for the troubles."

"So we find all the dragons we can and disable them?"

Will nodded. "At the moment, that's my plan. Here." He opened a door and waved her out onto the rooftop terrace. Closed for the winter, it was empty and barren, but it provided easy access to the near-identical one next door. Maddie scaled the wall effortlessly in her tied-up skirt, dropping onto Norris's rooftop as silently as if she burgled houses every day. Will felt clumsy beside her, his stiff evening wear hampering his movements. If he ripped the suit, maybe he'd use that as his excuse for fleeing the party.

Maddie hurried to the door into Norris's townhouse, shivering from the cold. "Do you know how to pick locks?" she asked.

"No." He'd read books on the subject and attempted to teach himself as a teenager, but he was no master thief. "Which is why I chose this entrance." He removed a flat screwdriver from his toolkit, threaded it into the gap between the lock and the doorjamb, and worked it back and forth several times. The door creaked, then popped open. "This door has been broken for years. Norris is too cheap to fix it. Sam and I used to break in like this to play with Kate and her brothers. In the days before they became poisoned with their father's vitriol. I wish they'd let Kate go off to college instead of leaving her with no hope for the future except to marry well. Sometimes I think she doesn't really hate me, she hates the world." Will held the door open. "After you."

The inside of the Norris townhouse was as dark as a tomb and nearly as cold as it was outside. The screeching of the dragons echoed from the walls, guiding Will and Maddie through the unlit corridors.

"He must have given most of his staff the night off,"

Maddie whispered. "But he must have an assistant or two to have activated the dragons."

Will nodded, then replied with a hushed, "Yes," in case she couldn't see him. He should have thought to bring a flashlight. Or a weapon.

His spine stiffened. Oh, God. What if this turned dangerous? What had he been thinking to bring Maddie into this?

And there was no turning back. She strode a step ahead of him, brave and determined. She'd never return to his house, no matter how he begged.

They found the first of the dragons sitting by an open fifth-floor window, baying out into the night air. Will grabbed the creature and flicked the off switch on its back. Working together, he and Maddie opened it up and removed the luxene fuel tube, rendering the dragon temporarily inoperable. One down.

Too easy. Will's sense of foreboding grew with every step they took further into the house. Something was sure to go wrong. They'd be caught, or one of the dragons would be equipped with an alarm or anti-theft device. He had to be mad to even be attempting this.

The fourth floor held a hooting, owl-like dragon, and the third floor a bellowing bear nearly as large as Maddie. Again, the machines were trivial to shut down and simple to disable. Will continued to fidget. Noise continued unabated, despite their successes.

His ears began to sting as they descended to the second floor. Maddie covered her ears with her hands, cringing.

"This is awful!" she cried.

Will could only nod. He pulled a handkerchief from his pocket, speared it with a screwdriver to poke a hole, then ripped off a piece. He rolled the small bit of cloth between his fingers, then plugged one ear with it. It worked. He ripped off more pieces, handed two to Maddie, and plugged his other ear. The muffling of the cacophony came as sweet relief.

Will reached for Maddie's hand. She gave him a squeeze, then threaded her fingers through his. They may have been unable to hear one another, and the minimal lighting limited their vision, but they wouldn't be stopped. Together they walked through another door, toward the source of the din.

Shafts of light from the street lamps outside lit the Norris's ballroom, revealing a flurry of activity. Several animal automata roved across the floor, howling and bellowing. One large, armored dragon repeatedly smashed itself against the wall that abutted the Ashton residence next door. Overhead, several flying creatures circled and dove, adding their own noises to the madness.

One of the flying dragons swooped low and Maddie slammed into Will, knocking him to the ground a moment before the dragon would have smashed into him. The creature sailed across the room and out an open window.

For a few seconds Will and Maddie lay on the ground, stunned, staring at one another. Dragons buzzed above them, and a second one found its way out a window. Maddie made a frantic gesture in that direction. Will couldn't hear her, but he knew she was thinking what he was. *Close the windows before it gets worse.*

They scrambled to their feet and raced toward the windows, heads ducked to avoid the flying dragons. As they ran, they grabbed any walking dragons within reach and shut them down. By the time they reached the windows, a third creature had flown out into the night. How many more had escaped before they arrived?

Will yanked one window closed, latching it securely while Maddie worked on the next window over. Outside, escaped dragons flew about wildly, causing pedestrians to duck and flee. How were they ever going to stop the things? Shoot them down? No one in the Ashton house hunted or practiced archery.

They closed the last two windows, then shut down the remaining walking dragons. Given the chaos outside, they could no longer spare the time to dismantle them fully. With only a couple of fliers left, the noise had diminished enough that Will pulled out one earplug. Maddie did the same.

"We'll have to knock them out of the air!" she shouted.

Will nodded. He grabbed the smallest of the shut down dragons, watched a flyer approaching, then hurled the one into the other, knocking it from the air. Maddie leapt to grab it and shut it off.

"Nice aim!"

Will shrugged. He wasn't wholly unathletic. "I play tennis." He scooped up the small, now-dented dragon and aimed for the last flying creature.

"Who goes there?" a booming voice called from just outside the door.

Dammit!

Will flung the dragon, hoping for the best. Maddie's biomechanical hand clamped down over his, her grip supernaturally strong. She didn't need to speak, or even look at him. He leapt to follow, moving with her as she ran to the window and threw it open. She released his hand, swung herself over the balcony, and disappeared. Below was noise and chaos and people running to and fro. All things that made him panic. But his family needed him. And he knew he would have Maddie by his side with her courage and daring. Will took a deep breath and hurtled himself over the balcony to the street below.

10

Maddie covered her head as a wailing dragon zoomed past. Five, maybe six of the things had gotten loose. They were so fast she couldn't be certain. Ahead of her, a snarling wolf-dragon blocked half the street, its jaws snapping at anyone who drew too near.

"Tennis, you said?" she shouted at Will.

"Y-yes." Among all the noise of the people and dragons and the mob of motorcars and carriages, Will had begun to look pale again.

"Fetch your racket. Knock them out of the sky." Maddie hoped the clear, firm command would keep him focused. "I'll tackle the walking dragons."

Will nodded and raced for his front door. Maddie eyed the wolf. Beyond it was an even larger dragon, with no visible off switch.

"Okay," she breathed. "Easy target first."

She approached the wolf, but its jaws snapped and it clawed at the ground, preventing her from getting near. Every time she tried to circle around, it followed. Drat. She needed to get behind it.

"Here, wolfy, wolfy," she called, inching closer. The creature snarled. Maddie took a step backward and it followed. "That's a good machine. Follow me, boy."

Bit by agonizing bit, Maddie edged her way back to the stairs of the Norris townhouse, letting the wolf get ever closer. It gnashed its teeth as she hopped up first one, then a second step.

Almost there.

The creature set its paws on the bottom step. Maddie darted up two more steps, then jumped, using the added height to get over the creature's head and onto its back. Her fingers found the off switch.

"Haha!" she cried, pulling out her screwdriver to disable it more fully.

Will appeared on his front stoop as she worked to open the wolf dragon, a racket and ball in his hands. In one fluid motion, he tossed the ball in the air and smashed it with the racket, sending it rocketing into one of the flying dragons. The bird-like machine clattered to the pavement.

Maddie's mouth dropped open. Will pulled a second ball from his pocket and took down another dragon, with the same effortless power and grace.

I play tennis, he'd said, as casually as one might say, "I like the color blue," or, "Nice day we're having."

He didn't play; he excelled. At least as well as his brother did at football. He was astounding. And she'd never known because he wasn't the sort to brag. Bookish Will Ashton had some surprising secrets.

A clicking noise overhead made Maddie look up. That awful woman with the bee-dragon was leaning out the open window above them, observing the chaos. The bee hovered beneath her, its eyes flashing and its insides clicking like a camera shutter. Will smashed a third dragon while the camera bee clicked and hummed.

"Damn that woman," Maddie muttered. How dare she turn this into a publicity stunt? Whether he was looking pale and terrified or showing off his athletic prowess, Will would not want the infamy sure to come from any mention in the papers. Maddie swatted at the bee, but it was too far above her head.

Focusing on what she could do, Maddie yanked the fuel tube from inside the wolf and poured the luxene onto the ground. A waste of money, perhaps, but it prevented anyone from powering up the dragon again any time soon. Her eyes lifted to her second target.

The beast was the size of a Saint Bernard, with a feline head and a hefty, rounded body. It roared like a lion whenever its mouth opened. Several party guests huddled in motorcars nearby, afraid to open their doors while it prowled in front of the townhouse steps. Maddie looked it over, trying to see where the off switch might be. She wasn't scared of this one. It was big and loud, certainly, but without claws or jagged teeth.

Another flying dragon tumbled to the ground. Will had gotten them all, it seemed, with the exception of the camera-bee. It was Maddie's turn to do her part.

She ran at the dog-lion-bear-whatever and leaped onto its back. With her skirts tied up, she easily straddled the creature, grabbing onto something that might have been an ear or a horn for stability. The dragon jumped and bucked, trying to throw her off, but Maddie squeezed her thighs together and held on. The dragon's body was smooth, with no buttons, dials, or switches anywhere. It jerked again and she teetered. Its roar reverberated off the surrounding buildings.

"I am so done with this," she snarled. She raised her screwdriver and plunged it down into the narrow gap between the creature's head and shoulders. Metal groaned. Sparks flew. The beast shuddered once, then sank slowly to the ground.

"What an appalling display of hoydenism!" exclaimed a female voice.

Maddie's head whipped around. The woman with the bee-camera snatched it from the air, bringing it to her chest and giving Maddie a triumphant sneer before ducking back inside. Maddie slowly dismounted. Will was at her side the moment her feet touched the ground.

"You are incredible," he breathed.

Maddie beamed up at him. A trickle of blood ran down his cheek, some minor scrape acquired during their mad dashing. She plucked the handkerchief from his vest pocket and gently dabbed at the wound. "So are you. And I will tell you just how incredible as I tend to this grievous injury that absolutely necessitates a quiet recovery location."

He took hold of her arm. "Follow me."

*

Maddie had her hands buried beneath Will's vest and her lips against his throat before the bedroom door snicked closed behind them.

"Incredible," she breathed, pressing another open-mouthed kiss to his neck, loving the shiver it induced.

"Maddie," he groaned. "God, Maddie you were brilliant." His fingers found the clasp of her jacket and he peeled it from her body. "The way you jumped into the fray, took charge… everything." His hand froze on the top latch at the front of her corset. "I've never seen anyone so beautiful, and it has nothing to do with this fabulous dress and the things you have hidden beneath it."

Maddie paused in her exploration of his skin, straightening up to look him over. His cheeks were flushed, his pupils dilated. She'd gotten his vest unbuttoned, and his shirt untucked. His tie hung at a strange angle, and his jacket was torn from their crazed dragon-chase.

"Nothing at all?" she asked, brushing his hand aside and flicking the latch open. His Adam's apple bobbed up and down as he swallowed hard.

"Maybe a little bit to do with those things," he admitted.

Maddie flicked open the second latch, holding the corset closed to keep her breasts from spilling out. "I'll take off mine if you take off yours, Mr. Tennis Stud."

He gave a bashful shrug. "I can't read books all the time."

"Good. Because right now, books are about the last thing on my mind." Maddie opened the last two latches and relaxed her grip, letting the corset fall to the floor. "Your turn."

Will yanked his jacket off with such force that he ripped it even further. The vest and shirt followed, fluttering to the floor, leaving him exposed to her view. He was slender, but toned, with clearly-defined muscles that allowed him to wield a racket with ease or to haul loads of books without a cart. Maddie's gaze swept over him, from his strong shoulders down to the grooves alongside his abdominals that disappeared into his trousers. She licked her lips.

Will reached for her, dragging their bodies together, bringing his mouth to hers. He kissed her deeply, fiercely, as his hands moved to caress her bare back, her belly, her breasts. Maddie moaned into the kiss, her own hands grasping greedily, feeling the flex in his arm muscles, the hardness of his lean torso. Her fingertips relished every touch, every texture: the tickle of his soft hair, the smoothness of the skin beneath, the ridges of muscle and bone. Up and down her hands slid, caressing his torso, his shoulders, his back. Her right hand couldn't feel the warmth of his skin as well as her left, but she let herself savor the difference in sensation.

Her hands skimmed down to cup his buttocks, pressing him into her tightly enough that she could feel the hard length of his arousal. *Ooh.* How would that feel beneath her fingers?

Maddie snaked her hands around between them,

stroking him through his trousers, first with her left hand, then her right. His groan was delightful, but her own body's reaction was even better. Warmth spread all throughout her. Wet desire welled between her legs. She burned for him.

She tugged at his trouser buttons, prying the garment open. Will never stopped kissing her as she freed his cock from the confines of his clothing, moaning into her mouth with every intimate touch. Her biomechanical hand curled around him, and she squeezed and stroked gently, not wanting to hurt him with her artificially-enhanced grip. Strange noises escaped her own throat. He felt incredible: soft skin against her fingertips, a rigid core beneath, throbbing against the flesh and metal of her hand. She was torn between wanting to touch him forever and wanting him inside her immediately.

"Maddie." His kisses moved from her lips to her throat, sucking the sensitive skin of her neck the way she had done to him only minutes before. "Oh, God, Maddie, is this… how far…?"

"All the way," she replied, with absolute conviction. "I'm ready if you are."

He leaned back enough to look her in the eye. "I've never gotten this far before." His words were matter-of-fact, entirely without embarrassment, and her heart thudded with a strange, unexpected joy that he could speak of such things to her without any nervousness or shame.

"Neither have I," she admitted. "But I've read books."

"I know."

Oh. Right. He'd seen nearly all of her reading material over the last six months, including that time she'd been perusing medical texts and stumbled upon *The Philosophy of Procreation and Sexual Intercourse.*

"Good," Maddie replied. "Then you will not be surprised

when I tell you I've come fully prepared for seduction. Before I left my house, I inserted a contraceptive sponge, dampened with a solution fatal to the animaculae of the semen."

Will's jaw dropped. "You were expecting this?"

"Hoping for it, more accurately."

His gaze turned to the bed. "I don't know how I ended up here, but damned if I don't like it."

Maddie didn't need any further encouragement. She grabbed Will's hand and together they scrambled for the bed, tugging and pulling at their remaining clothes until they lay naked and entwined, hands and mouths exploring flushed, sensitive skin.

"Like this." Maddie guided Will's hand between her legs, showing him where she most hungered for him. "Yes." Her eyes drifted closed as pleasure washed over her. His mouth came to her breast as his fingers stroked her. "Perfect."

Maddie arched her back, straining for more as the tension mounted inside her, twisting her hips into his touch to position him just right.

"Yes," she gasped. And then she couldn't speak. The climax trembled through her, robbing her of breath, of movement, of anything but the sheer force of ecstasy.

When at last she opened her eyes, it was to see Will leaning over her, gazing at her in wonderment.

"Fuck," he gasped. "Maddie. My God. Can you… can you do that again while I'm inside you?"

"I don't know," she admitted. "But I want to try."

Will bent his head to her neck, kissing slowly downward, worshiping every part of her with his lips as his hands once again caressed the sensitive flesh between her legs. Maddie spread for him, letting him settle between her thighs, shivering as his rigid shaft butted up against her sex. The tension had begun to rise inside her once again, and she clutched at Will's back, pulling him close, yearning for more.

He circled his finger over her clitoris the way she'd shown him, and she bucked beneath him. *Yes, yes. So close.*

Maddie's fingernails scraped over his skin. "Now," she moaned. "Please."

Will pushed into her, groaning his own pleasure, clinging to her as if she were his lifeline. Her name escaped his lips in a long, anguished cry.

Maddie soared. She rocked and thrust against him, taking him as deep as possible as he moved in and out, over and over, trembling and emitting raw, guttural noises. The orgasm shook her down to her bones, destroying her with bliss and leaving her undone, remade.

Will collapsed atop her, swore again, then murmured her name.

"Maddie." He rolled off her, then gathered her close to his chest, pressing kisses into her hair. "Maddie, my Maddie."

"I love you, too," she replied, the words out before she could even consider their implication.

He went completely still.

"That was a bit sudden, wasn't it?" Maddie admitted. Had she misjudged his feelings? Only an instant ago she'd been so certain of their connection. "It's only that almost from the moment I met you I've felt this… pull. A sense that you understood me. Whenever I had something interesting to tell, I would rush to the library because I wanted you to hear it first. I wanted you to be the last person I saw every night and the first every morning. I suppose that sounds silly."

"No." Will clutched her even tighter. "I understand you perfectly. Because I felt the same way." He squeezed his eyes closed. "God, how much time I've wasted. I love you,

Maddie Peters. Madly. Passionately. And I ought to have said something ages ago."

Maddie burrowed against him, her satisfied smile growing even wider. "You can say it now. We have time." She let her eyes drift closed, listening to the steady beating of his heart. "We have forever."

11

Will had to force himself out of bed to fetch his watch and check the time. The loss of Maddie's soft curves against him caused a physical ache in his chest. In an ideal world, he would simply flick off the bedside lamp and snuggle down for the night. In an ideal world, he wouldn't still be able to hear the distant murmur of a party he was supposed to be attending.

What he wouldn't give to crawl back under the sheets with Maddie and hold her all night. Hold her for the rest of his life.

He'd found a woman he wanted to marry. His parents would be pleased. Hopefully.

Will swore when he saw the time. They'd spent much longer than he realized making love and snuggling.

Maddie sat up. "What's wrong?"

"It's nearly midnight. My family must be wondering where I am. And my father is sure to be furious that I never greeted all those women he invited."

"You had more important things to do."

Will grinned, his gaze lingering on her naked body. Damn, but she was gorgeous. He wanted to make love again. "Indeed I did."

"I meant stopping those dragons."

"That, too." He stooped to gather his clothes. "We

should dress. I need to put in a brief appearance, much as I loathe the idea of returning to the party. And you need to return home eventually. I don't want you to become the subject of a scandal."

Maddie laughed. "We're going to be a scandal no matter what, Will. Leaping out windows? Fighting dragons in the street? An ordinary love affair sounds boring compared to that."

Will crossed to the bed to embrace her. "There is nothing ordinary about our love affair. It's the most extraordinary thing that's ever happened to me."

She beamed up at him and brushed a kiss over his lips. "Me too. Let's dress. Maybe we can dance, if you feel up for it?"

"I honestly don't know. Everything tonight was such chaos, and if the ballroom is as crowded as it was before…" He took a deep breath to calm himself.

Maddie laid a gentle hand on his shoulder. "I'll be there with you. Ready to dance, or ready to run away."

He clasped her hand and squeezed it, soft flesh and rigid metal. Beautiful to him, whatever others might think. And he was the same to her.

It took effort to release her and begin to dress. His suit coat was torn beyond repair, so he threw on a different jacket from his closet. It wasn't proper formalwear, but Will didn't care. When he was finished, he helped Maddie with her accessories and her hair. He didn't think it looked like it had before, but she was lovely nonetheless.

They arrived in the ballroom only minutes before midnight. The raucous, intoxicated crowd had gathered close to the massive wall clock that would count down the time to the New Year. Music played from the autogramophone, for the small percentage of the guests still dancing. Perhaps a dance with Maddie might be possible after all. Holding tight to her hand, Will started in that direction.

"William." His father's deep voice froze him in his tracks. "Where have you been?"

"Uh…" Will turned slowly, grasping for a reply that would neither compromise Maddie nor anger his parents.

"Norris was ranting," Will's father went on, not waiting for a reply. "Something about indecent behavior, tampering with dragons, and destruction of property. Said you were involved. I had to ask him to leave because he was bothering the other guests."

"He set all his automata to howling again," Will said.

"Yes, I heard the noise. But it didn't last long."

"Mr. Ashton and I found many dragons roaming loose and scaring the guests outside," Maddie chimed in. "We shut them down, naturally. I'm sure Mr. Norris was simply upset by the troubles his collection had inadvertently caused."

Will's father eyed Maddie with an assessing gaze. Her jacket was closed and her skirt down, leaving nothing potentially scandalous about her dress, but her style and accessories were certainly not high society fashion. "You are Miss Peters, I presume?"

"I am. It's a pleasure to meet you, Mr. Ashton."

He nodded. "Welcome to our home." He turned back to Will. "And where are the other young ladies?"

Will looked his father straight in the eye. "I have no idea. I invited Miss Peters, therefore her enjoyment of the evening is my priority tonight."

Will Senior stared back, his stern expression unwavering. After several silent seconds, his gaze dropped to Will and Maddie's entwined fingers, lingering there. "So, that's how it is, is it?"

"Yes," Will replied. His hand had begun to sweat where his palm met Maddie's. She gave him a reassuring squeeze.

"Thirty seconds to midnight!" someone shouted. A rousing cheer went up from the crowd.

Will drew Maddie into his arms. Her presence soothed away his cares about parental approval and fortified him against the noise and the crowd. "Madeline," he murmured. "I believe a New Year's kiss is reputed to bring good luck and strengthen a relationship. Would you do me the honor of granting me one?"

Her arms wound around his neck and they gazed, smiling, into one another's eyes. The crowd counted down the seconds. The clock began to chime the hour, but Will hardly noticed. He was lost to the taste of Maddie's lips and the ardent explorations of her tongue. He clung to her, letting the devastating kiss blot out the rest of the world, and in that moment, they were alone.

When at last Will opened his eyes and relaxed his grip on Maddie, it was to find himself in the midst of a wild mass of people laughing and cheering and making merry. With the exception of one highly disapproving father.

"William," his father said sternly. "We need to talk."

12

January 2, 1905

Maddie adjusted the trousers on her hips, patted down her pockets to check that she had everything, and buttoned her coat. She was doing this. It was a new year, she had a new lover, and her new life was about to begin. Much as she disliked causing pain to the woman who had raised her, Maddie couldn't remain here, hidden away. Nor would she act embarrassed by that silly photo in the newspaper of her astride the dragon, brandishing a screwdriver like a warrior-mechanologist. She wasn't embarrassed. She was proud, and ready to take charge of her own life.

Maddie slung her small bag of possessions across her chest and threw open the window. Her stomach gave a little nervous flip-flop. From her third floor window the ground looked frightfully far away.

Don't look down. You can do this. You jumped out a window only yesterday.

A window only half as high up, unfortunately. Taking a deep breath and pushing her shoulders back, Maddie lowered her makeshift rope out the window. Mrs. Hastings would be horrified as well as shocked when she discovered what Maddie had done with all the curtain ties, but it couldn't be helped.

Maddie climbed out the window and carefully walked her way down the wall, finding the entire process easier than expected without skirts swirling around her. She would stop in at Victoria's shop and thank her for the trousers. And perhaps buy a second pair.

By the time she reached the library, Maddie was walking with a spring in her step and a broad grin on her face. She bounded past the circulation desk, exchanging smiles with the woman working there—who no doubt had seen far stranger library patrons than Maddie in trousers.

Maddie's enthusiasm couldn't be suppressed. She had successfully escaped the confines of her godmother's townhouse, and now she had a proposition for Will. Or was *proposal* a better word? She shivered at the thought. A lifetime together. Not everyone had such an opportunity, and Maddie meant to seize it.

She found the research desk unattended.

Puzzled, Maddie made a quick tour of the stacks,

looking for a flash of red hair, or any sign of a cart, in case Will was shelving books. Finding no one, she returned to the desk, but still saw no sign of him. Not even an overcoat hung on a peg or slung over the back of a chair. A prickling of unease raced across her skin.

"Can I help you?"

Maddie turned to see a young woman in a blue dress. A pair of spectacles rested on her nose. One of the newer librarians, whose name Maddie had yet to learn.

"Er, is Mr. Ashton not yet in today?" Maddie inquired.

The librarian shook her head. "I'm afraid not. We received a phone call not long ago informing us that he is unwell and will not be in today. But I'm happy to be of assistance with any question you might have."

"Unwell?" Maddie echoed. Had he taken ill? Poor Will. It was probably that nasty cold that had been going around. She wanted to hold him and kiss his brow and bring him soup and tea to soothe his throat. But how could she? His father had appeared to barely tolerate her, which meant entry to the house was unlikely. And what of her plans? They couldn't proceed without him. She would have to take a room at a boarding house while she waited for him to recover.

But first she had to see him. He had to know where to find her. And she had to know his illness wasn't anything serious.

"Thank you, Miss... uh?"

"Taylor," the librarian answered.

"Thank you, Miss Taylor," Maddie continued, "but I won't be needing any help. I merely came to call on Mr. Ashton. I will send word to him at home."

"Of course. Have a wonderful day." Miss Taylor's eyes flicked briefly to Maddie's uncovered right hand. "Lovely biomechanics you have. My sister is a biomechanologist down in Savannah, so I know good work when I see it."

"Oh!" Maddie flexed her fingers and smiled. "Thank you." She gave the librarian a nod and hurried off to begin the trek to Will's neighborhood.

*

Will wasn't sick. Maddie knew it the moment she saw the crowd of reporters and photographers lying in wait outside the Ashton mansion. He was trapped.

Most anyone would have been unnerved to discover a horde of nosy people ready to bombard them the moment they stepped outside. With crowd anxiety as severe as Will's, it would be impossible to even open the door.

She had to get in to see him. Since the front door was the most straightforward option, she lifted her chin high and plowed into the fray.

She'd taken no more than two steps toward the townhouse when a voice shouted, "Hey it's her!"

"The dragon slayer!" another exclaimed.

The questions came in a furious rush.

"Hey, dragon rider, what's your name?"

"What's your connection to the Ashtons?"

"Are you young Will's girlfriend? How'd you meet?"

"Were you the lady he kissed at midnight?"

Maddie ignored every voice, every flash of a camera, pushing her way to the front steps, grateful again for the freedom of movement that came from wearing trousers. She hammered on the door with her fist, praying someone would open it.

The door swung open just enough for a burly man to peer out. "I'm sorry," he said. "The family is not receiving vis—" His head cocked to one side. "Oh, are you Will's girl? Come on in."

Maddie slipped through the door and the man closed it behind her, securing the lock before turning to face her. He had to be near six feet tall, with sleek black hair and golden skin. He grinned down at her, dark eyes flashing.

"I'm Alex Yuan. Will's friend and tennis partner. I live just up the street."

Maddie extended her hand for a handshake. "Your father's company supplied some of the joints in my hand."

Alex's big hand gave hers a hearty shake. "Excellent! I hope they serve you well. Will's in the library, if you'd like to follow me." Maddie followed as he started down the hall. "I stopped over when I saw the crowd outside. Sam and I have been trying to chase them off, but…" He shrugged.

They had very nearly reached the library when Will's father stepped out from the next room over. He marched straight to Maddie, a pinched frown on his face.

"Miss Peters. I'm afraid the family is not receiving visitors today."

The library door opened. "Father. Don't."

All eyes turned to Will.

"William, we talked about this," his father said. "You cannot pursue this relationship."

"It's none of your business," Will snapped. "We are both adults, and we have the right to choose our own future."

"I *may* have been able to overlook your indecorous public kiss as a mere holiday indulgence, but now? With that lurid photo in the paper and the things people are saying about you? About the family? It is intolerable. I cannot condone such an acquaintance."

"It's not a lurid photo," Will shouted, "and I don't give a damn what people are saying!"

"She's after your money, William."

"I most certainly am not!" Maddie snapped. Both men whirled to look at her. "Do you know why I came here? Do you? Well, apart from wanting to reassure myself that Will had not actually been taken ill?"

"Why?" Will asked.

"Because I have a plan. We go away together, you and I. A quiet, simple neighborhood. Along the new subway line, I thought at first, but then I realized the trains might be too crowded for you."

"Definitely," Will replied. "The mere idea terrifies me."

"Within walking distance of the library, then. I have some small amount of money to my name, enough to help supplement your salary until I can find work of my own. I'd like to become a researcher at the library or at a museum. That's it. That's all I want. Nothing big, nothing fancy. Just the two of us, together, doing the things we love."

"That sounds wonderful. I'll go pack."

"Absolutely not," Will's father growled. "Just think what the papers would say! You can't possibly mean to add an elopement to this disaster!"

"Yes. I can." Will's gaze locked with Maddie's. "Do you want to wait for me, or shall I meet you somewhere?"

"I'll wait. I won't leave you to face that crowd alone."

"Don't worry," Alex said. "Sam and I will help push everyone out of the way."

"William…" his father warned.

"You wanted me to get married," Will said flatly. "I won't do it in front of a giant crowd of people. Ever. Maddie wants to elope and I think she's brilliant. Don't panic. We'll be so boring, the papers will never want anything to do with us again. Librarians don't make headlines." He spun on his heel and walked away, head held high.

Maddie had never loved him more.

Will Senior stared at the empty place where his son had been, then finally turned back to Maddie. "I really don't know where I went wrong with that boy," he sighed.

Maddie's eyebrows rose. "Wrong? You didn't go wrong at all. He's a kind, intelligent, wonderful man. He simply doesn't fit in your world. So what?"

Mr. Ashton gaped at her. "So… I… I thought he would grow out of that library thing," he admitted.

"He's twenty-seven. I don't think he's growing out of anything anymore."

"No." Will's father sighed. "I suppose not."

"I hope you can come to accept his decisions," Maddie pressed on. "He does care very much for family. It's why he goes to your wife's party every year. Your blessing would mean a lot to him."

Mr. Ashton's eyebrows knit together. "You are a shrewd and persuasive woman, Miss Peters. I am beginning to see why he likes you."

"Thank you. I hope you and your family can learn to like me as well." She extended a hand.

Will Senior gripped it, stiffening when he felt the metal of her biomechanics. He glanced down, still holding her hand. "Well! This is some excellent craftsmanship."

Maddie felt a smile tug at the corners of her mouth. And Mrs. Hastings thought gloves were a good idea! Hah!

"You see?" Maddie said. "We do agree on something."

Epilogue

January 1, 1906, midnight

Damn, what a kiss. Will's entire body shook with the force of it. His arms tightened around his wife, sinking into the taste of her as fireworks exploded around him. She was sweetness and radiance, and deep, hot passion. Her lips and tongue coaxed groans from his throat, setting his body afire, warming him near to melting even as gentle flakes of snow drifted down to stick to his hair and lashes. When at last she let him up for air, he was certain all of New York was celebrating her performance.

"Well, if that isn't an omen of a good year, I don't know what is," he said, adjusting the thick quilt he'd wrapped around them to keep them warm on the snowy rooftop terrace of his parents' townhouse.

Maddie's laughter rang like a musical accompaniment to the fireworks bursting in the air. "You gave me two whole dances tonight, in front of all those people. I thought that deserved a significant kiss."

"Knowing I can ask to stop at any time and you'll help me escape does make it easier. Plus, I wanted a chance to watch Sam playing gallant knight for his shy Miss Linden. But I admit I was beginning to shake by the end of that second dance."

"I could tell." Maddie kissed him again, quickly but no less fiercely. "Thank you for a beautiful evening."

"Thank *you*." Will rested his head against hers, curling his arm around her waist as they looked out over the city. Electric lights twinkled below while fireworks continued to burst in the skies above. Out in the distance, too far away to see even from the rooftop, was their own modest house, quiet and comfortable, full of books and cozy chairs. The home of their dreams.

They watched the fireworks in companionable silence. There would be no dragon rampages tonight. Norris's antics had upset too many of his powerful neighbors last year, and he'd moved away in a huff, still blaming the Ashtons. The papers had hardly noted the occurrence, except to mention that his daughter may have run off to California.

She had. Will and Maddie had received a brief note, apologizing for the camera. Maddie had replied with a postcard with a simple message: *Go to college. You can do it!*

While Will vastly preferred the calm of this year's party, he would always remember last year with a smile, and all because of Maddie. Maddie his warrior princess. Maddie his book-loving research partner. His wife and his heart. Tonight she had worn another spectacular gown, this one a shimmering mix of blues and purples. The silk was smooth under his hand, and he stroked up and down, telling her without words that he was ready to caress the skin that lay beneath. She leaned into him.

"So, love," she murmured, her voice husky and enticing, "shall we retire to your old room for a repeat of last New Year's? Or would you prefer to relax in the library?"

Desire flooded Will's body. The quilt was too hot. His clothing was too hot. He couldn't wait to strip it all away. He turned toward the door, steering Maddie along with him.

"You know me, darling. I never say no to a library."

Be Mine

Be Mine

A Victorian Valentine's Story

Jacob Moreton, Lord Teage, goes to his wedding day not with joy, but burdened with grief and guilt. Can his new wife give him a wedding night beyond his wildest dreams and heal his fractured heart?

1

February 14, 1880

Once upon a time this would have been the happiest day of his life. Once upon a time he would have crowed his delight and danced for joy to celebrate his victory. Once upon a time he had been no more than Mr. Jacob Moreton.

Now he was Lord Teage, the seventh man to take possession of that name and its associated barony. He grasped his bride's hands before the altar. She was smiling. Something alarmingly like hope sparkled in those pale green eyes of hers. For an instant he froze, staring. Heat flashed across his skin. God, but she was beautiful. His every dream. His every desire. Beaming at him as if this union was the ultimate celebration of St. Valentine's feast.

He looked away. He couldn't bear it. What reason did she have to be smiling? She had no more choice in this matter than he did.

"I-I-I will," Jacob mumbled, because this was his duty. His penance. His punishment for wrongs that now could never be forgiven.

Octavia's fingers tightened on his. When she spoke her vows it was in a voice clear and firm, a far cry from his own sad stuttering. As if he needed the reminder that he didn't belong here, in this place, with this title, marrying this woman.

"Those whom God hath joined together let no man put asunder."

Sweat coated Jacob's palms. Was it too late to flee?

Would it make any difference? Everyone knew he was unfit for the role life had cruelly thrust upon him.

He leaned in and prepared to kiss her, because it was expected. Because if he couldn't even bring himself to kiss her, how was he supposed to beget an heir on her? A chaste kiss. A quick peck. Nothing, really.

It wasn't supposed to be like this. All the times he'd imagined kissing her, all the times he'd dreamed of kissing her, it had been magical. A brilliant, shining moment with stars spinning around them and a chorus of heavenly music ringing through the air.

He was taking too long. The hot gaze of the assembled crowd seared him. They probably thought he wouldn't do it. Maybe they even thought he'd never kissed a woman before.

He pressed his lips gently to hers. Simple. Easy. Mission accomplished.

But then Octavia kissed him back, and he was undone. She crushed her mouth to his as if desperate to taste him fully, her nails digging into his palm as she clenched his hand. Jacob's knees almost buckled. Her grip was the only thing holding him upright any longer.

And the stars. God, the stars. They were only in his head, but they danced around him in a dizzying array of joyful brilliance, rousing the inferno of desire that he'd tried for years to extinguish. He kissed her so hard and so long that he thought he might burn to ashes in front of the entire congregation.

The congregation. Dammit all!

Jacob jerked away, his breath coming in gasps, his lips tingling from the stupefying kiss. He'd kissed Miss Octavia Singletary. After eight long years of unsated desire, he'd finally kissed her.

Except she was no longer Miss Singletary. She was Lady Teage. His wife.

Octavia's eyes were half-closed, her own lips bright pink and parted just enough that if he kissed her again he could slide inside her. She sighed, the sound part satisfaction and part longing. Jacob's entire body tightened.

This was good, wasn't it? He ought to be pleased that she was passionate. That would make it easier to do his duty.

Easier to forget she was never meant to be yours.

He was a scoundrel. A thief. He refused to meet her eyes as they departed from the church and boarded the carriage that would convey them home for the wedding celebration. He wouldn't let one kiss undo his resolve. He was a proxy. A stand-in. He wouldn't let himself forget that. He wouldn't lay claim to what he didn't deserve. No more than was strictly necessary to do right by his family.

God help him.

2

Jacob leaned back in the leather armchair, sipping at his brandy and staring at the closed door that linked his bedroom with Octavia's. He needed to go to her tonight. He couldn't leave the marriage unconsummated. All day long, while he'd been shaking hands and accepting congratulations, his mind had been here. In this room. This moment. Dreading the wedding night he couldn't avoid. Dreading the fact that a part of him rejoiced at the mere thought of it.

I should just get on with it. How hard can it be? Get up, go in there, rut on her like the soulless bastard I am, and then go to bed.

He only had to do it enough times to get her with child. Then he could send her away to the country and not have to see her anymore. That would help.

Jacob snorted. As if anyone could send Octavia away from the city she loved. He remembered her stubborn streak. Her bold assertions of independence. That day she'd marched around the neighborhood wearing a women's suffrage sash was the day he'd fallen in love with her.

"But for family?" he said aloud, trying to convince himself. She'd retire to the country for family, wouldn't she? She was here, after all. Married to a man two years her junior who had a speech impediment and unsavory sexual habits. All because her parents had declared at birth that she was to marry the future Baron Teage. They'd meant Donovan, of course, but settled for Jacob. Octavia was twenty-six now, and the last thing her parents wanted was to have to ship her off to India to marry a military man.

He took another sip of the brandy. If he were a different man, he'd already have downed the whole glass and poured himself another. It seemed a good night to be three sheets to the wind.

But he'd seen the results of overindulging. A life of wild pleasure had killed his brother, and Jacob had vowed years ago never to let himself follow that same treacherous path.

The door opened.

Jacob nearly dropped his brandy. Octavia strode into his bedchamber as if she owned it, her auburn hair tumbled about her shoulders, her curves hidden only by a thin silk dressing gown. Bare feet moved silently across the room toward him.

"You're still dressed," she said, her beautiful face scrunching into a puzzled frown. "Well, partially dressed."

"I—" Jacob glanced down at himself. He'd stripped to trousers and shirtsleeves, but he was still fully covered and unprepared for bedsport. "I—"

Dammit. Forget stuttering. He couldn't even form a

coherent thought. What the hell was she doing here? Why had she been the one to come to *him*? Why did he like that?

Stop, he warned himself. He knew why he liked it and he wasn't going to let himself think about that. His fantasies weren't going to come true. He'd bed her quickly, be done with it, and go to sleep. Alone.

"Is something wrong?" she asked. "Are you displeased with me? You've hardly said a word to me all day, and you don't seem to want to touch me."

I want to touch you everywhere. I want you to touch me. I want you to shove me onto the bed and...

"I'm not much..." He paused, trying to fend off a stutter. "For talking. As you... know."

She didn't interrupt, even when he struggled to get the last two words out. Never once in their entire acquaintance had she ever treated him as stupid, annoying, or anything other than an ordinary man with ideas worthy of being heard. Another reason he'd always loved her.

"And touching?" she asked. "Aren't you supposed to touch me, now that we're man and wife?" A hint of pink stained her cheeks. "It was very nice when you kissed me."

"Octavia, I..." *Want to hear you moan with pleasure. Want to feel you on top of me, using me to fulfill your every wicked desire. Want to be your true one and only.* "This isn't right. We sh-shouldn't be here."

Her eyebrows lifted, then narrowed. "But it's our wedding night. Where else should we be?"

"It should have been..." He swallowed hard. "Donovan's wedding night."

Her frown shifted into a look of surprise. "Oh. Oh!" She crossed the room in three swift strides, and Jacob found himself enveloped in her strong arms, her soft breasts crushed against him, and her warm breath on his cheek.

"You must miss him dreadfully. I'm so sorry. I wish he could have been here."

Of course she wished that. Everyone did. Donovan had been dashing, charming, easy to talk to, and easy to get along with. He'd been adored by everyone he ever met. Including one-too-many pox-riddled whores.

"I know I can never take away your grief," Octavia said, "but is there anything I can do to comfort you?"

Jacob shook his head. This was already too much, sitting wrapped in her embrace. The temptation to give in, to let himself enjoy this, was near overpowering. He swallowed the rest of the brandy, letting the burn of the liquor distract him for a moment.

Octavia pressed a kiss to his cheek and released him. "If you ever wish to talk, I will always listen. Or if you need… something else. I'm here for that, too."

She walked around the room, examining his possessions and decor, waiting, he assumed, for him to reply. What could he say? *I'm sorry my brother's gone and you're left with me?*

"You have so much lovely art," she said, running a finger along the frame of one of his favorite pieces. "I'm sorry you will never be a museum curator now. I know it was what you always wanted. You would have done a masterful job of it."

Jacob's jaw became temporarily unhinged. No one else had even considered that he hadn't wanted this. Even his own family assumed he coveted everything Donovan had ever had. In reality, Jacob had never wanted any of it, except for Octavia. And for that sin alone, he was now living out his own personal hell.

Except that the woman in question appeared determined to make that hell as heavenly as possible. She smiled at him, a genuine, warm smile brimming with affection, and his heart skipped a beat. Damn, but she was beautiful.

"People forget, I think, that you've not only lost a loved one but have had your entire life turned upside down. I know it's been a year now, but have you had even a moment's peace? I can't imagine you have, what with taking on the title, and the planning for this wedding that seemed to go on forever. So many times I wished we could simply elope. Didn't you?"

It took Jacob several stunned seconds before he finally choked out, "Yes."

For years that had been his favorite fantasy. He'd plotted ways they might flee to Scotland and hide out until their marriage became legal. Or he'd imagined hopping a boat to France and touring all his favorite museums with her at his side.

"I thought so. But it's done, at last." She walked alongside his bed, letting her fingers brush the coverlet. "Would you like to go to bed now?" She paused at his bedside table, peering down into the small basket of silk scarves that rested atop it. "These are lovely."

Octavia lifted a scarf, letting it slide over her hands before weaving it through her fingers. Jacob's cock sprang to attention. Dear God in heaven, she had no idea how often he'd lain in bed, imagining her doing that very thing. He pushed himself up out of the chair and started for her, not certain whether he intended to grab her and kiss her with everything he had, or to steer her right back into her own room and never let her in again.

"Why do you have these?" Her eyes roved over the slatted headboard. "Ooh, do you tie your lovers to the bed?"

Jacob tripped over his own feet and nearly crashed into

her. "How—" he gasped. "How do you even know of such things?"

She shrugged, her lips curving into an impish smile. "I may be innocent, but I'm not ignorant. I have friends."

"But even married women of your acquaintance wouldn't… Would they?"

Octavia laughed. "Let me tell you something about girlfriends. True, serious girlfriends who will always be there for you. If one girl stumbles upon a book of erotic stories, she is honor-bound to share it with her friends."

Jacob's mouth opened, then snapped closed. He composed himself, then tried again. "I suppose boys are much the same way."

"So, do you? Tie them up, I mean?"

"No. Those are… u-unused."

"Ah."

"And you make it sound as if I have dozens of women at all times. I don't."

"Well, some. Not now, of course, but before. You are very handsome, after all."

Good Lord, every time she opened her mouth it was to bombard him with some new surprise. Nothing about this wedding night was remotely the way he had envisioned it. All he could do was follow along and see where she led him.

She frowned at him, letting the scarf flutter from her fingers. "You cannot be surprised by that. You *have* looked in a mirror, haven't you? Donovan may have had charisma galore, but you were blessed with all the beauty."

He was dreaming. That was it. He'd fallen asleep in the chair drinking brandy, and this was one of his fantastical dreams, where Octavia thought him more radiant than Apollo.

"But enough talking," she said. "It's time for bed, and

I've been waiting a very long time for this." She gave a firm tug on the sash of her robe and let it slide to the floor.

3

"Holy. God. Almighty."

Her cheeks turned pink at his swearing. "Oh, Jacob. I wish you could see the expression on your face right now."

He didn't. He was gaping like the lovesick fool he always had been, and probably looked like he hadn't a rational thought in his head. Which was the truth, unless you counted *Fuck her now!* as a rational thought.

"It's as if you're..." Octavia's words trailed off. Yet another thing Jacob hadn't anticipated. She always spoke with confidence. "Like you're in awe of every part of me," she finished breathlessly.

"I am." He was done for. Any hope of remaining detached, of not letting himself indulge in every glorious bit of her, had flown the moment she dropped her dressing gown. He was probably going to hell, but he would have his wedding night, and he would enjoy every goddamned second of it. He took a step closer to her, his fingers flexing, not knowing where to touch first. "Like that dimple in your chin."

"You like my chin dimple?"

"I love it. I want to... kiss it."

"Oh." The word came out in a half-whisper.

"Or the freckle on your left breast. Just here." He skimmed a fingertip over the tiny mark. The softness of her skin sent tingles up his whole arm. "I want to kiss that, too."

"Do it," she demanded.

How could he deny her? He bent to press his lips to the pale, perfect globes of her bosom. She gasped.

"Do it again. To the other breast."

Jacob obeyed, lifting his hands to cup and squeeze her breasts as he feasted on them.

"Kiss my lips again. Properly this time. With your tongue and everything."

"Bloody hell, you're bold," he marveled. This was nothing like he'd ever imagined. Beyond his wildest dreams. He put up no resistance when she grabbed his shirt and pulled him to her, kissing him more eagerly than anyone ever had. She opened to him, letting him explore and taste, swirling her tongue to mimic his motions until she had the knack of it and began to give all that she got and more.

She tore at his clothes as they kissed, snapping off buttons and popping seams. Her hands splayed against his bare chest, her fingers finding his flat nipples and coaxing them to hard points. Jacob fumbled with the fastenings of his trousers, anxious to be naked, skin-to-skin with her.

Octavia pulled back abruptly, breathing hard, her cheeks flushed and her pale green eyes shining with desire. "Into bed." They scrambled together onto the bed, where she pulled him down to her for another long, desperate kiss. "Tell me more places you want to kiss on me."

"Your palms. And wrists. And all up your arm." Jacob took hold of her hand and demonstrated for her.

"Where else?"

"Your shoulder and your neck." He sucked there hard enough to leave a love mark. "Then down to your breasts. Again."

He lingered this time, tasting her fully and teasing her nipples until she let out a low moan.

"What about," she panted, "lower?"

"Yes," he murmured, sliding down her body and peppering her belly with kisses. "You are delicious."

"Keep going."

"Mmm… Your thighs?" As his lips moved downward, his fingers stroked up the inside of her legs, sweeping over her sex and coming away moist with the evidence of her desire.

"More," she sighed. "I want more, Jacob. Lick my cunny."

He flinched, startled by both her demands and her language. "What the d-d-devil was in that book?"

"So many things. So many words. I think 'cunny' is a pretty word for it, don't you?" She tangled her fingers in his hair and pushed his head back down. "Do it, Jacob. Lick it. I want to feel your tongue. I want to scream like the women in the stories."

She spread her legs for him, and he settled between her thighs, stroking and tasting her, lavishing attention on the swollen bud where her pleasure centered. She groaned, her hips lifting, seeking more. She was divine. She writhed and whimpered, fingers clenching in the bedsheets, moaning his name. Jacob kissed and sucked and licked, his senses afire with her perfection, as desperate to bring her to rapture as she was to achieve it.

She cried out when the climax hit her, not a loud, sudden outburst, but a long, breathy mewl that began as a frantic squeak before fading and dying out as a gentle sigh of supreme satisfaction.

Jacob crawled up next to her to kiss her cheek. Her brow was damp, her limbs splayed. A pink flush had stolen over her face, her neck, and the top of her chest.

"Octavia," he whispered. "You are the most beautiful, erotic woman I have ever encountered. No one can compare. I love you. More than life." He sat up, running a hand through the hair she had thoroughly mussed. "I don't deserve you. I don't deserve this."

"What?" She snapped out of her reverie, pushing herself up on one elbow and fixing him in place with a stern frown. "What are you talking about? Of course you deserve this. You're a lovely man, Jacob Moreton. I know no one better."

He turned away from her, his lust squelched beneath the weight of his guilt. "I've stolen my brother's birthright. You were… meant to be Donovan's bride. Not mine."

"No."

Her response puzzled him enough that he turned back to look at her. "What do you mean, 'no'? You were. Your parents and mine planned it. Before I was even born."

"I know they did. But it would never have happened. I would never have married him. He was a philandering wastrel."

Jacob winced. "I know."

"He wasn't a bad man. He was sweet and kind and cheerful. He never met a soul he didn't love. Friends with everyone. But he had no sense. He saw life as one unending party. I don't know how you could ever think I would marry someone like that. Don't you know me better than that?"

"I thought you would do it, er, out of a sense of duty. To your family. Isn't that why you married me?"

"Of course not!" She scooted away from him. "You don't really know me at all, do you?"

Jacob squeezed his eyes closed, grimacing. His fairytale moment was over. No longer distracted by her wide-eyed sexual curiosity, she saw him for what he was. Unworthy.

The touch of her fingers to his arm made his eyes fly open. She leaned closer, gazing at him with sad eyes, her expression gentle. "That's wrong. This has nothing to do with me, does it? It's you. You're hurt. Grieving. Because of your brother? Or because people have treated you poorly?

Have they said hurtful things to you because you're different than him?

"No." Jacob shook his head. "Sometimes. They've a-always mocked my stutter. But this is… different. This is what *I* did. To him."

"To Donovan?"

He nodded, his jaw tightening. The guilt was eating his soul. If, indeed, any of his soul remained. Octavia deserved to hear his confession. She needed to know what sort of man she was shackled to.

"I wished for this," he whispered. "You were intended for him. And I wished him gone so I could have you."

She put her hands on her hips. The movement thrust her breasts out, but even that couldn't shake Jacob from his misery. "I don't believe for one moment that you wished your brother dead."

"No. Not dead. But gone. Stranded on a remote i-island. Accidentally married to a widow with fifteen children. Struck with the sudden need to become a cloistered, celibate monk. Something, anything to get him out of the way."

Octavia listened quietly, patiently, showing no signs of disapproval. The sweet, empathetic angel who had always had time for him. "Did you tell him any of this?" she asked.

"Yes. The day I-I left to study in Europe. My mother had started making plans for him to marry you and I was seething with jealousy. I told him he was wasting his life. Told him he was a w-w-worthless scoundrel who could never be good enough for you." Jacob swallowed hard. Tears filled his eyes. "I told him I hated him and slammed a door in his face. That was the l-last thing he ever heard me say."

Octavia embraced him and he collapsed against her, his body wracked by great, heaving sobs. She lifted a hand to stroke his hair, murmuring soothing words he couldn't hear through his weeping. Tears streamed down his face—tears he had never properly shed since that terrible day he'd arrived home to find his brother hovering at death's door, delirious and insensible of the world around him. Five days Donovan had lingered that way, while Jacob pleaded with him to recover, begged his forgiveness, swore to do right by him. He'd heard none of it.

"I'm here for you, love," Octavia consoled him. "I know I can't take away the pain, but I can promise you that he knew you loved him. Everyone knew."

Jacob only wept harder, crying until the tears dried up from sheer exhaustion and he slumped back down to the bed, still entwined in Octavia's arms. He had no idea how long he lay there. He dreamed that she whispered she loved him, that she always had and always would. His fantasy. Always a fantasy, but still he clung to it. In the dream, her words were soft, but fierce, insistent, and for the first time a part of him began to believe.

"I still don't deserve you," he sighed, opening his eyes to find those incredible, pale green orbs gazing down at him.

"Untrue. You made a mistake. Hurt someone you loved. You think I haven't? How stupid was I, trying to stall indefinitely? I let Donovan and my parents and yours think that in time I would go along with their plans, when in truth I was waiting for you."

He stared at her with the slack-jawed expression that he feared might become permanent if his married life continued on in this same, dumbfounding manner. "For me?"

"Yes, you. You weren't yet of age when I decided to marry you, and then you went to Europe to study, and I wasn't going to interrupt and ruin your career, so I waited and waited. But I should have said something. To them. To you. It was a bad decision. A terrible mistake. I'm sorry. I'm far from perfect, Jacob. I hope you'll still have me."

"Still have you? Bloody hell, O-Octavia, I don't think I could give you up if someone held a knife to my throat. You've turned my whole life upside down in a single evening and I… I think I like it."

She straddled him and kissed him hard, and this time he didn't fight the desire to forget that anything existed in the world but loving her.

"Good," she said, breaking off the kiss. "Because I have no intention of letting you go." She grabbed a scarf and slid the smooth silk across his cheek and down his chest. "What do you say to that, husband?"

"Tie me down," Jacob gasped. "Take me. Make me yours."

She trailed the silk down his arm, seized his wrist, and pinned it to the headboard above him. "Gladly."

4

Her mouth was everywhere. Jacob squirmed beneath her, arching into her touch, helpless before her sensual onslaught. His wrists strained against the bindings, but the silk didn't slip even a little. No one had ever tied him this tightly. He'd always made sure that one arm was loose, just in case. Octavia, though, had lashed him with knots that would make a sailor proud, and he'd allowed it. He was hers, to do with as she willed.

And it was glorious.

He groaned as her teeth nipped at his skin, her dainty fingers pumping his cock with vigorous strokes. He was going to come in her hands if she didn't relent soon.

That thought should have embarrassed him, he supposed,

but it didn't. She could bring him off any way she damn well wanted to.

He closed his eyes. He could still taste her on his tongue. Her scent filled his nostrils. Her lips were soft as the silk that bound him, her fingers strong and sure. He was helpless in her hands, but safe and content. His toes curled, orgasm a mere breath away.

Octavia let out a little squeal of surprise when he convulsed and spent on her fingers. Gasping from the sudden release, he opened his eyes slowly—only to discover her licking his jism from her fingertips, an expression of innocent curiosity on her face.

"How long before you can do it again?" she asked.

"I, uh…" She licked another finger and he sucked in an excited breath. "N-not long?"

She snuggled against him for a moment, toying with the hairs on his chest. "I'm going to kiss you down there," she declared. "Stop me before you finish again, because this time I want you inside me."

She was perfect. Absolutely, utterly perfect. Unafraid to say what she wanted and take it from him. Not in the least troubled by his desire to let her control and lead him. He still didn't think he deserved any of this, but he was thankful. He was blessed.

"I love you," he vowed, the moment her lips touched his cock. "I love you. So much." She took him into her mouth and he gasped. "I think…" She moved up and down, sucking and licking. His head spun. "Think you're perfect." She had only a vague notion of what she was doing, but she did it with such abandoned enthusiasm, that he was in real danger of disobeying her command and losing himself in her mouth. "For me."

She pulled off of him and clambered up his body until

they were eye-to-eye. "Yes. I am for you. I think I was always meant for you." She kissed him, adjusted her hips, and in an instant he was buried in tight, wet perfection.

"Fuck," he groaned.

Her eyebrows twitched mischievously. "That's what I'm doing."

She took her time, moving slowly atop him, accustoming herself to their union. Jacob rocked his hips in time with her movements, feasting his eyes on her bouncing breasts and parted lips. Her motions sped up, and she began to make little gasps of pleasure. He thrust harder and she gasped louder.

"Yes," she moaned. "Yes, Jacob, yes. More."

She bent over him, grasping the bedsheets and riding him as hard and fast as she could, her eyes glazing over, her head lolling to one side. A love goddess in the throes of ecstasy.

"Mine," she cried as the climax took her. "You're all mine."

"Yours," Jacob moaned, giving himself up to the bliss, the clenching walls of her tight passage wringing every last drop from his shuddering body.

She rolled off of him, unknotted the scarves, and snuggled against his chest, pulling the covers up over them.

She gave a sleepy sigh. "I love you, Jacob. I'm so happy to be married to you. I think maybe I'm the happiest woman in the world."

He held her close and stroked her lovely, auburn curls. Tears different than those he had shed earlier pricked at the corners of his eyes. "I think I'm the happiest man in the world."

Never in his life had he felt such joy and hope as he'd experienced in these last hours. Octavia would forever hold his heart—still fractured, but now pieced together, securely bound by her love.

5

Jacob woke from his first truly sound sleep in recent memory. The place beside him was empty, but still warm. Octavia was dressing for breakfast, he suspected. They had a few calls to pay before they departed on their honeymoon. A trip he was now considering extending well beyond the two weeks he had reluctantly agreed to.

He climbed out of bed and padded over to the washstand, where he found a St. Valentine's Day card and a brief note written in Octavia's florid hand. He picked up the note and read it.

> *Dearest Jacob,*
>
> *In all the excitement of the wedding, I neglected to give you a Valentine card yesterday. To make up for that, I am giving you one that I wrote four years ago and never delivered. I have other, more recent cards, and I will give those to you as well, but this one seemed the most prophetic. I love you, my heart. I am forever,*
>
> *Your Octavia*

Jacob set down the note and lifted the Valentine. Like many he had seen, this one was trimmed with lace and featured extravagant floral patterns and chubby-faced cupids. The bottom bore the words, "Be My Valentine." He flipped it over. She'd crammed so much writing onto the back that he had to squint to read her tiny words.

Dearest Jacob,

Thank you for attending my mother's party last night. It was a delight to walk the gallery with you and learn about art. I love that you want to work in a museum someday! And when I declared loudly that women should have the freedom to choose a bustle gown or a rational dress costume or a gentleman's suit or anything at all and not be criticized for it, you were the very first to defend me. I almost cried, I was so touched. Dancing in your arms, I finally understood why some people consider waltzing scandalous. I felt so excited, so wanton. And I liked it. I was happier last night than I ever remember. Happy to be with you. I woke up this morning realizing that I love you more than anything. I know you are only just twenty and too young to settle down, but I will wait for you, even though all I want to do at this moment is grab a rope and tie you to me so that you can never escape. Someday you will be mine. Forever. Until then, my love, I will content myself with knowing that in my heart I am always,

Your Octavia

"And I'm crying again," Jacob said aloud. He laughed and brushed away a tear. He'd cry every day for her, if it meant reliving this feeling. He thought his heart might burst from love of her.

He knocked on the door to Octavia's bedchamber, but got no response. Damn. She was already down to breakfast. He chided himself for sleeping so long, but only half-heartedly. He'd needed the sleep. And he wanted to be as alert and awake as possible today. He and his wife had much more lovemaking to do.

He grabbed something to wear and yanked it on with hardly a second glance. He skipped shaving and merely brushed his hair down with his fingers. He'd look a slob, but he didn't care. Octavia was waiting.

She hopped up from her seat the moment he entered the breakfast room and rushed into his arms. Her lips found his, and they kissed, Jacob cupping her face between his hands, exploring her with slow, tender motions, his love pouring out in this sweet, sublime joining.

"Thank you. For the Valentine card," he said some time later, letting her breathe, but still holding her clasped to his chest. "And thank you for last night. I may never feel truly worthy of you. But I'm no longer a-afraid to love you. Or to be loved. You make me happy. And that's enough."

Her hand caressed his cheek. "You make me happy, too."

"I was thinking that I'd like to… extend our honeymoon. Perhaps take a whole month? There are a number of museums I'd like to show you."

"That sounds lovely. Let's do it."

He grinned and gave her another quick kiss. "Wonderful. I'll instruct the servants to pack a few more things in our trunks."

She pressed her cheek to his, letting her tongue dart out to lick his earlobe. "Don't forget the scarves."

Love Is
in the Airship

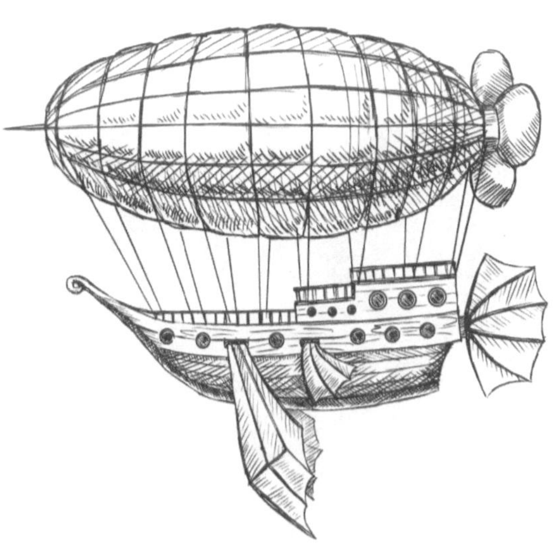

Love Is in the Airship

A Sass and Steam Story

Things to remember when fleeing your own wedding:

- mechanical serpents could lead you astray
- accidental kidnappings always involve the former boy-next-door
- sky pirates hold grudges
- sometimes all love needs is a second chance
- ♥♥ Happily Ever After. Guaranteed. ♥♥

Fleeing a wedding to a man she doesn't love, Euphemia "Effie" Werrington stows away on an airship, only to discover the ship's owner is the love who left her years before.

Charlie Wilson has been through a lot in the years since Effie's family sent him away, but despite his new piratical appearance, his heart remains as devoted as ever to the woman he left behind.

Pirates roam the skies and an angry family is hot on their tail, but the road to true love is never without a few bumps. Let romance take flight!

1

Spending her entire wedding day trapped in a shrubbery was the second-worst thing Euphemia Werrington could imagine.

Being discovered in said shrubbery and made to go through with the wedding would be the worst.

Effie carefully detached a portion of her skirt from the spiny bush. Choosing this location for her escape had been a grave miscalculation. In her defense, her judgement had been impaired. She defied anyone to make a good decision immediately after discovering one's fiancé embracing his mistress *in the church* on one's wedding day. Effie had clambered out the closest window, determined to flee as quickly as possible.

And now she was stuck in the shrubbery.

She worked her fingers between the smooth, white fabric and the prickly twig that had snagged it. She wouldn't let this dress be ruined. She'd designed it herself, and it was the one thing about this wedding that she didn't hate.

Except for the scratchy lace fichu. When Effie had revealed the dress that morning, her mother had taken one look at the low, scooped neckline and practically swooned. Apparently breasts were an affront to God. Which made no sense to Effie. If God had seen fit to give her a sizable bosom, shouldn't she be unashamed to display it? Shouldn't she be pleased with the beauty of her body as it was?

Her stepfather had said she looked like a Parisian tart. He would know. Not that Effie cared. She looked beautiful in the barely-there top and the leather corset *worn on the outside*. And fashionable, if you weren't a stuffy family from the English countryside.

Effie tugged the fichu loose and stuffed it into the shrubbery. The tearing sound as the delicate lace caught on the branches made her smile. She was done being a good girl.

She inched forward, pausing to free another bit of skirts. Not too much longer. She was still supposed to be dressing. She had perhaps a quarter hour left before anyone even noticed she was missing.

Something brushed against her boot. She glanced down and caught a glint of metal slithering off into the grass.

"Oh, no, Rusty!" She lunged for the mechanical creature, but her dress remained stuck fast, and she didn't dare pull any harder. "Rusty, stop!"

The snake-like dragon continued on his way, heedless of her cries. How had he come unwound from her waist? She must have bumped a switch while trying to maneuver through the shrubbery.

"Drat," she muttered, pulling at her skirts with even more haste. "Drat, drat, drat."

If only Rusty could hear and understand her voice. Effie always followed the latest news in dragon technology, and supposedly a professor in the United States had perfected voice controls. She was eager for such things to become commercially available.

Effie worked another snag loose, then another. Almost free. She watched the waving grass to track Rusty's progress. Too much further and she'd lose him.

"Oh, why couldn't I have gotten a chicken-shaped dragon, or one of those dog-like ones?"

Because you like snakes.

The way they moved about without any legs fascinated her. She enjoyed the way a snake could wrap around her neck or wrist. She could wear Rusty like a belt or a scarf and carry him anywhere.

The last tangled bit of her dress came loose, and she stumbled. The ugly veil that matched her discarded fichu toppled in front of her face, and she yanked it off and tossed it aside. Several hairpins came away with it. Effie shook the rest loose as she ran after her pet, letting her long, red locks tumble down. Freedom.

She raced across the open lawn, ten, twenty, thirtyish yards before she finally found her dragon wriggling away at top speed. She ducked and snagged the creature, his metal body cool against her hand. She flipped a switch on his back and he stilled.

"Thank goodness." She wrapped Rusty around her waist, comforted by his sturdy, but lightweight frame. "Now to get out of here."

Effie surveyed the area around her. She'd run nearly all the way to the treeline. She could hide in the woods, temporarily. She took a few steps further. Her gaze caught on an unnatural shape in the distance. Scooped, like a boat hull, perhaps? Curious, she plunged into the trees to take a look.

Another thirty or forty yards beyond, a small airship filled the entirety of a small clearing. Effie gasped in amazement, rushing toward it. The polished wood of the ladle-shaped hull gleamed, and the round balloon above was the same beautiful blue as the sky. Portholes of stained glass dotted the side and intricate scrollwork railings lined the deck.

"It's Charlie's dream ship!" She walked up to the vessel,

letting her hand slide across the smooth wood. "He would love this."

She jerked her hand away.

No. Stop thinking about him.

As if such a thing were possible. She'd been trying for three years to put Charlie out of her mind and she failed almost daily.

"It doesn't matter," she told herself. This airship mattered. It almost certainly belonged to one of the wedding guests. She could climb aboard and hide. No one would ever think to look for her there. What lady could climb in a wedding dress?

Effie pulled on the hidden ties in her waistband, cinching the front of her skirt up to mid-thigh. Legs free, she circled the ship until she found a place where small handholds had been nailed to the hull. Seconds later, she vaulted over the gleaming railing onto the deck.

A large chest sat along the starboard rail. Effie lifted the lid to find it half-full of some kind of folded cloth. Bedding? Curtains? Rugs? She couldn't quite tell, but it looked comfortable enough. She climbed inside and let the lid fall closed.

She snuggled down into the cloth, resting her head on her arms. She'd hardly slept last night, fretting over the wedding. She was safe for the moment. What harm could come from a little nap?

2

"I loved you first, and best!"

Charlie took another peek through the window. Hundreds of guests packed the pews of the little village church. A few men stood in the back.

"Stop the wedding! I object! No, no. Too ordinary."

He turned away with a grimace and resumed his pacing. "She's mine, dammit! You're not good enough for her!" *Too obsessive? Probably shouldn't swear in church.*

Honestly, he didn't know if this Lord Daycroft was good enough or not. Charlie had never heard of the man. They didn't exactly move in the same circles. Charlie had always been a step below the people Effie's family mingled with.

"Not that I'm bitter or anything!" he shouted, his voice echoing off the stone walls of the church.

He looked skyward, wincing as the bright sun hit his eyes. He flipped the protective filter on his monocle to its darkest setting.

"Pull yourself together, Charles Wilson," he told himself. "She doesn't want you. You've known that for years. You were an idiot to stop here." He withdrew his pocket watch and checked the time. "Work calls. And do you really want to find out if Effie's stepfather would make good on his threat? No. Get on with your life. And stop talking to yourself."

That wasn't going to happen. He'd been talking to himself for most of his twenty-three years. He plodded back to the Kestrel, muttering about how stupid he was. He had this ship. He had a flourishing career. What need did he have for a buxom redhead with a laugh like an angel and the untamed heart of a soaring falcon?

"Spain. Work. Good."

Charlie untied the moorings, scampered up the built-in ladder, and set the airship in motion. The Kestrel was a speedy little craft. In no time at all, she'd leave England— and Euphemia Werrington—far behind.

*

Clank.

Charlie flinched, yanked from the half-doze he tended to fall into when flying at night in good weather. Had he just imagined it, or had he heard a…

Clank.

"Not your imagination." The noise had come from over by the bin where he stored his bedding. Most nights, he liked to fly for five or six hours, then stop to sleep under the stars. Tonight he'd intended to go all night, pressed for time as he was because of his fool notion of trying to stop Effie's wedding. She'd be married by now, and probably in bed with…

Clank.

"Bloody hell," Charlie swore, not certain if he was talking about the unknown noise or the idea of Effie with another man.

A muffled rustling came from inside the box. Was there an animal trapped there? Or a stowaway? Who the hell would stow away on a tiny dirigible like the Kestrel?

Charlie hauled the lid open and peered inside. The ship was unlit, and the last vestiges of purple twilight were fading to black, but with his enhanced low-light vision he could see every detail of his surprise passenger. Mounds of white skirts. Tall gray boots with little, silver buttons. Mismatched stockings. Red hair tumbled all about. A body he would know anywhere.

"Goddamn," he muttered. "Effie?"

She sat up, rubbing sleep from her eyes and tugging up her dress where it had slipped down to almost completely expose one luscious breast. A snake-like dragon wound half around her waist banged its metal head against the side of the box.

Clank.

"What time is it?" Effie asked, groggily. "How long did I sleep and who…" Her eyes locked with Charlie's and went suddenly wide. "Charlie? My goodness. Charlie?"

"It's me," he replied, because what else could he say in such a situation?

"My goodness," she repeated. She scanned him from head to toe. "You look so… so…"

His jaw tightened. In the dim moonlight he wouldn't be as clear to her as she was to him, but she would see enough. She would see that he was changed. Inked. Scarred. Broken. Rebuilt.

"Go on," he snapped. "Say it. Everyone else does."

"I can imagine."

He didn't need to imagine. He heard the words every day. Freakish. Deformed. Unnatural.

"You look so…" She licked her lips. "Tantalizing."

3

Effie wondered if her expression looked as stunned as Charlie's did. She imagined it must. She couldn't seem to stop gaping. He was both the same and entirely different. His hair was still cut very short, and his face shadowed with stubble. Did he still keep the same routine of shaving only once a week? Or did his beard grow faster now that he was older? He wore a waistcoat, no tie, and shirtsleeves rolled up to his elbows, but his arms were significantly more muscular than she remembered. They were also completely covered with tattoos. In the dark it was difficult to discern what the designs might be.

Most peculiar of all, he wore a large, brass monocle over his right eye. A greenish glow emanated from behind the lens, the color eerily similar to the tube of luxene that fueled Rusty.

He noticed her staring and pushed the monocle up. With the lens out of the way, the green glow appeared more focused, like a dot or pupil in the center of his eye. His glass and metal biomechanical eye. A section of his face surrounding the eye had been replaced or covered with a steel plate. What on earth had happened to him?

"Traumatizing, did you say?" he asked. "You must have said traumatizing. I can't have heard you correctly."

"No. Tantalizing." He was. Exquisitely so. She had always found him attractive. Too much for her own good, according to her stepfather. Now these years apart had given him something more. A new, dangerous edge that set Effie's heart racing and her body tingling. New Charlie was an adventurer, and he called to all the wild impulses of her heart, longing to be let free.

She would have to be a fool to act on them.

"But never mind that," she said crisply. "What time is it, and where are we?"

"It's about half-past eight, and we're nearly halfway to Spain."

"Spain?" Effie almost choked on the word.

"Yes, Spain. Barcelona, to be precise. We're flying over France just now, and we should arrive by morning."

"But… but, why? How?"

Words failed her. They always did when she was surprised or upset or anything other than calm and happy, really. Charlie had always been the one to do the talking.

"Why, because I have an important business meeting. How is rather more complicated, but it has to do with the density of hydrogen as compared to air, steam engine propulsion, and—"

Effie folded her arms across her chest. "I know how a dirigible flies, thank you very much. But how are you here? And why were you there?"

Charlie's glowing green eye held her fixed in place. She couldn't see the color of his other eye, but she remembered it as a warm chocolate. Always twinkling. Always smiling. He wasn't smiling now. His mouth was set in the sternest expression she'd ever seen from him.

"I think what we should be asking is how and why are you on my ship?"

"I stumbled upon it, and it seemed a nice place to hide. I didn't mean for my nap to last, er, six hours." She felt the flush rising in her cheeks. "I've been very overwrought and tired of late." She swung a leg over the edge of the box and stepped out. "What business do you have in Spain? Are you a quilt merchant? Those blankets in the box were quite cozy."

"That is my personal bedding. I don't sell quilts. I sell airships."

Effie's mouth opened and stayed that way. "You... All those sketches...?"

"Yes. I've made a career out of my passion. I design the ships and oversee the construction. I'm to present my most elaborate and expensive plan ever to a client in Spain tomorrow. My business is based out of a small town in Scotland, but I have customers all over Europe."

Effie stepped to the rail and ran a hand along the gleaming wood. The exquisite craftsmanship had all the same loving care that Charlie had always put into his drawings. "You designed this?"

"Yes. And recruited many of the men who built her. We are a whole community based around airship fabrication.

A small, but close-knit group. I live in that village, now, Effie. My house isn't fancy. My neighbors and friends are craftsmen and farmers. We trade favors for goods and watch one another's children. It's nothing like the life you've always known."

No. Not in the slightest. But it sounded so lovely. Except for the one phrase that had stabbed straight to the center of her heart.

"You have children?"

Charlie's head tilted to the side and he frowned at her, his nose crinkling in that way it always did when he was puzzled.

"What? No. Why would you think… Oh, I see. I didn't mean anyone watched *my* children. Not yet, at least."

Effie stared down at the wooden planking. "Someday soon, though. I'm sure you must be married by now."

"No."

She looked back up. "No? But you have a sweetheart."

"Not that, either. What about you, Miss Werrington? Why aren't you married? Why did you run from your wedding?"

She shrugged. "I didn't love him. I don't even *like* him. He brought his mistress to the wedding, the cad!" She pulled a face. "I was doing what I was supposed to do. But I couldn't go through with it. I don't want to end up like Mother, stuck with a man she can't respect."

"She should try to divorce him."

Effie shook her head. "She is content to quietly tend to his needs and avoid conflict, even if it means she's ignored. I think she likes the solitude. People are different."

Effie's stomach rumbled, reminding her that she hadn't eaten a thing since shortly before fleeing the church. It was time she ate. She didn't want to throw her diet or her schedule off. She stuck her thumb into Rusty's mouth, and the snake bit down. A moment later, his eyes flashed yellow. Normal. Good.

"Effie? Did your dragon just bite you?"

"He tests my blood. You know I have the sugar sickness."

Even in the dark she could see his face blanch. "I could never forget that awful day you almost died. What do you need? Food? Medicine?" His jaw dropped. "Oh, fuck, Effie, do you need medicine?" He ran for the ship's controls. "I'll turn us around. Take you back home. Christ, Effie, why didn't you say anything?"

She rushed over to his side, grabbing his arm before he could pull any levers or spin any wheels. "Stop. I'm fine. Rusty carries enough for a week."

Charlie shook his head. "I should take you home. I can't even imagine what everyone is thinking. I've all but kidnapped you!"

Effie put her hands on her hips. "Listen to me, Charles Wilson. I won't let you destroy your business over this. And no matter whether you take me to Spain or back to England, I am *not* going home. Never. Good Girl Effie is gone."

4

Good Girl Effie is gone.

God, did he hope so. Because her reputation certainly was. Fleeing your own wedding in an airship with the former boy-next-door was not the sort of thing that could be hushed up. Even by someone with the sort of funds that Effie's stepfather had at his disposal. Plus, the man cared far more for his own reputation than for Effie's. Charlie knew that for certain.

Effie sliced off a dainty bite of Bacalao and sampled it,

chewing the salty fish slowly and thoughtfully. Her eyes drifted to the vegetables in aioli sauce sitting on the plate. Charlie had provided a variety of local dishes for their shipboard lunch, and she was determined to taste them all. Everything about Spain was new and exciting to her. She took it all in with wide eyes and radiant smiles. So eager for new things. So sheltered.

Much as he had been three years ago.

Effie flipped through his sketchbook as she ate, nodding at designs she liked. She had come along to his meeting that morning. He hadn't asked her to, but he hadn't said not to, either.

"I'm another designer," was all she had said, when his client gave her a curious look.

And she was. Charlie was certain that the astounding wedding dress she wore was her own creation. How many times had they sat together, swapping sketches and testing out new ideas?

"Oh, you should move ahead with this one," she said, gesturing at the book. "It's certainly not as elaborate as the ship that Señor Miron has commissioned, but I think it will be far more elegant."

"Not everyone is interested in elegant. I've noticed that many dirigible purchasers desire ships that will stand out in a crowd. Bright colors, highly ornamented rails, multiple types and colors of wood. That sort of thing."

Effie looked around the tidy and well-appointed cabin. It filled most of the hull, and he had furnished it with simple, but high-quality items. The table was sturdy, the sofa comfortable for reading or for sleeping on, and the bookshelves well-stocked.

"This ship is nothing like that. It's beautiful, and the workmanship is superb, but it's not ostentatious in any way."

"It's my masterpiece." There was no denying it. He'd put his heart and soul into this ship. He'd paid for it with an eye and believed it worth the price.

"I love it."

Charlie's breath caught in his chest. Three little words and any hope of hardening his heart against this woman evaporated. She was nothing like the Euphemia he'd told himself she must have become and everything like the Effie he remembered. Kind. Spirited. Affectionate. He made a pretense of slicing off some bits of his own salted cod to avoid looking at her. A fruitless attempt to save himself, he suspected.

"I'm a bit surprised you built yourself something so nice, though," she continued. "I would have thought you more likely to be too busy working first on projects for others." She released a little sigh. "Though I suppose I shouldn't pretend to really know you anymore."

She did know him. All too well.

"I didn't make it for myself. I made it for an extremely wealthy client. He had no specifications. Told me only to make it the best small craft I could devise. I worked out every tiny detail. Oversaw every aspect of the construction. Added a proper, flushing water closet."

"Which all airships should have, if you ask me. So, what happened? Did the client die? Did he not like it?"

"He loved it. And then he stole it."

"What?"

"He's a pirate, and he didn't want to pay. I was one man. Young, inexperienced, and alone. What could I do to fight him? He took the ship and flew away, leaving me sitting in the middle of a Portuguese airfield."

Effie leaned across the table, her eyes alight, her luncheon forgotten. "How did you get it back?"

"I enlisted the services of another client. A good customer, who had paid well for a fast, reliable craft. Also a pirate, and a sworn enemy of the man who took my airship. I joined her crew, and—"

"*Her* crew? A lady pirate?"

"Yes. *La Capitaine* is a brilliant and tenacious woman. I joined her crew and sailed with her after Redbeard—that's what people call him. We tracked him down, attacked his fleet, and stole back this airship. I suffered two broken ribs and lost an eye, but she's all mine now." He trailed his fingers across the wood paneling behind him. "As I think she was always meant to be."

"Goodness. And is that where you got all those tattoos? From the pirates?"

Charlie looked down at the web of gears, bolts, and other mechanical items covering his arms. "No. I got these done in Scotland. One of the men in our town is an accomplished tattoo artist."

"Do they cover your whole body?"

"You'll have to see for yourself." Charlie almost clamped a hand over his own mouth. Dammit, dammit, dammit. "I'm sorry. That was indecent. I would never want to imply that you would have an interest in… Just because we… I'm sorry."

"Yes." Effie looked down at her plate. "I suppose you are."

Charlie frowned. What did she mean by that? Did she think he was sorry she was here? Sorry to have ever met her? He wasn't, but he suspected she might be sorry to have met *him*. He'd almost ruined her life once before, and this debacle had the potential to finish the job.

"I should be getting back on deck, now. It's time we were going." He stumbled from his seat and hurried for the door.

"Charlie?"

He paused. "Yes?"

"Where are we going next? Somewhere exciting?"

"Only if you think Scotland is exciting. I need to be getting home to get this new project under construction and to deal with various other projects in different stages of completion. I'm happy to drop you off anywhere along the way, or arrange transport to wherever you wish to go." He'd do his best to see her safe and free.

"Ah." Her eyes dropped to her plate again.

Charlie scrambled up top, and tried to put all his energy into flying the ship. Other aircraft flew here and there above the bustling city, and the maneuvering commanded his full attention. Almost.

At least until Effie came up on deck and asked in her ever-curious voice, "Could you show me how to fly the ship?"

Charlie muttered half-a-dozen curses in as many languages. He'd learned *that* from the pirates.

He would give her anything she asked. He was every bit as much in love with her as he'd been three years ago. Maybe more so, now that she was fully embracing her independent streak. He cursed again and then gestured at the controls. "Be my guest."

The air was calm and she took to the simple controls well, and soon Charlie was scanning the skies instead of watching her every move. It was easier that way.

A glimpse of red caught his eye. He reached up and spun a dial on his monocle, zooming in on the distant spot. A dirigible. Small, though larger than this one. The sort that would have a crew of five or six and room for half-a-dozen passengers besides. The sort that so many aristocrats and wealthy entrepreneurs flaunted. It was headed straight for him and moving quickly. This time when he swore, it was in English, and aloud.

Effie spun to look at him. "What's wrong?"

"I think your family has found us." He pointed in the direction of the growing red dot.

Effie stepped away from the controls to peer over the rail, her lips pinched into a tight frown.

"But my stepfather's dirigible is green."

5

No amount of maneuvering could outrun the pirate ship bearing down on them. Effie didn't have to ask if she was correct in her assessment of the situation. Charlie didn't say a thing, and that told her enough. She remembered only twice when he'd gone so completely silent: the day she'd nearly died and woken to find him sitting at her bedside, pale as a ghost, and the night three years prior when he'd disappeared from her life.

He flew the ship to the best of his ability, but even as light and zippy as she was, the Kestrel was no match for a smuggling ship. Effie eyed the approaching craft. It sported a red, oblong balloon, painted with ostentatious gold swirls, like any pleasure boat. Coupled with an aerodynamic shape and powerful engines meant for outrunning air frigates.

She shivered. A confrontation was unavoidable. Would the pirates force them to land and evacuate the ship? Take them hostage? Kill them? Charlie had already lost a chunk of his face. She wouldn't let anyone do him further damage, whether that meant surrender or fighting. She needed a weapon.

The deck was empty except for the crate of bedding, coils of rope for tying down, and a few smaller boxes of provisions. She hurried down the steep stairs to the cabin below, grabbing everything that looked useful.

"Effie, what are you doing?" Charlie asked, when she returned with an armload of dishes and bottles. "I thought you were hiding down below to stay safe."

"And abandon you? Ha!" She spread her supplies across the deck. "The knives are too small and dull, but perhaps if we smash the plates or something glass the edges will be sharp enough to use as weapons."

"Against guns?"

"They have guns?" Of course they had guns. They were pirates. "Do you have a gun anywhere?"

"No. I'm a terrible shot."

"Damn." Effie's hand leapt to cover her mouth. She'd never uttered a curse word out loud before. She'd been very specifically told that she was never to use foul language. Even certain euphemisms had been forbidden. "Damn," she repeated, enjoying the cathartic freedom of no longer caring. And then, because she could, "Fuck!"

"For God's sake, Effie, this is not the time to practice your swears. Go below. Maybe they won't see you."

"They've already seen me. I can see them from here." She made a quick count. Four thugs and one nicer-dressed man with a long, white beard. "That man with the beard, is he the leader? Was his beard red, once?"

"No. They call him Redbeard because he kills so many people that his beard gets stained with blood."

Effie gazed straight into Charlie's eyes, brown and green, natural and mechanical, both hard and unblinking. "You're not joking."

"No. Go downstairs."

"Never." She picked up the biggest bottle she'd found below and smashed it against the deck, keeping the jagged, snapped-off neck as a weapon.

"That was my best brandy."

The prosaic complaint had an oddly calming effect on her. "Shouldn't you be drinking rum, like a proper pirate?"

"I'm not a pirate."

"No, but you look like one, and you had a lady pirate lover, and—"

"What? I did not!"

"No? But the way you talked about her…"

"She's a friend. There's been no one."

"No one? But…" The ship lurched as the pirate ship drew alongside, the hulls bumping. The four thugs hopped up onto the rail and leapt for the Kestrel's deck. "Not the time, sorry!" She raised her improvised weapon. "I'll keep them away from you."

Charlie abandoned the controls and ran for one of the small boxes, throwing it open and pulling out a wrench. "To hell with that, Effie! I'm keeping them off *you*."

The thugs charged. Effie screamed as one of the large men barreled straight for her. She swung the broken bottle neck blindly, scratching the attacker, but doing no real damage. The three other thugs all ran at Charlie.

"No!" Effie ducked away from the pirate's grasp, abandoning her shard of glass, and whipping Rusty from around her waist. She flicked a tiny switch as she slung the snake around, and he bit the pirate's arm and clamped down, hard.

The pirate yelped, and Rusty's eyes flashed green.

Effie danced from the pirate's grasping hands again, yanking Rusty back into her arms. "Your blood sugar is getting low. You should eat something."

The pirate growled something in a language she didn't understand, though she suspected it was some type of insult. He pulled a gun, but before he could raise it, Effie attacked with Rusty once more, swinging him with all her might.

The dragon's hard, metal head hit the pirate's skull with a thunderous smack, and the big man staggered. Effie hit him again, and he collapsed.

She whirled around, ready to help Charlie fend off the other attackers. Three pirates stood spread across the deck, one with a gun in hand. She saw no sign of Charlie.

Her heart skipped a beat. She screamed his name. If they'd thrown him overboard, she would kill every last one of them.

The pirates spun to face her. A sandbag came crashing down on one of them, dropping him like a stone. Effie looked up. Charlie hung upside down from a cable, the wrench in one hand, and various ropes wrapped around his waist and arms. He unhooked his legs, swung right over Effie's head, and dropped to the deck behind her.

Of course. He knew every bolt and cable and rope on this ship. He probably had defensive measures she would never have dreamed of.

Charlie yanked her backward as two more ballast bags dropped from above, but only one struck a pirate, and then only enough to make him angry. He waved his gun, apparently uncertain whether he wanted to shoot her or Charlie first.

Effie's eyes darted to the pirate she had felled with Rusty. The unconscious man still clutched his pistol in his right hand. Could she get to it in time?

Apparently not. The other man leapt at her, and she had only enough time to jump backward and avoid being crushed by two hundred pounds of sweaty pirate. She swung Rusty again, but this pirate was smarter and quicker than his companion. He dodged, caught Rusty in one of his beefy hands, and hurled the snake-dragon over the rail.

"No!"

Her shout turned into a scream of horror as Charlie dove after her pet, hurtling himself straight for the edge. His thighs hit the rail, his upper body pitching forward over top, and for an instant time stood still.

Effie's legs were pumping, but it felt like she wasn't gaining any ground. Charlie fell in slow motion, slipping further and further, until he caught himself with one hand.

"I have it! I have the snake!"

The world began to move again, and Effie grabbed hold of Charlie's shirt, pulling with all her might to help him climb to safety. A gun fired and she shrieked and nearly lost her grip.

"Don't shoot the girl, you arse," one of the pirates shouted. "With kettledrums like she's got, she'll fetch a fine price."

Charlie tossed Rusty up onto the deck, and the dragon slithered safely behind a box. With both hands and Effie's help, he hauled himself over the rail, falling to the deck in a heap. Effie positioned herself between Charlie and the pirates. If they wanted her alive, she could use her body to shield him.

She ought to have known better. She hadn't even opened her mouth to tell him to stay down when he darted out and raced for the helm, diving behind the control panel just as another gunshot rang out. The pirate with the gun started after him.

Effie shuffled sideways, moving toward the unconscious pirate and his gun, but keeping her eyes on the big pirate who stalked her. He smirked and made a half-hearted attempt to grab her, chuckling when she flinched.

"Don't you want to come with us, sweetling?" he mocked her. "I promise I'll take it nice and slow."

A bellow of surprise from behind her turned into a

shriek, followed by a muffled thud. Effie didn't turn. The pirate had made that noise, not Charlie. She could discover what had happened after she reached the gun and dispatched this last pirate.

"No, no, missy." He sprang for the gun. The ship lurched, causing them both to stumble. The pirate, unfortunately, stumbled right toward the gun. Effie backed away. "Now, just 'cause I don't want to shoot ya, don't mean I won't."

Effie continued backward, trying to draw the pirate away from Charlie. If he could fly the ship, maybe they could escape. Somehow.

The ship lurched again, and this time the movement was accompanied by a scream of absolute terror. Effie's head snapped around just in time to see a pirate's flailing hand slip away over the side of the ship. Over on the pirate ship, half a dozen more pirates had gathered, waiting along the rail for the Kestrel to drift near enough that they could swarm the deck. One man fired a gun in the direction of the helm.

"Take out the pilot, take over the ship," the pirate snickered. "They'll get him, and I'll get you."

Several more shots rang out.

"Charlie!" Effie shouted. He misinterpreted her fear for him as fear for herself and abandoned the helm, rushing toward her, wrench in hand, heedless of the possibility of getting shot. Her heart leapt into her throat.

The big pirate advanced toward her. She had precious little room left to back away. She took another step and staggered when she hit a solid wall. Make that no room. Time for plan B.

"You won't shoot me," she challenged.

The pirate laughed. "No?"

"No. Because you don't want to damage these." She gave her neckline a firm yank, and her breasts sprang free, the cool air immediately tightening her nipples to firm points. The pirate froze in mid step, his jaw hanging open as if it had come unhinged. Honestly, men were so silly.

Charlie charged across the deck, his boots pounding on the wood, but the pirate recovered too late from his stunned ogling. The wrench came down on his head in mid turn. His eyes rolled back in his head and he crumpled.

Effie dove at Charlie, knocking him to the deck, out of line of any gunfire. "That was so reckless," she chided.

"I should hit him again," Charlie said, not seeming to hear.

"Why?"

"He doesn't deserve to remember so perfect a bosom as yours." His eyes looked there and lingered.

She poked him in the center of his chest, as she had done so often those many years ago, then tucked herself back into her dress. "Let's crawl to the helm. We can avoid their guns and maybe fly away."

"No." He scurried along the rail on hands and knees, Effie right behind. "I need *you* to fly the ship."

"What? Me?"

He didn't answer until they had reached the helm and he had yanked on several levers, sending the Kestrel on a rapid and bumpy ascent. "We can't outrun them. But if I board them, I can disable them. All you need to do is keep her moving so the pirates can't board her."

"Board them? Are you mad?"

"Probably."

Effie grabbed his shirt. "You could be killed!"

"I know airships. If I do this right, they'll never even see me." He took her hand and squeezed it. "Do you trust me?"

She shouldn't. Who would trust a man who had

abandoned her without a word? And yet she did. With her entire being, she did.

She didn't even answer. She just tugged harder on his shirt until their lips collided and kissed him with everything she had.

"I love you, Charlie." She pushed him away. "Now, go."

6

Charlie opened valves, turned knobs, and loosened screws almost at random, doing as much damage with as little noise as possible. Fluid puddled at his feet. Escaping steam clouded the air around him. On the opposite side of the engines, he could hear Redbeard shouting commands at his remaining pirates, his fury evident even in the phrases that weren't English. Every angry word lightened Charlie's heart. Every angry word meant Effie was safe.

I love you, Charlie.

Her words echoed in his mind, an unending litany of joy. He'd never thought to hear those words again. He'd been so certain that they'd been no more than a lie, or at best a passing fancy. He'd been a fool.

He opened another valve, and then paused. Something about this boiler was off. He made a closer examination, brushing his hands against the metal, picturing the design in his mind.

Yes. It was off. Fatally so.

With a few, quick turns of his wrench, he disabled the faulty failsafe mechanism. He spun dials, flipped levers. Turned everything up to the highest setting.

"Bang," he whispered.

He moved as far as he dared toward the rail, looking for the Kestrel. The little ship maneuvered better than the pirate ship in such a tight space, but Effie's hour-long stint as pilot was sorry preparation for the task he had left her. The ship rose and fell as he watched, making boarding difficult for the pirates, but making no progress toward escape. Waiting for him.

"Ready on the ropes," Redbeard commanded. "He knows he can't escape. Hold her steady, and when he drops again swing over."

Damn. Charlie had to go now. Not only did he need to be off this ship before the boiler blew, but if those pirates made it across, he couldn't leave Effie to fight them alone. He inched closer to the rail, eyes locked on the bottom of his ship, waiting for her to descend again. He flipped his monocle to the special filter that helped him judge distance.

For an instant he thought he must be seeing incorrectly, even with the mechanical assistance. The ship was far too fast, the hull tipped too far forward. He cursed aloud. The numbers didn't lie. She'd put the ship into a nose-dive. A brilliant tactic, but a wildly dangerous one to a novice pilot. It was also his best and perhaps only chance to escape. He raced for the rail, knowing the pirates would hear him and turn, knowing he had only one chance to make the leap to his own deck. The tiny dial in his lens spun, flinging numbers into his mind that he could only pray he was interpreting correctly. He ran, leapt to the rail, and launched himself into the air, pulling his body into the tightest streamline he could.

He hit the deck with a bone-jarring crash. He would feel that tomorrow, he was certain, but now the pain was only a mild inconvenience. He scrambled for the helm, shouting for Effie to keep going.

"Charlie, something's wrong. The gauges have gone crazy."

He hopped up beside her and flipped one switch. The wind whipped through their hair and stung Charlie's uncovered eye. "This is good!" he hollered over the rush of air.

"Good?"

"Insane, but good!" Cables creaked, and the ship groaned in protest. No airship was made for this sort of wild descent, but Charlie knew exactly how much she could withstand. He stepped beside Effie, taking the wheel and pointing at the controls, showing her what to do and when. Little trembles of fear shook her body, but she kept at it, doing everything he told her as he righted the little dirigible and steered her as far from Redbeard's craft as possible.

Whether it was minutes later or tens of minutes, Charlie couldn't say, but when an explosion in the sky above them buffeted their ship, he let out a sigh of relief.

"Ship's dead. They'll either have to land or crash. We're safe."

Effie stared at him for a long moment, then flung her arms around him. He held her close, relearning her body, her warmth, her scent. "Time to go home," he murmured.

✦

Charlie fought to keep from dozing off as he landed the Kestrel in a secluded field in northwest France. He'd flown all day, with only a brief stop to drop off their unwanted captives. Every muscle in his body ached to lie down and sink into a deep slumber. Preferably with Effie in his arms.

After their escape, she'd diligently tidied up the ship, even making a careful record of all damage done during the pirate attack. He was in awe of her quiet efficiency and resilient spirit. His lips still tingled when he thought back to the way she'd kissed him. Fierce. Passionate. Ravenous.

"The couch down below is comfortable if you prefer not to sleep on deck," he said, pulling his bedding from the chest and spreading it out. "But it's a pleasant night and the blankets are warm."

Effie pressed up against him. "So am I."

"I remember. You didn't think I was really cold all those times I shivered so you would snuggle with me, did you?"

"I didn't waste time thinking about it."

He wrapped an arm around her. "Come snuggle with me, love."

He took off his monocle, she removed her corset and unwound her snake from around her waist, and they settled onto the pile of bedding. Their bodies fit together more perfectly than Charlie remembered. He rubbed a lock of red hair between his fingers. The time apart had only made her more beautiful. More desirable. More everything.

"You're incredible, Effie," he murmured. "I could lie here with you forever if you would have me."

She shifted to look into his eyes, studying his face in the darkness. "You could have had me. Three years ago. Why didn't you? Why did you leave?"

"Halston refused to let me marry you. Threw me out of the house."

Her dark-blue eyes narrowed. "He told me that *you* refused to marry me."

Charlie gaped at her. "And you believed him?"

"No. Not at first. But then you never answered my letters."

"I never received letters."

"Never? I wrote you every day for three months! I left them at your parents' house because I thought my stepfather might not send them on."

"I sent all my letters there, too, for the same reason."

"Drat. I mean, damn. He must have bribed a servant. I had no idea he was so devious. Or hated you so much."

"He didn't want even a vague family connection with a milliner."

"Your mother is a milliner who had enough money to move her family away from London's unhealthy air and allow her husband to leave his factory job to pursue his passion for botany. Her goods are worn by the most fashionable people in the world! I've designed dresses just to match her hats."

"Halston doesn't care. He told me if I said anything or came back he would disown you and smear your name so badly that you would have no choice but to walk the streets. 'Like the harlot she is.' That's what he said. I was terrified for you, Effie. And I was stupid. I should have done something more. I should have fought harder for us."

She laid a hand against his cheek, the tips of her fingers running along the transition from flesh to metal. "And I shouldn't have doubted you. I won't again."

Charlie pressed a kiss to her forehead. "I never stopped loving you. From now on, I'm going to prove it." He yawned before he could say more.

Effie brushed her lips against his. "Goodnight, Charlie. Sleep. I'll keep you warm."

He pulled her tight to his chest and let his eyes drift closed. No command had ever been sweeter.

7

Effie popped the last bite of orange into her mouth, licking the juice from her lips because Charlie was watching.

"Fruit and cheese is a very piratey sort of breakfast."

He neither moved from where he lay beneath the blankets nor looked away from her mouth. "Is it?"

"It seems it to me. I think you're a rather dashing pirate, Charlie."

"I'm an airship designer."

"With wild tattoos and a riveting night-vision eye."

"True."

"What about me? Do I make a good pirate wench?"

"Absolutely. The wenchiest wench to ever set foot on my pirate ship."

Effie couldn't help but grin. "Where are we going today? Your home in Scotland?"

"We will stop wherever you wish, Effie. You deserve the freedom to choose your own life. You don't have to do what your mother wants. You certainly don't have to do what Halston wants. And I won't pressure you to do what I want."

Effie set the last of her breakfast aside and burrowed underneath the blankets to snuggle against Charlie. "I thought we wanted the same thing."

His hand skimmed along her waist. "I like to imagine that we do, but…" He shrugged.

Effie nuzzled his neck and slid a hand between his legs, stroking his cock until it hardened beneath her fingers. "It seems we want the same thing. Just as we wanted the same thing that day beneath the apple tree."

He winced. "Oh, God, Effie, I was so awful and awkward that day. I think I did everything wrong."

She giggled. "Yes. We were fumbling and incompetent. But it was exciting and magical all the same."

"You were so covered in mud afterward that I had to carry you to your house and pretend I had found you injured and lying in a puddle."

"And I laughed so hard Mother thought I was hysterical and summoned a doctor." Effie pressed her face against

Charlie's chest, her body shaking with laughter at the memory. "Fortunately, we did improve our trysting skills."

Charlie's dexterous fingers found the row of tiny buttons in her bodice and popped them, one-by-one. "Drastically." He peeled the dress from her body, gazing admiringly at her naked form. "Extraordinarily, even." He pressed a kiss to the hollow of her throat and she sighed. "Let's see if we can remember all we learned together."

Effie tugged at the buttons of his trousers. "Yes, let's." She swiftly undressed him, pausing to examine the changes three years had made to his body. He was harder, more muscular. "Your tattoos only go up to your shoulders." She ran a finger along the edge of the design.

He nuzzled her breasts. "Mmm. Yes. Plenty of room for more. Perhaps you might pick your favorite location for my next one."

Her eyebrows twitched. "I will consider every option."

She wrapped her arms around him and brought them together, skin-to-skin—moist lips meeting, tongues tangling, hands exploring bodies too long untouched.

"Remind me again why I left you for three years?" he asked.

"Something about my stepfather calling me a harlot and us both being too insecure to believe we were truly wanted."

"Let's never do that again."

"Agreed."

He moved over her, and she lifted her hips to draw him in, matching the rhythm of his thrusts, riding with him toward the peak of bliss. Flying.

"My sky pirate," she murmured. "I should have known. Should have known we would always fly together."

Her eyes slid closed, her head lolled back, and she let the climax take her, clinging to him, unwilling to part until they were both fully spent. He groaned her name and went limp, rolling over to avoid squashing her.

"Damn," he murmured, pressing his lips to her temple. "That was Effie-ing fantastic."

She poked him. "Did you just use me as a euphemism for 'fuck?'"

"Euphemia-ism."

"Well, Chuck you, too."

They both burst into laughter, hugging one another close. "Whenever you wish, love. Whenever you wish."

✦

The sun hovered low in the west, heralding the end of the most glorious May Day that Effie could remember. Pretty white blooms adorned her hair, collected during their brief stop for a romantic picnic lunch. More flowers decorated her décolletage. Charlie had arranged them most particularly. Then crushed them with his amorous attentions. He'd picked her a new bouquet, but even the replacement blossoms now looked a bit squashed.

Which made them no less beautiful to Effie. This was a day of new life. Of new beginnings. She didn't know what tomorrow would hold, but she was up for any adventure that included embracing both Charlie and her newfound freedom.

She fished Rusty out of the dark corner where he'd crawled again and went to join Charlie at the helm. The joyful smile he'd worn all day had been replaced with a tight frown. He looked over his shoulder, adjusting something on his monocle.

"What's wrong?" she asked.

"What color did you say Halston's dirigible was?"

Effie looked off into the distance, but couldn't see more than a blurry dot on the horizon. "Green. Why?"

"Damn. There's a green ship back there. Just at the edge of my telescopic range. Been following us for the last hour at least. There's a regular spyglass in the box of tools, if you want to take a look."

Effie fetched the glass and peered at the dot behind them. Bright green balloon. Highly polished hull painted a darker color of green.

"Drat. That's him." She snapped the glass closed and looked at Charlie. "What are we going to do? I won't go back, no matter what they say."

"And I won't let them take you. I've been going over the calculations in my head and I don't think he can catch us. We'll be on the ground in under half an hour."

"Are we so close to your home already?"

"No, my home is about another half-hour beyond that. But I wanted to stop for dinner. And your next adventure."

Effie peered over the side of the ship. "What's here that's so adventurous? It looks like all fields and more fields. Sometimes houses." She spun back toward him. "Unless you mean to duel with my stepfather? You're not going to duel him, are you? You'd better not. You'll either die or go to prison, and I won't stand for that."

"No dueling. A quick stop at the blacksmith's shop. A nice dinner. A comfortable bed in an inn."

"Ooh, will we register at the inn as husband and wife under a false name? That does sound like an adventure. And did you say the blacksmith? Do you think he would be able to repair this switch on Rusty's back? It keeps getting accidentally flipped and then he crawls off into the nearest hiding place. Which is fine on a small ship or in a closed room. But outside he almost got away from me. If he were to crawl under a rock or down an animal hole, I could lose him for good."

Charlie chuckled. "We'll have him fixed. If not tonight, then I know craftspeople at home who have all the right tools and knowledge."

"Excellent. Just keep away from my stepfather and this can be the perfect day."

"That's my plan."

She turned back to the rail to watch their slow descent. By the time they touched down and had all the moorings secure, the distant dot of her stepfather's ship had grown into a large, green, clearly-dirigible-shaped dot.

"Charlie, Halston is gaining rather rapidly. I don't think we'll have time for your adventure. Perhaps we might do better to continue on. Or is there a good place to hide here?"

Charlie grinned at her. "No need to hide. He's too late."

"Too late?"

"Very much so." He held out a hand to her. "Effie, my love, will you join me on the adventure of a lifetime?"

She laced her fingers through his. "I think so, but to be absolutely certain, you'll have to tell me what this adventure entails."

"I'll give you two hints. One, this is Gretna Green. And two, you're wearing a wedding dress."

Effie laughed with joy, then did a little dance, pulling Charlie along with her. "You're right. He's much, much too late. Let's go get married."

Epilogue

Two years later

"I can't believe we were invited to this."

Charlie took Effie's hand and helped her onto the

roll-away staircase that had been pushed up to the Kestrel's rail. "Don't be silly. Of course we were invited. It's the royal debut of your dress."

"I'm sure we're only here because of your airships. This *is* the king's Spring Airship Gala, after all."

"True. But while my airships are nice, none of them are owned by royalty. Yet."

They descended together to the great, wide field packed with ships of all sizes and colors. Pilots in goggles and engineers in stained tunics mingled with lords and ladies in their grandest finery, talking of the latest innovations, the newest fashions, and grand plans for the future of air travel. Effie took it all in with wide eyes and happy smiles, another adventure for her ever-growing list.

She dazzled today in her floor-length blue gown. As always, the bodice was daringly low, and the skirts were full of hidden ties and hooks, ready to be cinched up should she need extra freedom of movement. Or if she merely wanted to show off her bright pink boots and mismatched stockings. Charlie's mother had made her a hat to match—a newsboy cap in the same color as the dress, with a big, pink rose on one side. As cute and unconventional as the woman who wore it.

"You must be Mr. Wilson of Wilson Airships," said a distinctly American voice. "Beautiful craft you have here. The only one I've seen to rival the Lasher ships."

Charlie and Effie turned to see a man in a crisp, black suit standing side-by-side with a woman in a dashing, knee-length purple dress.

"Evan Tagget," the man introduced himself, extending his hand.

Charlie's jaw dropped, but Effie didn't appear to care in

the slightest that one of the wealthiest men in the world had just introduced himself.

"My dress!" she exclaimed. "You're wearing my dress!"

"Which means you are Euphemia Werrington Wilson of Werrington Designs," the woman replied, spinning to show off her ensemble. "I love it. And Evan paid a fortune for it." She gave Effie a conspiratorial wink. "But if you really want to see something, come with me. The new Queen of Norway is wearing another creation of yours."

Effie teetered as if she were about to swoon. "Is she really?"

"She looks like a cloud, dotted with tiny embroidered airships."

"I can't believe it. I know I was *told* she would wear it, but I can't believe…" Effie clutched Charlie's hand and bounced. "Can you believe it?"

He gave her a squeeze. "Yes, love. I absolutely can."

Five minutes later, Effie stood before the fashionable and sporty Queen Maud, pink-cheeked from the praise of her dress design. Charlie missed most of the conversation, too wrapped up in his own discussion with Mr. Tagget about the potential of internal combustion engines. Hardly off the ship and already this day was a smashing success.

By the end of the gala, Charlie and Effie were clinging to one another, exhausted from hours of meeting and mingling with the world's elite. They scampered up to their ship and pushed the stairs away, ready for a moment alone.

"If Halston could see you now," Charlie laughed. "He'd be sorry he ever said a word against either of us."

"He'd never be invited. Not with Drusilla flaunting all her scandalous affairs. Which she might be doing just to spite him."

Charlie nodded. Effie's stepsister had married Lord

Daycroft, Effie's ex-fiancé, and by all accounts the couple despised one another.

Charlie put an arm around his darling wife, grateful as always for the blessing of a true, loving partner and companion. "As incredible as today's adventure was, I don't need parties full of royalty to consider my life a full and happy one." He bent and pressed a kiss to the place above her heart where she'd tattooed their entwined initials between a pair of wings. "All I need is you."

Effie's fingers unfastened his shirt buttons, exposing the ink that matched her own.

"Us," she corrected.

Of Barmaids
and Bicycles

Of Barmaids and Bicycles

A Potions and Passions Story

Spying, sarcasm, and swords: All in a good night's work.

In this bonus epilogue to *How to Seduce a Spy*, a last minute assignment goes slightly awry, leading Henry and Elle to a wild night of magic, mayhem, and a most unusual duel.

"Tonight? Impossible."

Henry shook his head, his shoulders slumping in disappointment. It had been too long since he'd had a thieving assignment and he was itching for the thrill of some nighttime crime. But he had family obligations, and he'd sworn years ago not to be reckless.

Ayleston stroked his beard. "If not you, then who? With Harris unavailable…"

Missing several fingers after meeting the sharp end of a blade.

"You are the only retrieval specialist near enough to Rivenstoke's home to take his place. I'm afraid we have no alternative."

"You could give me a few days' time. If Rivenstoke is truly selling state secrets he will have taken security precautions. Doors will have the best locks. Windows could be barred. He might even have guards. I can't break into a house with no knowledge of these things. I need to learn the grounds, the layout of the house, the number of servants, family members, and guests to expect… Why am I bothering telling you this? You know all this. I can't do it. It's impossible."

"Harris provided us his notes."

"Notes?" Henry frowned at Ayleston. "He makes *written* notes?" Good God, what were they teaching their spies these days?

"He left us notes, and they will provide you the information you need. It must be done tonight at Rivenstoke's weekend party. We have reason to believe that he intends to leave England by steamship at eight a.m. tomorrow morning, papers in hand."

"And who knows what other information he's keeping in his head to pass along. Damn. Why don't you just arrest him?"

"No proof. We need those papers."

"So I steal you the papers."

"An anonymous benefactor leaves us the papers, which we will then act upon immediately."

"You should just bloody arrest him," Henry muttered.

"High treason is not a charge to be taken lightly. We want clear proof and as much of it as we can obtain. We need those papers, and we need them to be fetched tonight."

Henry sighed. "What do you want me to do?"

"We have a carriage waiting outside. You will go to Rivenstoke's weekend party this evening as Harris. The two have never met, so the deception should be simple. Join the party. Mingle with the other guests."

"Sounds thrilling."

"You don't have to like it, Ainsworth, you only have to do it. During the night, sneak into Rivenstoke's chambers and steal the papers. They may well be kept on his person, even when he sleeps. Drug him with a potion, if necessary, to keep him from waking. Go tell your wife you're leaving and then meet me in the carriage. I'll have all the notes you'll need."

"This is a terrible idea."

"You will be well compensated."

"Which makes it no less terrible."

"But it might allow you to send your son to Eton."

Henry shrugged. "I was educated at home. I don't see much purpose in fancy schools."

Ayleston glanced heavenward, exhaling heavily. Even

at thirty-one years of age, Henry still felt a rebellious thrill whenever his elders made that expression.

Ayleston started for the door. "I suppose I should be thankful you are doing it at all."

"Yes, you should. Because it's a terrible idea and something is bound to go wrong. Which means I'm your best choice. I do, however, have a family event tomorrow morning at ten a.m. here in town. I have no intention of missing it. So don't expect me to be following Rivenstoke to his ship or lingering at the party or any other such nonsense."

"As long as you get those papers." Ayleston jammed his hat onto his head and stepped out the door.

"Oh, one question," Henry said. "Harris's knife fight wasn't related to all this, was it? Because I prefer to keep all my limbs attached."

"No, it was a bar fight. He got into an argument over a woman."

"Ah. Perhaps he needs a reminder of the first rule of spying. Never sleep with the barmaid."

✳

"Never sleep with the barmaid? Really, Henry?"

Elle stepped into her husband's arms and he pressed a kiss to her cheek. "To be fair, you were an *ex*-barmaid. And I took quite a bit of convincing."

"You are incorrigible."

One corner of his mouth ticked up in a mischievous grin. "And yet you love me anyway."

"I do. Though occasionally I do wonder..."

"What the hell you ever saw in me?"

"You mean aside from your kindness, bravery, intelligence, eccentric humor, respect for women, devotion to family, solid work ethic, independent spirit, and love for everything that I am?"

"Damn. I'm quite the catch, apparently."

"You are. But I do wonder if I'm equally as crazy as you are. Because I believe I will be joining you on this particular adventure."

His smile faded. "How much did you overhear?"

"Not enough. You're going to a party and it's a terrible idea."

"That sums it up well enough."

Elle took a step back to stare into his eyes. "It will be dangerous, I gather."

"I expect so. Rivenstoke is said to be highly intellectual, has won awards for marksmanship, and likely knows we are on to him."

"And, yet are you going to take the assignment regardless."

"Someone has to."

She nodded. "Yes, I think I had better come along."

"Toss a couple party dresses in a trunk and we can be off. We'll stop and drop off the children at Emma's."

Elle folded her arms across her chest. "Henry, Emma is preparing for Lily's party tomorrow morning."

"Exactly. The distraction of extra children is precisely what she needs to give herself a reason to step aside and let her servants handle the preparations. Otherwise she'll try to do everything herself and be a flustered mess."

Elle considered that a moment, and had to concede that he was probably correct. "Very well, we'll drop them at Emma's." Because she certainly wasn't letting Henry run off on this mad mission alone. Not when she had knowledge and skills that could protect him.

Three hours later, a steam coach pulled to a stop in front

of Rivenstoke's yellow brick leviathan of a country home. A Mr. and Mrs. Harris alighted, only to be nearly run down by a trio of mad bicyclists flying across the drive. Several more followed further behind, the riders red-faced and breathing hard.

"Damn," Henry muttered. "They're having bicycle races and we missed it. Perhaps I can challenge the winner. Though it looks like they're all on those new-fangled safety bicycles. Takes away half the fun. I'd like to see them run that same race on ordinaries."

Elle took hold of his arm and leaned close. "Because what this mission needs is self-inflicted danger."

"It needs excitement. Because tonight I'm required to mingle and present some semblance of normalness. It's going to be excruciating."

Elle patted his arm. "You poor thing. Why don't we go in and dress for dinner. Perhaps a few moments in the privacy of our bedchamber will fortify you for the task ahead."

His eyebrows twitched. "A long few moments. Dressing for dinner can be quite an involved process."

"Indeed. I have many layers of undergarments that must be just so. I may need help with them."

"I will happily inspect each and every detail of said garments."

She gave him a quick kiss as they ducked inside. "I thought you might."

✳

"Excellent, isn't it?"

Henry only nodded, desperately trying not to choke and cough as the liquor burned down his throat. He turned away from Rivenstoke to hide his watering eyes and flushing cheeks, letting his gaze fix itself once more on Elle.

She looked spectacular tonight, in a pale green gown that she'd purchased on their last visit to Paris. Her gift to herself. Bought with her own earnings. He was so damn proud of her and the life she'd made for their family. If only he could be dancing with her instead of chatting with Rivenstoke, on the verge of blowing their cover because the real Harris was noted to be fond of a stiff drink.

"The lady in green caught your attention again?" Rivenstoke asked. "She has a quiet sort of beauty. Easy to overlook, but a fine treat for the sharp-eyed."

Henry toyed with the remaining liquid in his glass. This man was dangerous, observant, and too interested in Elle. "I suggest you keep your hands to yourself. She has ways of dealing with presumptuous men."

Rivenstoke only laughed. "Don't like competition, eh? Bold of you to bring your mistress along for the weekend. Though I doubt anyone other than myself knows that there is no Mrs. Harris."

Henry didn't flinch. "Is that so," he replied dryly.

"Indeed. She's quite elegant. Carries herself with confidence. Wherever did you find her?"

"Paris."

"Naturally. An actress?"

"Barmaid."

He chuckled. "Well, she knows how to play the lady, regardless. I wouldn't want her mingling with my own wife, of course, but she's a pretty enough thing to brighten a party."

Henry contemplated smashing his half-empty glass in Rivenstoke's face. "If you'll excuse me, I think I'd like to ask her for a dance."

"Of course. You've hardly taken your eyes off her all

evening." He nudged Henry with his elbow. "Looking forward to a nighttime romp?"

He'd already had an afternoon romp, but he wasn't about to divulge that to scum like Rivenstoke. He nodded to his host and hurried toward Elle.

"Learn anything?" she asked, sliding into his arms for a waltz.

"He's shrewd, arrogant, and suspicious of us. Dangerous as hell."

"I'm glad I came, then."

"So am I." His worries about her safety couldn't outweigh the benefits of her assistance and the comfort of her presence. "Still not lying about wanting to take you on all my missions."

"Any changes to your plan?"

"No. Potions are ready?"

"Always."

Playing the besotted husband—his favorite role in life, along with doting father—carried Henry through the remainder of what would otherwise have been an appallingly boring party. To his vast relief, it also saved him from having to sample any more of Rivenstoke's revolting beverages. He hung with the revelers to the end, when they staggered, drunk or exhausted, to their beds.

"Be careful." The warm breath of Elle's whispered words tickled his ear, and her soft lips grazed his cheek. She pressed a small vial into his hand.

Henry tucked the potion into a waistcoat pocket. No more words. No more sounds. He answered her with a quick kiss and slipped into the dark corridor.

The hall was silent, lit only by scattered potion lamps, their tiny circles of golden light little defense against the heavy shadows of the moonless night. Henry picked a recessed corner and lounged against the wall, necktie undone and empty brandy glass in hand.

Half an hour ticked by, during which three people walked past without even noticing him. Ten minutes more and the house was still as death, the practiced footsteps of a spy not even a whisper on the plush carpeting.

Henry made his way quickly from the guest wing to the family wing, following Harris' notes. Memorized, of course. He knew better than to keep anything incriminating on his person. The notes were thorough and accurate. Either Harris had been in the house before, or he had a connection on the inside.

A flash of movement caught Henry's eye the moment he stepped into the family wing. Ducking back into the shadows, he watched as a man in servant's clothes approached from the far end of the hall. The man paused, adjusted some bit of decor in the middle of the hall, then continued on. Henry slipped around the corner, counting the seconds and listening to the man's footsteps.

Thirty seconds passed. Forty-five. Fifty.

Henry dared to look again. The servant had turned around, strolling in the opposite direction. Patrolling.

Damnation.

Time to improvise. Henry checked his pockets for potions and selected the one he wanted. Moving as fast as he dared, he picked his way down the corridor. The guard paused again at some random spot, pretending to tidy something else. He spied Henry approaching and froze in mid-turn, but Henry had already broken into a run. He sprayed the man in the face with the potion, catching him before he could tumble to the ground, unconscious.

Henry dragged the sleeping servant to the end of the

hall, leaving him in the darkest convenient location. One problem solved.

He reviewed the notes in his head, counting the doors to locate the room he wanted. He pulled a second potion out of his pocket, unscrewing the cap and attaching a needle-thin nozzle to the round, rubber bottle. A few squeezes of the bottle, and the lock filled with the potion. Wisps of icy smoke rose from the keyhole. Henry waited the ten seconds Elle had instructed, then poked his largest pick into the lock. The innards of the mechanism crumbled with only a single jab. He turned the handle and the door swung easily open.

No lights brightened the bedchamber, and no fire burned in the hearth. Henry slid silently toward the bed, hoping that Ayleston's information was accurate, and Rivenstoke did, in fact, keep the papers on his person at all times. It would make the search far easier.

A sleeping figure in the middle of the bed made a snuffling noise. The bedsheets rustled as he shifted and then settled. Henry crept closer. He'd had to use half of his sleeping potion to take down the guard, but a faceful would keep Rivenstoke unconscious long enough for Henry to find the documents and leave.

Elle was waiting for him in the room. She would have everything packed and ready. They'd abandon the dummy trunk and carry the two smaller bags that contained their belongings.

The room was so dark that Henry could hardly make out the human-shaped lump beneath the blankets, but the spray potion had a wide enough coverage area that his aim wouldn't need to be perfect. He pointed the bottle in the direction of the soft breathing and pulled the trigger.

Ten seconds he waited again before withdrawing Elle's

pocket torch. He would keep it on the lowest setting, but he needed the tiny bit of light to find and verify the documents. He flicked the switch and pointed the beam at the bed.

Fuck! The sight before him stunned him so much that he nearly said the word aloud. *Fuck, fuck fuck!*

Snuggled down among the blankets, sleeping away the remainder of his potion with a smile on her face, lay Lady Rivenstoke, her blond hair curling around her peaceful face.

Damn Harris and his stupid notes. He'd sent Henry to the wrong bloody room. Now Henry was stuck with no sleeping potion, no lockpicking potion, and no idea which room he actually needed to enter.

He had two options: return to his own room and hope Elle had the ingredients and time to make him a new batch of potions or try the next room down with normal lockpicks and hope that he could get the papers off Rivenstoke without a sleeping potion.

I knew it. I knew this whole mission was a bad idea.

He'd go back to Elle. Rivenstoke would be a light sleeper. Entering his room without a potion would be the last resort. Henry flicked off the torch and hurried for the door, opening it slowly to prevent any squeaking.

"There he is!"

Henry sprang back, his hand going for his pistol. The servant he'd sprayed stood in the hall, wide awake.

What the everloving hell?

Elle's potions never failed. Never.

"That's the bloke that sprayed me," the man said, pointing a finger in Henry's direction.

Lights flared. Rivenstoke stepped into Henry's field of view, eyes ablaze with fury. Leaving the gun in his pocket, Henry stumbled out into the hall, feigning drunkenness.

"G'evening, Riverstone," he slurred. "What're you doing

up so late?" He staggered across the hall, banging into a small table hard enough to send a decorative vase crashing to the floor.

Rivenstoke stalked up to Henry and grabbed him by the shirt. "What the hell do you think you're doing here?"

Henry shoved Rivenstoke into the servant-guard, knocking the man flat on his back and causing him to let out a yelp of surprise. A door two rooms down creaked open and a head poked out. An audience. Perfect.

"Can't a man go out for a walk without being shouted at?" Henry asked in a too-loud, still-slurred voice.

"That is my wife's bedchamber," Rivenstoke snarled.

"You don't say."

"I will ask you one more time before I kill you, what do you think you are doing here?"

Failing my mission, apparently.

"Sleeping with your wife, obviously."

Rivenstoke's eyes swept the hall. Decorative weapons from ancient to modern covered the walls. None, fortunately, would be a match for Henry's pistol, and while Rivenstoke may have had papers concealed in his nightclothes, Henry didn't think he had a gun.

Rivenstoke's gaze finally returned to Henry, his lips curling into a nasty sneer. "Very well, then. Since you have insulted my honor and hers, I will meet you outside in the field just behind my house at dawn. Bring your pistols and have your affairs in order."

A duel? Shit. Elle was going to kill him.

Henry abandoned any pretense of drunkenness and met Rivenstoke's glare with a frosty smile of his own. "I'm afraid I can't do that. If you make the challenge, you are honor bound to allow me the choice of weapons."

"Fine." Rivenstoke waved a hand at his collection. "Choose."

Henry gave the walls a quick once-over and picked his favorite from the bunch. "Swords." Rivenstoke's smile broadened. Damn. Was the man an expert swordsman, too? Probably. "On bicycles."

The haughty smile vanished. "What?"

"Swords on bicycles. That's my choice. I'll see you at dawn." He pushed past Rivenstoke and the gaping lookers-on, hurrying for his room. He had a few hours to rest and regroup. To make a plan for snatching some incriminating papers in the midst of a duel. And to try to explain to Elle just what the hell he had done.

✳

Elle brushed a lock of hair back from Henry's forehead. How could he sleep at a time like this? Military training, she supposed.

He looked peaceful in his sleep. Younger than his age. Innocent. Not like a man who goaded treasonous lords into absurd duels. She sighed, giving a little shake of her head, then pressed a kiss to his cheek.

She slipped from the bed to check on the potion that sat steeping. Almost done. She was taking no chances. Henry would have the best possible vitality potion she could make and multiple health potions in his pockets. She would keep an array of defenses at hand for when Rivenstoke inevitably cheated.

No more than two minutes, Henry had said. The guard must have taken a powerful preventative to have woken so quickly from her sleeping potion. A general antidote wouldn't suffice. He must have ingested a specialized stamina potion designed specifically for remaining alert and awake. Either Rivenstoke was a potions master in his own right, or he worked closely with one. He would go to the duel magically prepared.

Elle dipped her finger into her potion and touched a drop to her tongue to check the potency. Perfect. Rivenstoke might be skilled and ruthless, but he had no idea who he was dealing with.

"Elle Deschamps Ainsworth," she said, as if introducing herself. "Ex-barmaid. Shop owner. Potions Master. Spy partner." Over on the bed, Henry began to stir. "Lover to the craziest man in England."

Henry sat up, looking not at all as if he'd been sound asleep seconds before. "Who is he? I'll duel him, too."

Elle sat beside him on the bed, handing him the vitality potion. "I don't imagine you've come up with a better plan while you were sleeping?"

"Afraid not." He drank the potion down, grimacing as he swallowed. "Ugh. That burned almost as much as Rivenstoke's gin."

"It will strengthen you against any injuries you might sustain."

"Good. Because I'm likely to crash the bicycle at the very least. I intend to make as big a spectacle as possible."

"Not especially stealthy of you."

"No. But when word of this spreads, I want everyone saying, 'drunk fool at party causes duel on bicycles,' and not, 'spy attacks prominent figure in his home.' I should change."

"Change?"

Henry began to strip off his shirt. "Into something more sporty. Have to look the part, you know, and Ayleston left me that god-awful suit of Harris'. If I'm going to suffer stab wounds, I'd prefer not to bleed on my own clothes."

Elle squeezed her eyes closed and rubbed her temple.

"Joking is better than panicking," she murmured. "Joking is better than panicking."

She opened her eyes and watched Henry pull on the ill-fitting gray tweed with quiet efficiency. He lifted and twisted his arms, checking for freedom of movement. Potions went into pockets, his knife into his boot. His pistol he tucked into the back of his trousers.

He picked up a wide-brimmed straw hat and plopped it on his head, tilting it to a rakish angle, and the serious spy again became the impish boy. "How do I look?"

"Ridiculous."

"Excellent."

A knock sounded at the door, and Henry opened it to reveal a bleary-eyed footman.

"You Harris?" the man asked.

"I suppose I must be," Henry replied.

"I'm t' lead you out to the field. You have a man to be yer second?"

Elle slung her potions bag across her body and stepped up to Henry's side.

"She's right here," he replied.

The footman's eyes widened. "A woman? You sure you're not still tanked up?"

"'Course I am," Henry slurred. "Just had a drink, di'n' I, love?"

"*Évidemment,*" Elle answered with an exaggerated sigh. This she could do. He'd play the fool and she the exasperated wife. The footman only shook his head and motioned for them to follow.

Rivenstoke awaited them in the grassy expanse just beyond his gardens, wearing a scowl as black as his monochromatic suit. A pair of equally rigid and somber men flanked him, hands clasped behind their backs. Half-a-dozen bicycles and as many swords lay neatly arrayed at their feet.

"Harris," Rivenstoke sneered. "How good of you to join us." His gaze flicked to Elle. "Has she come to beg for your life, or is she eager to become your widow?"

"She can hear you perfectly well and she speaks fluent English," Elle snapped.

Rivenstoke's scowl transformed into a lascivious grin. "I beg your pardon, my dear. Rest assured, I will be happy to comfort you after I cut your lover down." He turned back to Henry. "Pick your weapon."

Henry wasted time turning over every sword and examining every bicycle, babbling to himself about weights and balance while Rivenstoke looked on in annoyance. As much as Elle hated Henry's casual acceptance of danger, she couldn't suppress her pride and admiration for his intelligence and skill. The duel hadn't even begun and already Rivenstoke was on edge, while Henry remained cool and relaxed.

The additional benefit of Henry's stalling manifested in the sudden appearance of a dozen more houseguests, roused during his noisy departure. They hurried over, many still in their nightclothes, to watch the madness unfold.

"Enough," Rivenstoke barked. He grabbed a bicycle and hauled it upright. "We start this now or I run you through where you stand."

Henry kicked a sword up into the air and caught it deftly by the hilt. "Not very sporting of you, old man. I thought this was a contest of honor." He righted a bicycle and swung a leg over it.

Elle grabbed a bicycle for herself, tying up her skirt to reveal the trousers she wore underneath. Rivenstoke's seconds snickered at her. One man called her a whore, while several other onlookers cheered their approval of her scandalous behavior.

One of the black-clothed men motioned for Henry to take up a position opposite Rivenstoke. "Fifty yards apart," he ordered. "When I give the signal, ride toward one another with swords drawn." He tossed Henry a derisive look, then turned to Rivenstoke. "May the best man win."

The two combatants backed their cycles up until they were approximately the correct distance apart. Elle rode alongside Henry, ready to render assistance at any moment. He still wore his insolent grin, but the slight narrowing of his eyes revealed his deadly serious intent. Their eyes met and they nodded to one another. Partners.

Rivenstoke's man raised his hand, and Henry readied himself, one foot on the pedal, the other on the ground, poised for a race. Elle slipped two potions from her bag: her best healing potion and a defensive weapon.

"Go!" the man shouted, dropping his arm.

Henry and Rivenstoke took off. Elle clutched her potions, kicked her cycle into motion, and prayed.

*

Henry veered sharply at the last instant, his sword catching nothing but air and his cycle skidding to an ungraceful stop. The crowd jeered and booed. Rivenstoke cursed him.

"Again," Rivenstoke's helper commanded, gesturing imperiously. Good on him to seize some brief enjoyment from his position of power. Everyone here looked to be enjoying the spectacle, in fact, with the exception of Rivenstoke. And probably Elle. She shadowed Henry's every move on her bicycle, ever watchful.

Henry took up his position a second time, considering his next tactical maneuver. Rivenstoke had made only a half-hearted attempt to strike him on the first pass. Feeling him out. This time they would come to blows.

They flew at one another again, the tires of the bicycles kicking up bits of dirt and grass. Henry didn't swerve away this time, nor did he launch an offensive of his own. He parried Rivenstoke's attack, his whole arm vibrating with the force of the blow. The man was furious. He was also the better swordsman.

Henry, though, was the better cyclist. He swung his bicycle around to avoid a second thrust of Rivenstoke's sword, losing his hat in the process. Straw crunched as Rivenstoke flattened the unoffending headgear beneath his tires.

"You owe me two pounds and ten for a new hat."

"To hell with you, Harris," Rivenstoke snarled. "I'll give you one final charge and then we do this like real men."

Henry drew his cycle alongside his enemy's so that no one else could hear his words. "Real men don't try to start wars for financial gain." He whirled around and rode off to his starting position.

One last charge. Rivenstoke would make a serious attempt to kill him this time. Henry checked the healing potions in his waistcoat pockets. He didn't even need to look at Elle. She would be ready and she could ride almost as well as he did.

"Go!" Rivenstoke's man called.

Henry took off, pedaling furiously, holding the sword only for show. The cycle was his real weapon. With no more than a yard remaining between the two bicycles, Henry cut sharply to the right, skimming past Rivenstoke's unprotected left side. Henry kicked out with his left foot, landing a solid blow to Rivenstoke's back tire and sending both bicycles spinning into a spectacular double crash. Henry tucked and rolled, abandoning the sword and drawing his pistol in a single motion. He tucked the gun into his outside coat pocket and scrambled to his feet. It was unlikely anyone still believed him drunk at this point, but insane was equally effective.

"Oy!" he exclaimed, addressing the gathered crowd as much as his adversary. "I think I've stabbed myself. First blood to you, Rivenstoke!" Henry walked toward his enemy, extending a hand. "I trust this settles the matter? Let me be the first to congratulate you."

Rivenstoke's tumble had been far less graceful than Henry's, and he had yet to pick himself up off the ground. Henry's position blocked him from the view of any onlookers. The crowd never saw Rivenstoke draw a gun of his own, nor did they see Elle dump a potion in his face as she pedaled by.

"Rivenstoke?" Henry called, continuing the show. He knelt beside the now-unconscious man, shaking him with one hand and searching for concealed papers with the other. "You all right, old chap?"

He had something hidden beneath his shirt. Henry tugged at clothing, digging for it. "Damn. He must have hit his head."

Henry's fingers found the edge of the slim pouch and yanked, breaking it loose. He stuffed it inside his own coat, along with all the crumpled receipts and notes from Rivenstoke's pockets. He rose to his feet and returned to his bicycle.

"Well, that's that, I suppose." He glanced at Elle. "We ought to be going now."

"I agree," she replied.

They grinned at one another and raced off toward the house, to the shouts and applause of the other guests.

✦

The speedy steam car carrying Ayleston's courier zipped past, much faster than the chugging locomotive where Elle and Henry had secured themselves a private compartment.

"Hidden in plain sight?" she asked.

Henry nodded. "Crumpled up in his front pocket among utter rubbish."

She turned from the window and picked up the pouch that Henry had found beneath Rivenstoke's clothing. "What did he have in here, then?"

"Love letters from his mistress, it seems."

Elle removed a paper from the pouch and scanned it. "Ooh. This is quite explicit. She has some interesting things she wants him to do to her."

"Oh?" Henry shrugged out of the too-large coat, wincing. The shirt and waistcoat below were stained with blood.

Elle tossed the lurid letter aside. "Henry!" She dug in her bag for the healing potion that she'd already put away. "Did you really stab yourself?"

"Afraid so. It's not bad."

"It's bad enough. Let me look."

He sat still and allowed her to remove his clothing and examine the wound.

"Truly, it's nothing to be concerned about," he said. "It hardly even hurt when it happened. Your vitality potion works wonders."

"It's dangerous and still bleeding a bit," she scolded. She smeared a thick salve over the wound and made him drink a potion. "You are supposed to be careful."

"Maybe I only wanted you to undress me and run your hands all over me."

Elle cleaned up, stowed her supplies in her potions bag, and set it aside. "You know full well that all you need do is ask if that's what you're after." She discarded her outer layers of clothing and straddled his lap. "I am always happy to oblige."

Henry's arms wrapped around her, drawing her close for a kiss. "We're going to arrive at Emma's party all pink-cheeked and dishevelled, aren't we?"

"It won't be the first time." She brushed her lips over his. "Mmm. Nor the last."

Elle replied with a deep, long, lingering kiss. "I love you, Henry Ainsworth, Notorious Bicycle Duelist."

"And I love you, Elle Ainsworth, Scandalous, Trouser-wearing Potions Genius. You are my perfect partner."

She clutched him to her breast and kissed him again. *Truth.*

✳

From the *London Morning Herald*

HORRIBLE HOUSEGUEST.

A prominent figure became a combatant in a most unusual duel after an inebriated—or possibly mad—houseguest insulted his wife. When satisfaction was demanded, the guest, one Mr. H—, insisted upon a contest of honor employing both swords and bicycles. It is unclear whether the cycles or the swords were meant to be the primary weapon, as both proved largely ineffective. The duel ended when both parties crashed, sustaining painful, but not life-threatening injuries. Mr. H—, having stabbed himself with his own sword, turned tail and fled, accompanied by a trouser-clad Frenchwoman rumored to be a barmaid of questionable virtue. The host was assisted back to his home to recover. He has declined to comment on the incident.

LOFTY LORD LESS THAN LOYAL?

A certain Lord R— has disappeared following an altercation at his country home. Conflicting reports state that he has been imprisoned or that he has fled to the continent. The reason for his departure, however, is agreed upon: R— was in possession of documents of a shockingly subversive nature. The editors of this paper are confident that Her Majesty's civil servants will see that the man is brought to justice, if, indeed, such a thing has not yet happened.

Hannah Wells
Is Not Impressed

Hannah Wells Is Not Impressed

A Mad Scientists Society Story

It's time.

The latest scientific exhibition for the people of Detroit is hopping, and Doctor Hannah Wells is ready to reveal the design for her time-traveling cycle. Or, rather, she would be ready if the conman in the next booth over would stop spouting nonsense to the whole room.

As Hannah wavers between ignoring her neighbor and refuting his lies, she befriends a trio of eccentric scientists who help her find her voice. And as she shares pieces of her own story and reminisces on her first time-travel adventure, she's reminded that there's no need to impress everyone. Because wherever—and whenever—you go, the right people will be impressed with you just as you are.

Detroit, Michigan
April 23, 1893

"You think it'll actually work?" asked a mousey scientist. (With his messy hair, slightly rumpled tweed suit, and green-tinted glasses, the chances of the man pursuing any other profession were, in the learned opinion of Dr. Hannah Wells, infinitesimally unlikely.)

One of his companions, a tall man in a bespoke suit, considered the blueprint that was the focal point of the display. (This man was also a scientist, judging by the screwdriver tucked into his breast pocket where a handkerchief ought to have been.)

"Not in a million years."

The woman with them (also wearing a suit, and therefore likely also a scientist), nodded her agreement. "I'd give it about a fifty percent chance of doing absolutely nothing, and another fifty percent chance of it bursting into flames."

Hannah coughed to stifle a laugh and quickly looked in the opposite direction. Enough people considered her unprofessional merely based on her sex. Getting caught eavesdropping wouldn't be a good look. Even if the "time machine" display next to her own booth was little more than a child's fantasy sketch. And its creator hadn't even bothered to show up on time to the expo.

She smoothed down her skirt and picked up her journal. Her neighbor's folly would be her own gain when the interesting trio of scientists moved along to her display.

They wouldn't be so dismissive of *her* time vehicle, and she would wager that she had an answer for any question they could throw at her. (Unless, of course, they got into deep mysteries such as "What is time?" or "Is the universe just an ever-twisting loop of possibilities?" If they wanted to get into that sort of talk, she'd claim them all as best friends and set up a meeting over drinks.)

The bespectacled scientist stepped toward Hannah's booth, and she turned to smile at him.

"Hello. I'm Dr. Wells, and I'd be hap—"

The main doors to the exhibit hall flew open with such a thunderous bang that the easel holding Hannah's schematic wobbled. She flung out a hand to steady it, fumbled her journal, bumped the table holding her fuel cell prototype, and whacked her elbow on the wall behind her.

"F-f-fiddlesticks!" She bent down to retrieve her diary, muttering a few of Bel's favorite curses under her breath.

"Oh. Are you, um, okay?" asked the scientist.

As Hannah collected herself, a booming, gasping voice cried out, "S-sorry. Beg pardon. So sorry, ladies and gentlemen."

(The speaker had to be fake-gasping. No one could be that loud and out of breath at the same time. Hannah craned her neck for a look.)

"Please excuse my tardiness." The speaker was bent over, hands on his knees, as if winded. "I've only just returned from an… unexpectedly arduous journey. If you'll give me a moment to make my way to my booth, I'd be happy to share the story of my time machine."

"You absolute fucker," Hannah whispered.

Her nemesis had arrived at last.

✳

~~March 7, 1893~~ Day 1

Adjustment complete. Commencing travel test.

Ooh. Well, something is happening. Cycle is trembling. Hard to write.

Oh my goodness.

Oh my goodness!

Ohmygodohmygodohmygod!

I've traveled. I'm somewhere. I don't know where, but it's very different. Dark. Could be night. My hands are shaking. I hope I can read this later.

Okay, sorry for not being scientific. Here's what happened:

The cycle began to shake. I became quite disoriented, not exactly like fainting, but similar enough that I almost tried to dismount so I could lie down. Before I could even swing a leg over, my senses began to clear. I looked around and nearly toppled over in astonishment.

I've done it! I've traveled.

Now to explore the area a bit and see when and where I am!

(Note: This is why I styled my machine after a tricycle. Wherever I go, the machine goes with me. I've already set the dials for a return trip in case I encounter any dangers.)

✳

"Given the success of my small-scale tests, I knew the time was right—pardon the pun—to take the machine on its maiden voyage," said Dr. Pompous Bastard.

(His real name was Jefferson P. Hawthorne, or maybe it was P. Hawthorne Jeffries, or something to that effect. Regardless, Hannah had decided that Pompous Bastard was more apt a moniker.)

PB, as she was now thinking of him, leaned against the wall next to his dubious schematic, legs crossed casually and arms flailing as he regaled the audience with his story. He'd gathered quite the crowd with his raucous entrance and disheveled appearance. He wore no coat, and his white shirt was stained with grass and dirt and torn in a few places. One of his cuffs was missing entirely, and a reddish-brown stain beneath his right knee could have been blood. (Or food residue.) Several days' growth of beard darkened his jawline, and once-slicked back blond hair now hung in limp strings around his ears. Unsurprisingly, PB was encroaching on Hannah's territory, enough that she'd had to move her easel to protect her own exhibit.

She scowled (no one was looking at her) and wrinkled her nose. Any conman worth his salt knew how to dress and act the part, but did he have to *smell* like unwashed socks? Hannah fetched a vial of perfume from her handbag and discreetly sprayed it in his direction.

"I loaded the box with my travel kit and set the dials for the year two thousand eight hundred ninety three, exactly one thousand years in the future."

"Thank you for doing that very complicated math for us," Hannah murmured.

A snorted half-laugh made her glance over her shoulder. The woman in the suit was watching the spectacle with her arms crossed. She gave Hannah a nod of sympathy.

"I can't begin to put into words the feeling of flying through time," PB went on, "but allow me this poor attempt. There was a sensation of motion, both in and out of the box, though I had not budged from my seat. Slow, at first, which made me think it might be my imagination, but then ever increasing in speed. I saw the outside world rushing past, cities rising and falling, acorns growing to mighty oaks in the blink of an eye, the landscape around me changing so rapidly I could not take it all in. When the machine came back into focus and everything went still, I knew I had completed my journey. I exited the box and set off to find the local populace and bring them greetings from the 19th century."

"You just walked away from your time machine?" Hannah blurted. She nearly clapped a hand over her mouth as heads turned. How could she have been so foolish? She had no choice but to soldier on. "You left the machine unguarded and sought to introduce yourself to strangers? Strangers who almost certainly have a completely different set of social customs to your own and may not be able to communicate with an English speaker from our time?"

The whole premise was absurd. Outrageous. Only a white-skinned man of certain means would have the audacity to assume any place at any time would welcome him with open arms. It was too bad his time machine was a fake. Hannah would have liked to suggest he travel back to the time when giant monsters roamed the earth.

PB laughed. "But of course, my dear. How else was I to learn anything of this future world?"

Observation? Scientific measurements? Photographs? Having an actual plan?

"I'm not your 'dear,'" Hannah spat. (Not the most well considered response, perhaps, but honestly? "My dear?" Ick!)

He smiled, the smarmy bastard, and returned to his tale.

✳

Day 1, continued

It is definitely night here at the moment, but the moon has emerged from behind the clouds and my eyes have greatly adjusted. I am in a grassy field that could be part of a farm or wilderness. The air is cool but not frigid, temperature and humidity both in the normal range for Michigan in the spring. The readings from my astrolabe support this conclusion. I am not far from home in terms of distance, only in time. The sky glows off to the west, suggesting lights from a city or other occupied location. I will approach cautiously and observe.

The city is in sight! Or, a part of a city, at least. I am concealed among bushes, peeking through the fence that encloses some variety of transport station. Despite the hour, a steady trickle of vehicles comes and goes, much like at a train depot or a harbor. The primary difference is that these vehicles fly!

I'm struggling to look away. The sight of every vehicle rising above the earth sends a new thrill through me. The smallest craft are perhaps the size of a bus, but many are at least the size of a house! They are curved and sleek, fashioned primarily of metal. The mechanism by which they fly is unclear, but it is neither balloons nor wings.

Given the darkness and the distance, my observations of the people at this venue remain vague. Most look to be dressed in working garb of jumpsuits or shirts and trousers. Hair color and skin color vary, as they do at home. I see no obvious evidence of division of labor by sex. Could it be that in this future time people are not separated into categories such as men and women or Black and white? How refreshing!

I think I will attempt to move closer to the facility's entrance. I should like to get a look at the text on their signs. From afar I can pick out some familiar words, but others elude me. They must speak a dialect of English, but the printing isn't identical to ours, and pronunciations may also have changed. Maybe I can get close enough to hear a bit of conversation. Regardless, I will continue to record m—

"Care to explain what you're doing snooping around the spaceport?" drawled a superficially casual voice with an unfamiliar accent. "And why you're riding that… velocipede?"

Hannah twisted around and stared up into the very pretty (and clearly annoyed) face of a woman in a crisp, dark uniform.

"Eep!" was all she managed.

✳

The crowd around PB had grown to include most of the attendees of the science fair and some of the exhibitors as well. The three friendly scientists now stood guard around the perimeter of Hannah's space. The woman gazed avidly at Hannah's schematic, within arm's reach of the easel, should anyone bump it. The tall man lounged against Hannah's table (or appeared to, though he didn't seem to be resting much, if any, of his weight on it). His lanky limbs were sprawled, preventing others from moving in closer. And the dark-haired man with the green spectacles was elbowing or bumping particularly tenacious encroachers while repeating that he was "terribly sorry" and "so clumsy." Hannah had slipped each of them her calling card.

"So, wait," drawled Tall Scientist, waving a hand at PB. "You could understand their language, just like that? But it wasn't English?"

"It was a simplistic language," PB replied. (Pompously, of course. The reader should assume that everything he says is pompous, regardless of any other adjectives used.) "As I said, Dr. Franklin, they were very childlike people, these future earthlings."

"Right, sure. But if I go to… say, Norway… I can't understand the children any better than the adults."

A few people chuckled.

"And what is your reasoning for describing them as 'childlike'? You said only that they were small and seemed delicate. But according to your tale they had a city and a culture, albeit different from ours. Care to explain further?" Dr. Franklin looked smug.

(*Dr. Franklin, creator of the mechanical man!* Hannah realized. Which meant the other man was Dr. Finch, nee Jekyll, and the woman was Captain Nemo of the undersea ship!)

"I'm wondering why they looked so different from us," Nemo mused, without turning from her perusal of Hannah's diagram. "You can look at any Greco-Roman statue and see that people don't change so drastically in such a timeframe."

"And consider those preserved bodies they've pulled out of bogs in Europe," Finch added. "They're estimated to be even older, but have been mistaken for recent burials."

PB's smile was so tight Hannah could almost hear his teeth grinding. "My journals contain much greater detail on all these topics, naturally. I'd be happy to share them with interested parties after the fair concludes. Now, as I was saying…"

Hannah rolled her eyes. So did her three new sort-of-friends.

✳

Hannah clutched her journal to her chest and did her best not to glance down at the controls of her time vehicle. She wouldn't flip the switch to send her home unless absolutely necessary. She could deal with one surly woman. What sort of scientist would she be if she ran off at her first encounter with a future person?

"I beg your pardon," she said. "I mean no harm. I am a

scientist and I was merely observing your… What did you call it? Space-port?"

The uniformed woman walked a full circle around the time machine, her ponytail swaying as she walked. She had a confident gait Hannah couldn't help but admire. And there was something captivating about her dark eyes—even though she was frowning.

"Okay," the woman said, "WTF is this? Some steampunk cosplay shit?"

"I'm sorry. I don't understand those words."

"And chill with the Shakespeare voice, go'm?"

Hannah blinked rapidly as her brain tried to parse the woman's odd pronunciations and unfamiliar words. "Er… I'm three centuries removed from Sha— Never mind."

"Astral work, though. Looks real." The woman poked at the machine's control panel.

Hannah yelped and slapped her hand away. "Do you mind?! This is delicate machinery!"

The woman took a step back and put her hands on her hips. "Look. Whatever game you're playing, take it somewhere else. Snooping at the spaceport's gonna get security involved, and if they call the forcers in, there'll be lockdown and I won't be able to fly my ship outta here."

Fly my ship.

Hannah's eyebrows shot upward at those three tiny words. "You have one of those vehicles? You're an aviator?"

"A pilot, yeah. Now yeet yourself outta here before someone worse than me finds you."

Hannah flipped her journal open and began to scribble. "Might you, perhaps, allow me to observe your vehicle up close before you depart?"

The pilot's eyes went large and round. "Are you actually insane?"

"Only for a moment, of course. I won't disrupt your work. Please? It would be wonderful for my notes."

The two women stared at one another for several seconds. Then the pilot shrugged.

"Eh, what the hell. Why not? You're cute and I haven't done anything illegal in a few weeks."

Hannah briefly considered the folly of following a strange woman who used foul language and claimed to do illegal things, but the lure of discovery was too strong. Besides, if this woman had meant to hurt her, she would have had plenty of opportunity already.

"Oh, thank you! That's most kind of you, Miss…?"

"Bel."

Hannah extended a hand. "Very nice to meet you, Miss Bel. Or is it Captain Bel? I'm Doctor Hannah Wells."

"Just Bel, Doctor." She gave Hannah a brusque handshake. "C'mon then." She gestured for Hannah to dismount.

"Oh, I can't leave my machine."

Bel sighed. "If you want to see my ship you have to walk, go'm? No one's letting you take that thing inside."

Hannah bit her lip. "Well, I…" She hopped off the cycle, secured it to the fence with a simple chain lock, and took a steadying breath. "Lead the way."

✳

"I just can't believe that not a single person thought you were insane, or dangerous, or—" Hannah had been trying to keep her mouth shut, she really had. But with the other scientists around her bombarding PB with questions, the words slipped out before she could stop them. "Or simply not worth their attention," she finished, determined to stand her ground even if the whole crowd scowled at her.

"Exactly," Dr. Finch chimed in. "Seems a bit peculiar if you ask me. I can hardly go anywhere without *someone* thinking I'm odd. Can't imagine showing up in the future and expecting to be welcomed with open arms. What made you so confident, Mr. Thorneson?"

"Hawthorne. It's Dr. P. Jeffery Hawthorne. And I must say that the future people I encountered showed a great deal more civility towards me than you have here today. Which illustrates my point about the downfall of our civilization. Lack of manners. Lack of traditions. Lack of—"

Dr. Finch interrupted, "Yes, yes. I have a story all about that moral purity nonsense and how it can harm one's sense of self worth as well as one's respect for others. But that's for another time. The story I actually want to hear is from Dr. Wells."

"Hear, hear!" Dr. Franklin joined in. "Great idea. Let's compare time travel experiences. What better way to do science than to collect as much data as possible. So tell us, Dr. Wells, how was your first encounter with a future civilization?"

Nemo turned from the easel and looked pointedly at Hannah's journal where it lay on the table. She gave a subtle nod.

Hannah picked up the notebook and flipped to one of her earlier entries. "Day 2," she read aloud. "In any scientific endeavor, one must consider that failure is a possible—even likely—outcome."

*

Day 2

In any scientific endeavor, one must consider that failure is a possible—even likely—outcome. After all, it is through repeated failures that we learn. We weed out irrelevant data. We learn where to direct our attentions. Each failure points us closer to the truth. Because what is Science if not the process by which we form greater understanding of Creation? An understanding that we may never entirely achieve, but for which we will continue to strive.

Failure is not a... well, a failure.

Oh, who am I kidding? I didn't fail scientifically. My machine works spectacularly, in point of fact. I failed myself. I failed to behave in a rational manner and follow my own rules. I broke my promise to remain seated on my machine for the duration of my travels. And now I'm trapped on a star ship en route to a "transit station," whatever that may be. Though I am curious how it will be different from the "space port" we left hours ago.

Bel has not apologized for departing while I was aboard the ship. She says only that she had to leave when she had a "window."

To be fair, I shouldn't have lingered so long on the ship. Maybe I wouldn't have if I hadn't seen the helm with its beautiful array of buttons, dials, switches, and lights. So much like my time vehicle and yet so different! I wanted to touch everything!

I couldn't do that, of course, for many reasons, so I settled for watching Bel make her preparations for flying. I must have been rather transfixed, staring at her elegant hands and the swiftness with which she moved them over the controls. She is obviously a pilot of much skill and experience.

And I believe she may have forgotten about me while engrossed in her work. She began speaking with someone about her departure preparations — a male voice that must have come through a telephonic device. Many of the words were foreign to my ears, so I confess I was not listening intently. It was only when the star ship moved beneath my feet and I let out a startled cry that she turned to look at me.

By then it was too late for me to disembark. I am now sheltered in a small passenger room, awaiting an apology I am unlikely to receive.

Conclusion: People will be people. In my time and the future.

✳

"And you believe *her* story?" PB scoffed. "I suppose it's no surprise she goes hying off on a bicycle from the looks of her, but travel to the stars? A woman piloting a flying ship?"

Nemo loudly cleared her throat.

"The captain has a point," someone in the crowd called out.

For the first time, PB lost a bit of his swagger. "You… drive a boat."

"A submarine," Nemo corrected politely. "That travels to depths previously unknown to humanity." She smiled at Hannah. "Please continue, Dr. Wells. I'd love to hear where you went and how you made your way home."

✳

Day 2, continued

I should further describe the ship for my records. It is not unlike a cargo train or ship at home, with the bulk of the vehicle comprising space for storing goods. (I don't know what sort of goods Bel is transporting. The crates are unremarkable boxes of wood or steel, various sizes, with no discernible writing on them.)

There is an engine room of sorts at the middle of the ship. The technology is entirely foreign, and I had no more than a moment's glance at it. At the front of the ship is the control room, with a seat for the pilot and many, many instruments. Again, the technology is mystifying. I would love to have time to study it in detail, but that is far outside the scope of this mission. (Not that flying on a star ship was within the scope of this mission, but here I am. I will make the best of it.)

The crew/passenger rooms are between the control room and engine room. There is a small ~~kitchen~~ galley and a lavatory with bathing facilities. All very clean with a lot of metal surfaces and rounded edges. (So no one jabs themself on a sharp corner if the ship bounces? Or an aesthetic choice?) The sitting rooms are carpeted, however, with fabric-covered walls. Very soft and cozy. I am sitting in a comfortable armchair with deep cushions. A small table/desk stands beside it, and across from us is a couch, just large enough for a person of my stature to nap on, if needed. If we continue on much longer with no sign of our destination, I might—

A pile of clothing landed in Hannah's lap, startling her from her writing. Her pencil tumbled to the floor as she blinked up at Bel.

"Figured you might like a change."

Hannah fingered the cloth. Sturdy cotton, it seemed. Possibly the exact same dark blue uniform that Bel wore. "I am comfortable for now, but thank you."

"You're welcome. That couch pulls out into a bed, by the way, and there's food in the galley and all the facilities are operational. Feel free to shower if you want."

Hannah gaped. "H-how long do you expect me to remain on this ship?"

"Well, 's eight hours out. Usually four or five for the cargo transfers, if customs doesn't put up a fuss, then eight hours back. Could be a bit more waiting for a window in and out if the station is crowded."

"I—" Hannah's jaw worked up and down but no sound emerged.

Bel's gaze flicked to the couch bed. "We could find stuff to do, if you're bored, go'm?"

"You mean sleep?" Hannah frowned at the couch as her brain processed Bel's words and tone. "Oh! You're propositioning me."

Bel chuckled. "You're funny. But, yeah, I'm 'propositioning' you. I've seen how you've been eyeing me, so just wanted to tell you we can fuck if you like. Or not. Whatever."

"Uh, not at the moment. But… thank you?"

"So polite." Bel's grin was alarmingly captivating.

Hannah tried not to squirm. How was she supposed to sit there like everything was normal when her mind was now exploding with prurient thoughts? When she'd set off on this journey, she'd neglected to consider that the Free Love movement might have had some effect on future populations. Not that this was a bad thing. Far from it. But she hadn't been prepared for open discussion of casual Sapphic relations. In her mind, such things sat firmly in the realm of fantasy. Fantasies she only ever considered in the privacy of her own bedroom.

Bel sprawled on the couch, long legs stretched out and one arm draped lazily across the back. "Tell me, Dr. Hannah Wells, where are you from?"

"Pardon?"

"Never seen anybody here dressed like you 'cept in a movie. And all those polite phrases and the way you pronounce words. Sounds like a high-class affectation. Is it a Southern thing? Northeastern? Or is it like a religious sect? Am I being insulting? Shit."

Hannah adjusted her posture, then wondered belatedly if she had only made things worse. "I'm from Detroit."

Bel snorted in disbelief.

"It's true. You're simply asking the wrong question. My 'affectation,' as you termed it, is temporal rather than spatial. I am from Detroit. In 1893. What year is it here?"

Bel considered Hannah for a long time. Hannah held herself rigid, refusing to react as Bel's dark eyes lingered on everything from the laces of her boots to her once-tidy coif.

"Okay. Possible. It's 2143, if you want to use the pre-stellar calendar."

Hannah scrambled for the pencil she'd dropped. "Two hundred and fifty years! Excellent. Do you mind if I write that down?"

"Be my guest, Doctor. I've got nothing better to do for the next several hours than look at your pretty face and try to decide if I've lost my mind or if you really are a time traveler."

Hannah scribbled down the date, then paused, her pencil still touching the page. "I think… I think this might help convince you."

She handed Bel the journal.

* * *

"If you appeared inside the transit station, you'd know immediately what it was. People walking about with luggage, cargo carts rolling by, kiosks selling food and drink, shops for both necessities and luxuries, advertisements splayed on the walls."

Hannah waved her hands excitedly as she talked. She had the rapt attention of the entire room, and it seemed the more eyes that focused on her the more animated she became. (She was determined to call it excitement and not nerves.)

"It was like a massive train station. Even the glass and steel construction would be familiar to anyone who knows of the Crystal Palace and similar structures. The difference was in scale. Fifteen levels in all, with a main corridor that must have been a mile long. There were moving sidewalks for pedestrians and elevators at regular intervals."

"Have you no creativity for your lies?"

"Oh, for f—" Hannah cut off the expletive and faced PB for what she promised herself would be the last time. "It's a functional building. The function isn't going to disappear because the vehicles have changed. And if you'd stop interrupting, maybe I could get around to describing the additional differences?"

"*You* interrupted *my* story! I saved a primitive people from—"

"Shut your damn mouth, sit down, and let the real scientists talk or I'll have my friends throw you bodily out the door, go'm?"

Oops. She hadn't meant to channel Bel. People were gaping at her. She'd be a scandal. But somehow she didn't care anymore. Not with the crowd hanging on her every word and three equally scandalous scientists grinning and nodding. They had her back. They really were her friends now.

She cleared her throat and continued. "Perhaps the most obvious difference between the transit station and our train depots or seaports—well, aside from the view of the stars out the windows—was the enormous number of moving picture screens, of all sizes. They were… Yes? Did you have a question?" She gestured at a woman who was frantically waving her hand.

"Have you brought anything from the future back with you? Anything you could show us?"

Besides a tendency to use foul language? Hannah's face heated. "Ah… well…"

✦

Day 3

Well. I can now comment on the overnight accommodations of the transit station. The room I presently occupy is much like any hotel back home. A bed, a desk, a chair. It has a private washroom, which is the best thing I can say about it. The decor is bland, the bed is hard, and the "window" is actually a moving picture screen with a short film of mountains that plays over and over without end.

Yes, I'm being harsh. I have to vent my ire somewhere, and it seems more productive to do it here than to rail at Bel, who is key to my return home. I have intentionally remained here in the room while she went out so I would not lose my temper at her. If I wasn't reliant on her for transportation back to my time machine, I wouldn't hesitate to give her a piece of my mind. It's her fault I'm in this mess.

I can't complain about the clothes, however. The uniform she provided me has plenty of different sized pockets where I can store my belongings. I have swiped the pen (it has a button on top to extend or retract the tip, which makes a satisfying click when you press it) and stationery from the desk as a safeguard in case something happens to my pencil or journal.

Ah. Bel has returned. I will do my best to be polite. Maybe.

"I got food." Bel withdrew several paper containers from her bag and spread them on the hotel desk. "Didn't know what you liked, so there's a few things." She took one of the containers for herself and perched nearby on the edge of the bed.

Hannah examined the food. There was a salad, a meat and rice dish, a diced vegetable soup, and several small packages of unknown items that vaguely resembled chips or crackers. She picked up the salad and a fork.

"This is fine. Thank you."

Hannah rubbed her thumb over the fork as she prepared to dig into her meal. The smooth, glossy surface didn't feel like metal or wood. She paused to examine it further, testing the weight (very light!) and flexibility (slightly bendable, and the material would spring back into shape when she released the pressure.) A tine snapped off as she repeated the test.

"Oh!"

Bel chuckled. "Don't tell me they didn't have forks in 1893."

"Of course we have forks!" Hannah scowled at the broken utensil instead of at Bel. "But they're higher quality than this… brittle material." She reached for a spoon and flexed it until the bowl broke apart from the handle.

"Plastic. And don't lose those bits. They go in the recycler. Last thing I need is to get a trash violation."

Hannah smiled sweetly. "If only we were on your ship, on our way back to Detroit."

Bel tore open one of the food packages. She crunched her way through several orange-colored chip things before she replied.

"How was I supposed to know I'd be flagged for a search? Hasn't happened in ages."

"But it *has* happened before."

Bel crunched another chip and shrugged one shoulder.

"Because you're a smuggler," Hannah continued.

"Not right now. I'm not syrup-brained!"

"I see."

"Look, Miss I'm-Gonna-Trespass-at-a-Spaceport-in-

My-Time-Machine, you don't know me and you don't know my world, so cut the judgey looks. 'Let he who is without sin' and all that fuckery."

"You're right. I don't know your situation. My apologies."

Hannah turned her attention to her salad. There was so much she didn't know here. But she did know Bel, or at least a few key things about her. Bel was straightforward and competent. Kind. (No one who didn't care would have warned Hannah about snooping or bought her more food than necessary just so she could pick what she liked.) She was clever and prickly and interesting and… Oh, rats. Hannah just liked her. Quite a lot, in fact.

It was so difficult to stay mad at someone when they were feeding you and you were terribly hungry.

When only a handful of leaves remained in the bottom of the paper bowl, Hannah finally let her gaze return to Bel. "So, what do you smuggle?"

"Huh?"

Bel's brow furrowed, then slowly smoothed out as she appeared to process the question. Hannah understood the feeling. Sometimes her brain was just too full to take in everything. Other times, it was moving too fast to stop and listen. She had no "quiet time" in her head the way some people claimed to.

"Oh, you know, the usual." Bel waved her fork. "Plastic. The higher quality stuff that hasn't been through the recycler a million times. Booze, obviously. Anything with high taxes on it."

"Ah." Not so different from Hannah's time, then.

"Puts coins in the bank so I can smuggle the good stuff. Books, media, medicines, scientific research—whatever the high-ups don't want people to read or share."

"The government is corrupt? Or the robber barons?"

Bel huffed a small laugh. "Always. History repeating itself, as usual. Make the people into obedient little workers so the elite can profit from it."

Hannah listlessly prodded the remnants of her salad. "Oh, dear. I had hoped the future would be better."

"Nah. Humans gonna human."

"You are a pilot, though. It appears there is more equality between the sexes? And from your… offer, I gather that Sapphic relations are unremarkable in your culture?"

Bel gave a curt nod. "The problems aren't gone, but it's not like your time. Two steps forward—"

"One step back. You still use that saying?"

"Yup. Though sometimes it feels like one forward, two back. Or three and two. Eight and eight. You get my meaning."

"I do. What was it you said? Humans will be humans? And most of us are only trying our best. You smuggle, but have your reasons for it. I try to be sensible, but I can't suppress my curiosity. Also, I stole the clicking pen."

"The what?"

Hannah showed Bel the pen, clicking it a few times.

Bel laughed. "Keep it. The hotel doesn't care."

"You're sure? It's very, well, satisfying."

Click. Click. Click.

"I'm sure. The pen is yours, Doctor. Be a rebel."

Their eyes met. Mirth shimmered in Bel's dark irises and her lips curved into a kissable bow. Heat crept up Hannah's neck. She shifted her chair a few inches closer to the bed.

"Is that a challenge, Captain?"

Bel's communication device sang a jaunty tune, and she dug it out of her pocket. "Hold that thought. This might be our ticket home."

Hannah clicked her pen again in demonstration. "It's quite a soothing feeling and sound. And the retractable tip avoids lost caps and accidental ink marks, so you can see why these pens would be popular in future times. The outer casing of the pen is of a material called 'plastic.' I have been told that it can be created from crude oil and other similar materials, but in 2143 most of it comes from mining and refining plastics discarded in the twentieth and twenty-first centuries. And before you ask, no, I am not recording specific details of technologies in my journal. I believe much more study is necessary surrounding the nature of time travel and the possibility of contaminating the past with the future or vice versa."

"One of the leading theories is that contamination isn't possible," Dr. Franklin said, belatedly raising his hand. "Because whatever you're going to do in our time is a thing that already happened in the future. Sorry, I don't want to take all your time. Do you want to go get a drink after and we can chat about it?"

"Yes, come to our club," Dr. Finch jumped in. "They have good tea if you don't mind the autokettles."

"And good whiskey," added Captain Nemo.

Hannah grinned at the trio. "That sounds lovely, thank you." She addressed the crowd. "I'm sure you all have additional questions for me as well, but please don't forget the other scientists here exhibiting today. The room is full of fascinating discoveries and important inventions, and I would hate for anyone to miss out. I will be here at my table for the duration of the event if you'd like to look over my schematics and notes or speak to me individually. Although my voice won't hold out forever, I'm afraid. We scientists are often solitary, quiet sorts, as I'm sure you know."

The crowd chuckled.

"Thank you so much for your attention, and I hope you have a wonderful time exploring the rest of the exhibits."

Hannah took her seat with an air of finality and pocketed her journal and her pen. Goodness. She'd done it. Stood up for herself and her work. Things would be different from now on, for better or for worse. People would know her name, that was certain. Whatever happened, she couldn't say she regretted it, even if she became the latest scandal for the newspapers.

"We'll see you later for that drink," Nemo said, as she and her friends headed away.

Hannah waved.

The crowd dispersed slowly, but eventually the expo settled into the usual up-and-down flow of passersby. Hannah clicked her pen and let her mind wander, calmed by the steady rumble of background voices.

Naturally, it was PB who broke her reverie.

"Bitch," he growled, during a lull in the traffic. "You're as much a liar as I am. A noise-making pen as proof? It probably doesn't even write."

"I'm not interested in your opinion, so if it's all the same to you, I'd rather not converse. Believe me or not, I really don't care. I know what I've done and seen and I don't need to prove myself to you or to anyone."

And she didn't. She really, truly didn't. Anyone who mattered would listen to what she had to say and treat her with respect, no matter what she did or didn't accomplish. And it was enough. Hannah Wells was enough. All on her own.

She smiled to herself and clicked her pen again. In the end, the right people always found her.

✴

Day 3, continued (or is it Day 4? I have lost track of time. Lacking sleep and without the usual sense of where the sun is in the sky, I can't say if it's day or night.)

We are en route to Detroit. I have shut myself in the same chamber as before. Bel was busy for a time, checking over the new cargo and piloting us from the transit station. I expect her to visit again when she is able. It seems that once the ship is on its proper course through space, it flies itself with little supervision. (To those of you in my time developing self-driving steam cars: Don't give up hope! Look where your work will lead someday!)

I'm not sure whether I will let Bel in or send her away. I had been genuinely prepared to kiss her at the hotel. I have since had time to reconsider.

(Side note: When I get home I must remember to write up a fresh copy of these entries that omits some of the personal details I have recorded here alongside my scientific observations. This journal will be kept private and, in the way of such autobiographical musings, published or destroyed by those who come after me. Is there a Society of Sapphic Scientists? If so, I will leave it to them in the event of my death (whether timely or untimely).)

Where was I?

Oh, yes, Bel. Now that I am firmly on the path of returning home, I think it wise to distance myself from her. I will never see her again, and I already like her quite a bit more than is prudent. Kissing her (or beyond) will only intensify these romantic inclinations. I know myself. This is not the sort of acquaintanceship that could remain casual on my part. I believe

I was doomed the moment she offered me my choice of foods. Certainly from the moment she told me to keep the pen.

I will therefore keep every further interaction entirely professional and make our inevitable parting as painless as possible.

Hannah had barely settled down on the couch-bed when the door opened. Just her luck. Bel would decide to appear *now*, right when Hannah had convinced herself to get some sleep. She sat up, grunting as her body protested. She knew full well that a few hours rest here and there wasn't sufficient for her physical or mental well-being. But did she listen to the part of her brain telling her so?

"You never do," she muttered.

"Did you say something?" Bel asked. "Sorry to be gone so long. Space debris. Had to stay at the helm. Did I wake you?"

"No, I only lay down a moment ago." Hannah glanced at Bel but didn't make eye contact. "I thought I would sleep until we reach Earth."

Now there was a phrase she'd never imagined she'd utter. When this was over, she would either have an entirely new perspective of the world, or the whole adventure would fade to the unreality of a dream.

"It's been a busy few days," Bel agreed. "I see you changed back into your own clothes."

"Ah. Yes." Hannah smoothed a wrinkle out of her skirt. "Can't go home in your uniform. I'd be deemed a bicycle-riding hoyden." She pressed the toe of her boot into the carpet, rubbing the pile one way and then the other, watching the subtle shift of color. "Actually, I *am* a bicycling-riding hoyden, but people can't tell that from looking at me, so they leave me alone. If they even notice me. I'm not especially remarkable, after all. Don't let me keep you. I'm sure you have important things to do. I'll just go to sleep."

"Oh, no. Not on your life, Wells. You think I don't know what you're doing?" Bel laughed. "You think I haven't tried self-deprecation? Avoidance of conflict? Talking about anything but actual feelings? Been there, done that. I've had therapy. Lots of therapy. I know all your tricks."

Hannah looked up and met Bel's eyes for the first time since she'd entered the room. "Therapy? For what? Have you been ill? Please tell me it wasn't that awful electro-therapy? Or any of those other things they do to 'hysterical' women. Are you—"

Bel held up a placating hand. "No, no. Nothing bad. Forgot you don't have therapy yet in your time. I'll explain it later. My point is that I know you're trying to push me away and I also know that won't help either of us. For my part, if I'm never going to see you again, then I'm going to take all of you that I can get, g'om?"

None of the words tumbling through Hannah's brain made it to her mouth. Her body hummed with awareness of the woman standing across from her. Bel's mouth was set in a hard line, her forehead creased. Memories flashed through Hannah's mind of all the times she'd heard a man tell herself or another woman that she was "prettier when she smiled."

Fools.

A static, smiling facsimile of Bel could be pretty. The real Bel was nothing short of radiant. Her beauty lay in her defiance and her strength. In her confident stance and the subtle nervous tic in her jaw. In the kindness that lurked behind her cynicism. She could be brash and demanding or patiently understanding. Perfectly imperfect.

Like me. The real me, not the sensible-voice me.

Hannah squared her shoulders and lifted her chin, bringing a slight smile to Bel's lips.

"Ah. There you are. How about it? Wanna steal a moment, pen thief?"

Hannah sprang to her feet.

And then they were kissing, arms wrapping around each other, lips and tongues clashing. Hot, messy, perfect.

They tumbled onto the bed, landing in an awkward tangle. One of Hannah's legs hung off the edge and something (probably a hairpin) was poking into her shoulder, but she didn't dare break the kiss. She gripped Bel's waist, tugging at her shirt until a tiny corner of it pulled free from her trousers. Hannah slid a finger through the gap, finding the smooth skin underneath.

Gods above, Bel was delicious. Hannah squirmed, trying to worm her hand further beneath Bel's clothes. She needed more. So much more.

More lips. More skin. Everything she could possibly get before their time ran out.

She jerked away.

"Wait!"

Bel propped herself up on one elbow. "Did you change your mind?"

"No, no. I just..." Hannah put a hand to her hair and another pin fell out of her coiffure. "We have time before we reach Earth, correct? A few hours at least?"

"Yes."

"Right. Good. So why am I trying to wolf down a gourmet meal instead of savoring each bite? We should take things slower."

"A gourmet meal, am I?" Bel arched an eyebrow. She let herself fall back onto the bed, spreading her arms wide. "Well, then. Come and devour me."

Grinning, Hannah clambered up from her awkward position. She hiked up her skirts and knelt to straddle Bel's legs. First order of business was to finish what she'd started with the shirt. She worked it free from Bel's waistband and pushed it up just high enough to reveal a narrow patch of skin. Her fingers itched to delve beneath, but she forced herself to settle for the lightest of brushes over the exposed flesh. When Bel let out a tiny sigh of pleasure, Hannah knew she'd chosen correctly.

She took her time undoing the shirt's bottom button. Bel held perfectly still, the picture of calm except for the slight pinkening of her cheeks. Oh, this was going to be fun.

Hannah moved on to the next button, grazing the small patch of newly revealed skin as she did so. Next came the third. And the fourth. Each bit of Bel was as soft and lovely as the last, and Hannah catalogued a freckle here, a dimple there, all the natural creases and imperfections of a body in use. Simply gorgeous.

She quickened her pace once she reached the lacy edge of Bel's undergarment, curious what women wore in these future times. She was Dr. Wells, scientist, after all. Even during sex.

"Is it common for women to wear short stays like this in your time?" The garment (in a pretty burgundy color) appeared to be fashioned primarily of tightly woven cotton with a lace overlay, shaped to cup the breasts without either lifting or compressing them. Hannah couldn't see any boning, nor did she feel any when she trailed a finger along the edge of the material.

"My bralette? It's comfy. Works really well for me, but as you can see I'm not the most endowed in that area. You'd likely want something more supportive for everyday wear." Her gaze flicked to Hannah's chest. "But there are lots of choices for people with different body shapes and sizes. Bras of multiple styles and materials, corsets like you would wear, substances that just stick to your skin and hold things in place."

"Fascinating. Do you mind if I make a note of that in my journal? After we're done here, of course."

Bel chortled. "I should have known you'd be like this in bed. You're astral, Doctor. Please, write down anything you like."

"Thank you. Now, how does one go about removing this bralette of yours?"

Bel wriggled out of her shirt, then yanked the bralette up and off. She tossed both garments aside.

"My turn?"

The words didn't register for several seconds. Which honestly wasn't Hannah's fault. No one should be expected to pay attention when there was so much lovely skin on display. By the time she opened her mouth to reply, Bel had a firm grip on her waist.

"Yes, I sup— Oh!" Hannah landed flat on her back.

Bel gave her a cheeky grin. "Good thing we're going slow, because you have a lot of tiny buttons."

"They're quite normal buttons. My whole wardrobe is like this."

"Mm-hmm." Bel fumbled with the first couple of buttons before finding her rhythm. "And you've got a corset or whatever under here, so I don't even get to feel your skin yet."

"Er, that's the corset cover next. Then the corset and then a chemisette."

A bit frustrating, Hannah had to admit. She did want Bel's hands on her. But she also could enjoy observing the process and admiring the naked breasts swaying above her.

"Insanity," Bel muttered.

"Well, I'm very sorry, but we don't have your fancy washing devices in my time. Without the proper undergarments, I would be scrubbing clothes nonstop or heaping endless work on some poor laundry girl who I'm sure earns too few coins as it is."

Bel's answering grin sent another rush of heat through Hannah's body. "I like you indignant. Don't ever change."

Hannah couldn't form a reply. Bel didn't seem a romantic sort of person, but those words!

Don't ever change.

Had anyone else said anything half so supportive in her life? She lived in a world that constantly demanded change. Change how you look. Change how you act. Change who you are. Endless pressure to fit, to conform.

Bel, though.

Bel urged her to be herself. Even applauded her for it.

Hannah grabbed for the ties of her skirts and began unknotting them. If Bel liked her whole, uninhibited self, that's what she was going to get. A few tugs and a shimmy, and Hannah kicked her legs free from everything but her drawers.

Go fast, go slow, go fast again. Here she was, being impulsive and capricious, and she wasn't going to apologize for it.

Bel certainly didn't seem to mind, in any case. She nudged Hannah's legs apart and knelt between them.

"Stars, are you wearing that weird old underwear that's split open in the middle? I could have just crawled under your skirts at any time and had my mouth on you?"

Bel didn't give Hannah time to reply. Nor did she say another word, her lips and tongue too occupied with a thorough exploration of Hannah's quim. Bel was an attentive lover, responding to each of Hannah's gasps and finding all the spots that made her back arch. Occasionally, Bel would make a small hum of satisfaction, as if Hannah's pleasure were her own.

Hannah wove strands of Bel's hair around her fingers, not quite pulling, but pinning her in place. "Please. Please, Bel."

She needed. God, she needed. Bel worked her clit with delicate sucks, keeping her hovering on the edge. She was so close. So, so close. She panted and writhed, her fingers buried in Bel's dark tresses, hip jerking.

And then it hit. Hannah cried out, her vision going white like the stars all around them as she rode out every last wave of orgasmic pleasure.

Eventually her breathing even out and she pried her eyes open to find Bel smiling down at her.

"Hey, gorgeous. Enjoy yourself?"

"I did. And now I'm going to enjoy you."

Bel—sweet Bel, wonderful Bel—happily ceded control to Hannah, letting her reverse their positions and strip away the remainder of their clothes. Hannah began with her fingers, then her mouth, watching Bel unravel bit by bit. She delighted in every taste of arousal, every touch of warm skin. Bel didn't vocalize much, but her body contorted, and she pleased with her hips and her eyes, until coming apart in one, long shuddering climax. The cool, collected pilot. Undone by something as human as feelings.

She was glorious.

"We're funny, aren't we?" Hannah asked. "People, I mean."

Bel frowned. Her dark hair fanned out around her in disarray. Her eyelashes fluttered. "Because we have weird conversations during sex? That might be a you thing."

"No," Hannah laughed. "And yes. The way we feel and act. Think or don't think. We're so messy and beautiful and it doesn't matter if that's now or in the past or the future. We're all simply… us."

"Yeah. Yeah we are." Bel opened her arms. "C'mere and give me a kiss."

They snuggled for a while, then went for another round of sex. This time it was slow and lazy, less about reaching climax and more about enjoying their bodies and basking in the warmth and closeness. Hannah could have continued for hours.

They only broke apart when a beeping alert summoned Bel back to the helm. They helped each other dress and exchanged a final, quick kiss.

This is it. The end.

Hannah joined Bel in the control room, but they didn't speak. In a daze, Hannah jotted notes about the landing, the Earth as seen from afar, and other sights that should have held her full attention. Mere seconds seemed to pass before they bumped gently onto the tarmac.

The end. Time to wake from the dream.

"Hey. Before you go."

Hannah's head jerked up. Bel held out a small, squarish device, similar to the one she used to communicate with people elsewhere.

"This is just a basic burner phone, but it can contact me anywhere on Earth or at the transit station. Y'know, if you're ever in the area again."

Their fingers brushed as Hannah accepted the device.

"Thank you. I'll… be sure to keep that in mind as I'm traveling."

Bel winked.

*

Hannah smiled as she closed her journal. Those early days of traveling had been quite the adventure, hadn't they? She'd filled nearly half the book since then. Maybe by this time next year it would be full. Maybe she could even reserve a larger space at the exposition and bring her time cycle.

"Remarkable!" a man exclaimed.

Hannah looked up, but the word wasn't directed at her. PB was telling his story again, and had gained himself a listener, apparently. She wasn't going to comment on the inconsistencies in his tale. Another few minutes and she'd begin packing up.

The fair had been much calmer after the earlier crowds had dispersed. She'd greeted the occasional interested viewers, answered a few questions, and posed for two photographers. A good day, all in all. Maybe she'd be in the newspapers after the morning's kerfuffle, but maybe not. Sensation, scandal, or side note—she was proud regardless.

Hannah put away her journal and her pen and checked her watch. Twenty minutes until the official end of the event. Twenty minutes until she went out for a drink with three of the most interesting scientists in the city! Who else could be better company?

She gazed off into the distance, a soft smile playing on her lips. Well, maybe there was one person…

"Hey, you!"

Hannah jumped.

As if summoned, Bel swaggered up to the table. "Told you I wouldn't miss it!"

"Oh?" Hannah made a show of looking at her watch again.

"Okay, I got the time off a bit. That thing's fiddly! But

I did get a cute video of you sitting there thinking. Wanna see?"

Bel touched her phone screen to start the moving picture. Hannah leaned over to watch.

"I took a panorama of the whole room first, then it'll zoom in on you."

"Oh, it's lovely. Thank—"

A strangled noise came from over Hannah's shoulder. PB had moved in for a look and was now staring, mouth agape.

"That... It can't... I..." His gaze darted between Hannah, the screen, and Bel in her twenty-second century apparel.

Hannah let him sputter, saving her attention for her partner. "I'll be packing up in a moment, and then I've been invited for drinks with fellow scientists. I'm sure they'd be happy to meet you, if you'd like to join us."

"Astral. I'm in." Bel closed the video and pocketed the phone. A sly grin spread across her face. "Because with you, Doctor Wells, any time's a good time."

The End

About the Author

Award-winning author Catherine Stein believes that everyone deserves love and that Happily Ever After has the power to help, to heal, and to comfort. She writes sassy, sexy romance set during the Victorian and Edwardian eras. Her stories are full of action, adventure, magic, and fantastic technologies.

Catherine lives in Michigan with her husband and three rambunctious kids. She loves steampunk and Oxford commas, and can often be found dressed in Renaissance festival clothing, drinking copious amounts of tea.

*

Visit Catherine online at
www.catsteinbooks.com
Join her VIP mailing list for exclusive bonus material and book news.

Instagram
@catsteinbooks

Facebook
@catsteinbooks

Also by
CATHERINE STEIN

Potions and Passions

The Earl on the Train - Book 0.5

How to Seduce a Spy - Book 1

Mishaps & Mistletoe -
A Holiday Novella -Book 1.5

Not a Mourning Person - Book 2

Once a Rake, Always a Rogue - Book 3

Love at Second Sight - Book 4

Sass and Steam

Love is in the Airship - Book 0.5

A Shot to the Heart - Book 0.75

Eden's Voice - Book 1

What Are You Doing New Year's Eve? –
A Holiday Novella - Book 1.5

Priceless - Book 2

Dead Dukes Tell No Tales - Book 3

Arcane Tales

The Scoundrel's New Con - Book 1

The Spinster's Swindle - Book 2

Mad Scientists Society

The Courtesan and Mr. Hyde - Book 1

The Electrical Affairs of Dr. Victor Franklin - Book 2

Courting Captain Nemo - Book 3

Lords of Dystopia

Earth Earls are Easy - Book 1

Other Books

Mating Habits - Book 1

Idle Nature - Book 2

My Heiress, 'Tis of Thee

Boy Meets Earl/Her Fair Lady

Available at your favorite online retailer.
www.catsteinbooks.com

✳

Thank you so much for reading!

If you enjoyed the book and are so inclined,
I would love for you to leave a review.
Happy readers make an author's day!

I love hearing from readers, so feel free
to contact me on social media, or email:

catherine@catsteinbooks.com

✳